THE
POLAR PROTOCOL

THE
POLAR PROTOCOL

ICE AND FIRE

WILLIE HIRSH

HILDEBRAND BOOKS

an imprint of W. Brand Publishing

NASHVILLE, TENNESSEE

Hildebrand Books an imprint of W. Brand Publishing
j.brand@wbrandpub.com
www.wbrandpub.com

Cover design by designchik.net

Polar Protocol /Willie Hirsh — 1st Edition
Available in Hardcover, Paperback, Kindle, and eBook formats.

HC: 978-1-956906-59-2
PB: 978-1-956906-60-8
eBook: 978-1-956906-61-5

Library of Congress Control Number:
Release date: July 11, 2023

Contents

AUTHOR'S NOTE

O n June, 14, 2023 Israel declassified the hypersonic missile interceptor development named SKYSON-IC, the first in its kind in the world. I predicted the need of the interceptor development in this book without knowing who would be the first to deploy it.

The compelling argument of defense agencies always will be, where to invest in future development. This development can take a decade to complete, which is how long it took Israel to develop.

Seeing the restlessness in the world with hypersonic missiles being used in the Ukraine war with Russia and hearing other countries like China, North Korea, and Iran, announce the hypersonic missile operational is like watching a volcano about to erupt.

Although Polar Protocol is a work of fiction, it shines a light on the realities of global geopolitics with its defense challenges serving as background for the story.

The new Israeli Interceptor will be displayed in Eurosatory, the international defense and security exhibition for land and air in Paris, France, late July 2023.

CHAPTER ONE

February 24, 8:15 AM
Lockheed Martin, Space and Engineering Technology Facility
Lone Tree, Colorado

After passing the security gate, the middle-aged man turned off his new Ford Expedition and parked in one of the VIP visitor spots reserved for the morning event. With unimaginable power, an explosion blew the SUV into the air like a feather, disintegrating and shredding the metal into unrecognizable pieces. What was once a luxury SUV vehicle, the pride of the American Auto industry had been forcefully dissipated into debris, landing on the cold February asphalt of Lockheed Martin parking lot.

The target was its driver, a rocket scientist defense contractor on his way to the event. Now only a few burning pieces scattered here and there serve as witness of the brutal terrorist attack. What's left of the scientist's body after being engulfed in flames, fueled by his highly combustible winter clothes gave him no chance to survive.

A momentary eerie silence swept the area as a secondary gas tank exploded loudly, creating shock waves that rocked the security booth from its anchored foundation. The security guard fell onto the concrete floor a few feet away from his original post gasping for air, disoriented, and dazed.

The security guard quickly regained consciousness and pressed the emergency panic button on his Apple Watch. He hoped it could still send a signal from his wrist. The Bluetooth connection to the main building security office miraculously received the signal, which automatically dispatched the local authorities who showed up within minutes through the facility's twisted iron gate, now laying on the asphalt. The alarm continued to obnoxiously blast its warning.

First responder vehicles dispatched from the closest fire station wailed in the background. The fire trucks extinguished what was left in the soot-covered parking spot, struggling with the fire to prevent another catastrophe by it spreading to the other parked vehicles and nearby building.

Three police cars surrounded the area that held the remains of the Ford Expedition and its victim from a safe distance, barricading it with yellow tape and awaiting the detectives to begin the investigation of a possible domestic homicide.

Employees emerged from the building gasping in total shock, holding their heads in their hands in disbelief.

The top-secret development meeting taking place in the conference hall, was obviously canceled with its keynote speaker dead in the parking lot.

"What happened?" they all asked, panicked and upset, searching for anyone who could shed light on the incident.

"Is anyone hurt?" asked one and another piped up repeating the question.

"Yeah, there was a man in the car!" exclaimed one man who always seemed to know more than the others.

It was pure chaos, while all watched the gruesome scene as the driver's flesh was consumed by the fire exposing his bones.

"It was definitely a bomb!" one man shouted to his colleagues who stood in the distance. "It was a freaking bomb!" He looked at the vehicle in shock. "Oh God, I know this man! Who the hell would want to kill anyone here?" he yelled loudly knowing there was no answer to his emotional question.

"This definitely will trigger a major FBI investigation," said one woman.

"Who said it was a bomb?" yelled another man.

"Whose car was it?" a woman asked emotionally.

For the paramedics, there was nothing more they could do to help. They examined the twisted skeleton when the fire was out and shook their heads.

Simon looked preoccupied. He had never seen a horrific scene like this before. Lumbering toward the paramedics with heavy steps, he shook his head in disbelief at seeing the destruction the explosion had caused. He showed his detective badge and immediately asked without formality in a low authoritative tone, "How many were there?" He sniffed.

The chief paramedic turned toward Simon and raised his eyebrows. Then he shook his head and with pursed lips said, "Just the driver, no one else was in the car! Nothing much to save here." His voice was sad.

"Identification?" he asked squinting at the police sergeant next to him. His voice was cold and tough like the Colorado winter.

The thin police sergeant, his uniform too large for his body, looked up at Simon's face which hovered nine inches above his and replied without emotion, "The car is registered to John Gregory. Fifty years old. Lives in Arizona!" Then he pulled his shoulders back and licked his upper lip, puzzled.

"Could anyone confirm the victim's identity? He could have loaned the vehicle to someone else, for example!" Detective Simon glanced at the person's records printed from his police car computer, and gazed intensely while making a surprising comment, "Wow, he drove ten hours here?"

A slender tall man in a gray suit and a red tie approached quickly toward them, his distressed face was confused and grim. He stopped near Simon, who assumed the man must be a high-ranking Lockheed Martin executive.

"Oh my god, my god!" he howled "No . . . no, no, no!" He continued sobbing and holding his head in his hands. A colleague came closer and held him tightly helping him compose himself. It seemed he recognized the twisted Arizona license plate.

"Who's in charge here?" he asked, exasperated, looking for an answer from the police who were chatting and taking notes.

"Detective Hardly," Simon introduced himself quickly and showed him his badge. "And you, sir, are?"

"I'm the general manager of this facility," he replied and continued. "Mark . . . Mark Markovich." He handed him a business card, shaking his head with true sorrow, his lips pursed.

"Can you, by any chance, identify the person in the car? I know it might be a hard scene for you, sorry about that, but it will help us to crack this fast!" Simon said in a business-like police manner.

"I recognize the license plate from Arizona. The car is registered to John Gregory, our top scientist from Courtland Alabama Missile facility!"

"With a license plate from Arizona?" asked the detective.

"Yes, he moved there a couple of months ago, when the hypersonic missile facility in Alabama opened last year."

"Sorry, my condolences, sir!" he could not find the right comforting words and felt awkward.

"Yes . . . yes detective, it must be him, we expected him. John was the speaker of the defense department conference regarding his missile program!"

Mark nodded his head. His eyes were open wide when he said, "I just spoke to him half an hour ago. He called me from the hotel, and he said he was heading out in five min–"

"Sorry sir, seems he was very close to you." Simon managed to say with deep sympathy and put his hand on Mark's shoulder.

"You don't understand Detective Hardly . . . he was our lead scientist, working with us on a very important and classified military hardware development. It's a huge setback for our military missile program. The conference today was the last step before testing our equipment on a real target. The first thought that crossed my mind was, 'Was this an accident or a terror attack execution style?'" His words trembled, and his lips quivered while the nerves in his cheek twitched.

"I don't think it was an execution. Who would be the enemy? The Russians? Besides it's unethical and against the Geneva Accord to go after civilians!"

"I guess you don't know our enemy! They will do anything to stop us. We reported to the FBI a few times regarding suspicious people scouting the facility with telescopes from a distance, and no one bothered to check," he sounded frustrated.

"I'll bring this to the appropriate agency and the FBI. It's not good!" Simon squinted and coughed lightly.

"Hard to explain the immensity of this loss to our country's national security. He drove here from Arizona enjoying his new Ford Expedition, he stayed in the Hill Wind Hotel nearby, and then this happened!" The manager stretched both hands forward and gasped for fresh air. His emotions were chaotic, spinning in his mind like a tornado. He could not manage to keep his thoughts straight and controlled. He jumped from subject to subject quickly and his face looked distressed.

"Sorry, sir! Are you OK if I ask more questions? Did you mention a hotel?" Detective Hardly snapped his first lead from the general manager on John Gregory in the last few minutes. The deceased had parked his car in an open hotel parking lot which could be accessed by anyone with no security protection, other than the standard security cameras that saved the recordings for ninety days. From the hotel, driving for about ten minutes, Simon connected the facts immediately. *The car was new and not defective, the cameras should be able to detect if anyone tampered with the car, this will be a game changer,* he thought.

The squad team was taking samples of everything they could find trying to find traces of explosive materials that triggered the explosion and put them in the sterile plastic bags with care.

Simon signaled the paramedics to assist with Mark's emotional state and calm him down.

"What a loss, what a loss!" Mark kept mumbling swaying his body back and forth when he was put into an ambulance for treatment of shock.

"Anything new?" Simon asked his assistant who was taking notes and photos documenting the scene from different angles.

"Other than two damaged cars," said the sergeant, "we have many smashed windows and cracked windshields. Looks like a powerful blast. More signs that the man was followed and targeted by terrorists."

"Keep looking, Sarg!" exclaimed Simon. A passing thought made him ask aloud, "Who might be behind it and what's the motive, is our first question to answer. If you are right sergeant, then the bomb was probably planted in the hotel parking lot overnight."

"Not sure. It could have been planted in Arizona and detonated via remote control from a distance, or just mistaken identity," the sergeant answered Simon's sentence with his opinion.

"If so, why make the trip from Arizona to Colorado? It's easy to trace someone who took the trip. Perhaps the assassins are looking at us right now, you never know!" Simon thought out loud.

"It's been an hour . . . hard to find anyone sixty miles from here but–" the sergeant twisted his body uncomfortably insinuating he might go the extra mile and ask neighboring agencies to put up roadblocks and check for any suspicious behavior. Then he said, "You might be right, perhaps he is watching us!" He looked around and all he could see were media field reporters crowding to the reporting stage assigned away from the security booth.

"Doesn't hurt, sergeant, to put up roadblocks. Go ask the hotel to retrieve the surveillance video recordings and images from the cameras right away. We might get them, sooner than later," he exhaled heavily and covered his face with his scarf.

"Right away, detective. I will also report to my superior, perhaps he will call the FBI!"

The sergeant cut out immediately and called his dispatcher on the radio.

The general manager, loaded with relaxants, exited the ambulance with the aid of a nurse. He was still talking to himself, mumbling words in disbelief. His phone rang. He answered.

"Yes sir. Yes . . . yes, John Gregory is gone!" he exclaimed on the phone.

"What was the victim's position in the facility? Sorry if I asked before but I–" Simon could not complete his sentence, the manager put him on hold.

"I told you already, he was our lead scientist. Brilliant mind. He was the one who saved America with his innovations time after time, for thirty years. The rest is confidential. I can't talk about it now. I am sure you know what Lockheed is doing isn't . . ." the spasm in his cheek hit him again and he sighed deeply with unbearable stress.

"Yes, a major defense contractor–" whispered Simon as he adjusted his sunglasses.

Mark's raspy voice answered laconically, "Yes, like F-35 for example and on and on . . ."

"How many visitors other than the victim were invited to the conference today? Was it confidential?"

"Yes, it was a confidential invitation, and about a dozen guest speakers other than him. The rest are our Lockheed Martin engineers and scientists' teams, developing the hypersonic missile."

"I imagine it's a huge loss." He shook the man's hand in sympathy and support for his loss.

"Loss?" He shrugged. "You can't imagine, detective, without the victim's ingenuity, we are set back weeks, months, years. He oversaw the new Hypersonic Interceptor Missile Program and was developing its counterpart at the same time."

"I am not a scientist but understand the gravity of the situation. I am sure the FBI will get to the bottom of this tragic event," the detective replied and frowned.

Media vans with their satellite antennas and communication gadgets started broadcasting from the crime scene. No doubt someone was watching and saying to himself "mission accomplished". Media swarmed the area displaying their TV station logos, looking for breaking news and starting their unsubstantiated speculations.

In the distance was also Ron Hill, an expert military blogger and military magazine reporter who was invited to cover the Lockheed Martin conference event, perhaps the only one in the crowded group of reporters who had an invitation in his pocket.

"News travels fast," Ron murmured seeing the congested media parking spot and watching the low hanging morning sun in the east, hoping for warmer weather. He tightened his coat and pulled his stocking cap down. It was a very cold morning.

CHAPTER TWO

Patrick Stevenson was briefed by his administrative assistant, Victoria Harper. The young energetic woman was very effective and hardworking. She stood just inches away from the CIA director, her boss.

Patrick, an Ex-Rear-Admiral, had a long list of career moves: navy fighter pilot with a long combat experience in the Gulf War and the war on terror versus Al Qaida and the Taliban in Afghanistan, squadron commander, wing commander, top navy intelligence officer. He was offered to work for the CIA as the head of the Iranian desk during the nuclear negotiations with Hayatullah's hard regime. He sealed the director's deputy position after the agreement was signed. Then he captured the top seat after his boss resigned, taking the helm of the NSA. Patrick felt comfortable in the front seat running the most notorious intelligence agency in the world, the CIA.

Patrick, in his mid-fifties, with short thin white hair that he refused to dye, had a short lip-long mustache "adding to my toughness" he used to say. Wearing glasses was not the tough look he wanted, so he maintained a short, half-inch narrow beard under his bottom lip like a buccaneer, perhaps making him look more like a man someone would listen to. Despite his many exhausting years in the navy, he carried his tall body like an athlete half his age, with energy to work around the clock with no break.

"That's all for now!" Victoria exclaimed as she was about to go back to her desk behind their shared wall.

"Patch me in with Dan Schmidt," Patrick said politely and examined her as she walked out wearing a black tight jumpsuit emphasizing her athletic curvy body.

Victoria kept her "upper thirties" age confidential. She looked much younger and felt the same. Many men were mesmerized by her blue eyes, pouty lips, and Audrey Hepburn-like face. She was a talented individual and got her job with Patrick through her late husband who was an Air Force general assigned to the Pentagon then later became a senator representing his state.

Many times, she asked to be recruited by the CIA to train as a field agent and was declined, despite her high security clearance as wife to the former Air Force general. After her husband's death in a car accident, she made sure to be seen at all the Pentagon and political events she was invited to, socializing and enjoying her limelight life. Perhaps her "stray cat" survival skills as an orphan, adopted at a young age by a British family, helped her navigate life. Or maybe it was because she was only two years old when she was separated from her older brother, who since disappeared without a trace, that kept her relevant in the close circles of Washington.

Her immigrant parents who fled after the collapse of the Soviet Union, died early from a disease, but they told her it was a car crash like her husband's. She was educated at home by her adopted parents until she was ready to attend college where she met her husband, who was deployed in Britain for one month with the Strategic Air Command as a B-2 pilot.

At the local bar next to the Air-Force base, one glance from her captivating eyes was enough for the B-2 Pilot to ask her to join him back in the US; it was love at the first sight. When his deployment ended, they flew back on the bomber and got married shortly after, in a ceremony that was remembered by many for years.

Then, Victoria opened an interior design studio and got contracts to design most of her husband's air force colleagues' and politicians' homes and military offices.

Her interior design business closed, and Victoria asked her husband to help her get a meaningful job in one of the military departments with his high-profile connections. At one event they met with the previous CIA director, and he agreed to hire her as junior administrative assistant to one of the desk officers in the agency. She went through another security clearance. She was clear after six months of waiting.

Victoria advanced to be the director's assistant though there were rumors that she might have advanced due to her romantic relationship with the ex-director, which they both strongly denied.

Patrick was loyal to his motto that the end result was more important than the methods. Victoria was an energetic and intelligent woman, and he took his schedule and job very seriously.

"I'll get you Dan," she replied behind her back walking out from his office with a convincing smile and a V sign with her fingers.

Patrick paid close attention to one note on the briefing she had placed on his desk pertaining to Lockheed Martin scientist John Gregory, who was killed that morning in an explosion.

"WOW!" Patrick exclaimed. "That's an escalation," he mumbled, waiting for FBI Director Dan Schmidt to get on the line. "A new war," Patrick murmured softly and adjusted his glasses.

Dan Schmidt was on a flight to Colorado to get involved in the investigation of the dead scientist; it just didn't sit very well with him. "It is fishy," he said as he ordered his plane to get ready for an immediate departure.

A slightly heavy figure, especially in the upper chest, Dan was never worried about his health and never changed his way of life. His celebratory lifestyle resembled someone who lived each day as his last; however, no one could run the FBI better than him.

His margarita glass was on his table, shaken slightly due to the light turbulence; he held a cigar despite the FAA rule forbidding smoking even in the FBI private planes. Dan's phone buzzed, and he recognized the special ring tone from a secured number. His buddy Patrick, "the obnoxious one", as he used to call him. He let it ring for a while, a pissing match, a childish game he played with the CIA director.

Finally picking up the call, he listened to his friend on the speaker without the usual greeting.

"You had a triple heart bypass–six stents–you smoke like a chimney, and eat bacon with six eggs for breakfast daily?" Patrick scolded remembering their friendly breakfast meeting in Georgetown two weeks ago. "You are deceiving the creator, Dan!"

"I take prescription drugs. Let the doctors worry about me. Besides what do you care; you're a big blob of fat yourself!" he always replied with a mysterious smile as if cheating death.

Patrick chuckled. "Yeah, you can say that, Dan!"

"When the CIA calls me, it means the wheels in your mind are already spiraling into a black hole! Manipulating spy games again, Patrick?" He slammed right off the bat, and chuckled loudly, exhaling the blueish cigar smoke into the small plane cabin.

"Einstein was right then!" Patrick replied and giggled. "You know why I am calling, Dan?" Patrick skipped his normal niceties and with a firm and clear voice said, "Dan, this might grow legs beyond your territory and responsibility of the FBI, so we need to be on par with all the info you can share with me. It's not a competition anymore."

Dan scoffed, "News travels fast I see, is 'Hulk' involved yet?" He used the secret service's code name for the president.

"Of course, cut to the chase Dan. We are all getting the briefings the same time as Hulk," he said sarcastically. The humming of the jet engines in the background added to the somber feeling of the call.

"John Gregory . . . what else do we know about him?" asked Patrick as he fixed his mustache in his desk mirror.

"Are you on speaker?" scolded Dan.

"Not anymore . . . from what we already gathered from the field, General Duke whom you know and Mark Markovich the general manager of Lockheed Martin are not happy dudes right now. This will slow down the final development of our hypersonic missile and its killer Interceptor deployment."

Dan got serious sipping from his margarita with pursed lips. "What's on your mind, Pat?"

"I have a briefing with Hulk later, he will cross me for answers. I need to tell him what killed John Gregory and if this is a new tactic, or how can I stop the SVR and China from waging war on our scientists? He will put all of his weight on both of us! Who killed the scientist?" asked Patrick, a question that he could put several answers to, like perhaps a targeted terror attack. His loud voice set the tone for this conversation.

Dan chuckled loudly. "C'mon Mr. Spy Daddy! Take it easy, you know the answers old man, a gas tank of a new SUV will not explode in a parking lot, so what's left?" Dan rubbed his hazel eyes slightly and extinguished his cigar in the huge ashtray, the only ashtrays in use on a plane in the Western Hemisphere. "He was on someone's list, Pat, guaranteed, I'm sure of it. It's a professional job perhaps using Semtex for the bomb which might be traceable!" he exclaimed. "We can trace where the Semtex came from you know an–"

"Do that Dan, perhaps domestic terrorism. We need to move on that fast, confirming it's a bomb will open a new can of worms!"

"We need to clean the backyard Pat, probably whoever did it didn't work alone yo–" Dan sighed.

Patrick snorted and shot back, cutting Dan off in the middle of his sentence. "From my perspective you might be right to think it was a terror attack and perhaps Gregory is not the last one on the list. Reminded me of the attack on the Iranian nuclear scientist to slow their nuclear program down!" Patrick inhaled.

"Exactly! That's the point, to slow us down . . . this is like an attack on our missile development program Patrick!" Dan growled on the phone changing the subject. "The Pentagon just announced that the Russians are using their hypersonic missiles in the war on Ukraine, where have you been? Only I see the connections?"

"I see the connection Dan, loud and clear. The Russians do not want to see us dwarfing their military advantage, so, it's easy to attack our science progra–"

"Exactly!" Dan yelled. "By killing our development scientist!" Dan sounded uptight and geared up to tackle the issue from this angle.

"It's a new global whirlpool of bloodshed. I see what's going on in Ukraine, they push the Russians' backs against the wall, which causes the Russians to attack us with their sleeper spy network. I am worried they will start using tactical nuclear war heads. Anyway, what your plans?" asked Patrick as he heard Dan grunt a nasty word.

The airplane cabin chimed, signaling the plane's descent into Centennial Airport. The captain announced they will be landing in about twenty minutes.

"My plans . . . well, first I need to know if it's an inside job, Pat. We locked off the parking lot and there are two dozen dogs sniffing for chemicals or whatever other explosive materials were used for a bomb. After ruling out any collaboration from Lockheed Martin employees, we will then branch out. Look Pat, this can take time and should not slow you down!"

Patrick inhaled deeply and said, "It's a good start buddy, but how will you interrogate 850 employees?"

Dan sighed. "We will concentrate on the guest list first, who was invited to the conference event. The employees went through an annual security clearance; they are on the low probability list but y–"

"Remember, the least suspected are to be interrogated first."

"Thanks for reminding me of my job, Patrick," Dan chuckled. "This is not my first rodeo, you know?" he added sarcastically.

"Just saying, Dan. I will have my agency poke around to see if there is a foreign agency behind it!"

Dan sighed and said, "Don't be surprised if it comes from your agency. The entire world wants to see us down on our knees, Patrick. Russia, China, and even North-fucking-Korea have the hypersonic missile, everyone except us, and that fact keeps the White House up all night!"

"We do have it Dan. It's in the works and will take time to resolve its technical bugs, however clear for service it's another issue . . ."

"Not operational for at least two years, Pat. The world will be burned a couple of times over by then. So, what will they do? They grab whatever they can, Crimea, Ukraine, and perhaps we are a target too!"

"It makes sense, Dan. I hope, if this is an assassination, it will trigger a big domestic espionage chase after the killing cells. That is what I am worried about."

"Look at the fucking Israelis; they gun down the Iranian's nuclear scientists one by one. Doesn't it look like the same footprint to you?" Dan gasped. "Clear this with Hulk today. Get his clearance!"

"We need to gather more intel; the Israelis might know something as well. They always do, those bastards."

Dan cut Patrick off abruptly upon seeing the news on CNN. "Russia used the new missiles to attack Mariupol factories and the nuclear power station. It's a muscled-up show, to make us look vulnerable and helpless. We can't defend ourselves against that missile!"

"Well, we are vulnerable!" Patrick erupted. "That should be the smoking gun, your motive, go for it!" he said in a loud growl.

"Sure, your CIA will be sucked into it too, Patrick!" He chuckled nervously and then he changed the subject. "I am landing soon, I guess you will be on your way to meet Hulk!"

"Yes, the White House is all over the assassination case, very worried, especially if it's an inside job!" Patrick exhaled stressfully and continued, "This matter is on the situation room agenda, plus he wants to cover the war progress in Ukraine and discuss what Hulk is preparing as a military assistance. OK, keep me briefed on your findings Dan, please!"

"Will do. Take care!"

The captain announced that they were on final approach reporting the destination weather info, just before the line disconnected leaving both Dan and Patrick with the weight of the world on their shoulders.

Mole. Scientist dead. Ukraine war. All this must have a common denominator, Patrick thought. He must connect the dots, but his brain had started going in circles. He must come up with a plan.

CHAPTER THREE

February 24, 2022, 3:15 PM
The situation room, the White House.

The Department of Homeland Security along with the rest of the Cabinet assembled in the situation room with the president, who appeared very tense and concerned. It was not enough that he had the entire nation scrutinizing his Covid-19 policies and performance, along with the zillion mutations and the Covid-22 pandemic; it never seemed to stop. And now, the murder, on top of the war in East Europe plus the Chinese threat to invade Taiwan, putting the plant into absorption alert. *The worst time to be president and the leader for the free world,* the president thought.

"Can someone stop the world? I want to get off," the president stated and examined all the faces as he walked into the room. "The world is getting all fucked up guys!" He took off his Ted Baker jacket and flicked a nearly invisible hair from his white shirt. He removed his red tie and put it on the table ready to tackle the world's complicated issues. His arrogant Chief of Staff behind him, locked the meeting room door, and walked away to his other White House duties.

It was afternoon, after exhausting marathon meetings, the president was not in the mood for more bad news.

"I just met with the new French ambassador who submitted his credentials," he reported calmly to no one in the room particularly. He sat down at the head of the long conference table shaking his head. "The French believe that Primankov is eyeing Georgia and Latvia after Ukraine while asking the Chinese to finance their war and provide them with attack drones," he growled, visibly upset, then he yelled to the White House butler who was still in the situation room clearing empty liquor bottles. "Hey Walter, can you please bring the leftover refreshments and food from the ceremonial room? They hardly touched the food there." The butler, from a distance, mumbled under his breath. "I don't need the media to investigate me for wasting White House food, so I'm recycling it," the president said sarcastically, and everyone laughed.

"Anyone have an idea how to fix the world?" He shook his head saying it with all seriousness. Everyone chuckled not sure if the president was joking or not. "Looks like Europe's war, from what the Pentagon is telling me, is a ten-year war, or even worse, World War III. We need to tailor our strategy carefully. First financially, then the military upgrade needs, and lastly, what our allies need." The president threw it all in decisively on the table, and his palm landed on the table with a thud. It was with that gesture that Patrick knew the real meeting had started.

"Indeed sir, indeed. Looks like the Russians are raising their heads lately and there must be a reason for it!" said Cody, the chubby Secretary of State who looked like an Idaho potato on a good day. Cody's navy-blue jacket and matching tie he always wore were too short, but he was a brilliant diplomat with experience in global and foreign affairs. "President Primankov is very restless and shows evidence of defiance toward NATO expansions as our deterrence factor is not as effective as it used to be," he said waving his extinguished pipe in his right hand.

"Are we pushing Primankov into a corner Cody?" the president asked, surprised. "Are we provoking him? We shouldn't!"

"We are not. It's his old soviet era ideology that Ukraine is part of Russia and that's why he annexed Crimea to start with. If we want to stop the war, we should give him a reason to stop it, and not by military means. Right now, it looks like he is not progressing the way it was planned, and Ukraine is not losing either. Rumors are that both countries lost hundreds of thousands of soldiers in that war. Ukraine is asking for more military assistance!"

Cody inhaled deeply as if smoking his pipe, checking the facial expressions of his colleagues in the room. Most nodded in agreement trying to analyze the Russian dictator's profile along with him.

"Yes, we already know the new axis of evil," the president mumbled. "I am more concerned about what advancements they are planning ahead of us, and I get a grim picture." He stared at Cody looking for his help. "Iran is collaborating with Russia, for example!"

"The Russians confiscated a large area of coal, gluten crops, and resources to fuel its military machine. It's a new kind of war, Mr. President!" Alvin Nelson the secretary of defense intervened with much confidence. An ex-Marine top officer turned to politics in his state of Alabama. His baritone voice would have been well-suited as a voice for a science fiction monster character; his voice compelled everyone to listen.

"What does that mean Alvin?" the president shot back. "What has that got to do with our discussion?"

"The gluten crop shortage will push many countries into a famine. Sixty percent of the world's sunflower seeds and a large percent of the gluten supply comes from Ukraine. Russia will stop exporting gas to Europe and will cause an unrest in European democratic governments. Russia will take advantage of separatist's groups in Europe to cause chaos and start anti-government riots in Europe," Alvin said as he lifted his eyebrows showing his intense brown eyes.

"Good point," said Cody, who concurred with his defense secretary. "Last night it was reported that $400 billion in Crypto currency evaporated in a puff of smoke. This will affect the stock market and if you ask me, the Russians' hands are in the mixing bowl."

"I heard Russia has the force to start WWIII, training forces to conquer the North Pole when the ice melts!" the president erupted with his concern about this global threat. "And NATO has zero desire to fight nor is interested in getting involved!" he howled loudly.

"NATO is awaiting your signal, Mr. President!" explained Alvin. "The Russian tactics are to carry out a linear war. They will fight step-by-step, confusing everyone. First, they had the Pro-Russian separatists starting riots and *voila* just like that, they conquered Crimea like a real-life chess game. When Crimea happened, the previous administration had no clue what was going on . . . until . . . until it was all over," Alvin, looking grim, leveled his eyes on the Cabinet team, then stiffened.

The president took back the helm and said, "We should have a different response. First, what can we do to avoid escalation?" He then asked, "Secondly how can we deter Primankov from going nuke? Does this revolve around the fact that they have the hypersonic missile, and we don't?"

Patrick knew the critical fact that disturbed the president and everyone in the defense department. He knew all about it and thought it was time to speak up. "The moment the Russians begin disinformation propaganda and spreading contradictory information about the war, you know they are planning something big. We should not give the impression that the Russians can win an all-out war against us only because we don't have an operational response to this hypersonic missile sir. We should make sure he is not desperate enough to start with nukes," Patrick looked at everyone in the room, judging their reactions.

"He is not there yet; he is only threatening–" the NSA director, Marcus Barbour jumped in, but was cut off by President Rufus who stared at Patrick as he hung his head. Then, raising his chin, he locked an intense stare with Patrick.

"Marcus, you, and Patrick combine your expertise and come up with a plan. Think about how to stop or slow the Russians down. Make them busy with something else . . . without having the consequence of landing boots on the ground. We need to be one step ahead of them the whole time. Send a strong message because we don't want to start teaching Russian as a first language in schools," Rufus scoffed, hoping their ingenuity and creative minds would find a solution, then he stared at Patrick again. "Patrick, your thoughts. Fast!" he hollered, and the chatter subsided.

"Sir, we have a technological gap. I am sure that Russia is arrogant because their hypersonic missiles are being successfully utilized in Ukraine for the first time. They've gained confidence and that's not good! We need to sabotage them and that's my department. All I ask is for carte blanche use of all our military resources collaborating with my plans, and I'll make the Russians believe they won't win if they escalate this war further!"

"Before I grant you permission to execute your plans, can you shed light on how you would do that?" Rufus furrowed his brow.

Patrick paused and cleared his throat; his brain was racing fast. After a deep inhale he proceeded. "So far, we have a murdered scientist at Lockheed Martin. This is an escalation of a different level to slow us down from completing our hypersonic development program. They want to spread fear among our defense scientists, so we will retaliate the same way with a twist!"

"That sounds frightening!" the president gasped. "Go on!"

Patrick decided to skip further thoughts, wondering if the president was reading his briefings from the same morning at all. He pursed his lips; his racing thoughts were deeply rooted in the world of espionage.

The Cabinet members do not have to know everything he does or thinks. *The walls are listening too.* They might chatter the plan accidentally at a gathering of friends or at a political event. So, he shared with the president a piercing stare. The president got the hint and refrained from asking any further questions of Patrick.

The door opened following a short knock and White House Chief of Staff Stanley Spanapolous walked in, dragging behind him the White House butler. He nodded politely to the Cabinet members and led the butler to the credenza with the silver trays of leftover food from the ceremonial room. Then he left a few briefing notes on the table in front of the president, the ones the president hadn't had a chance to read yet.

"Holy Mother of God, Primankov attacked the nuclear power plant causing a radioactive leak?! And this note is for you, Patrick, from Dan!" The president handed Patrick the note.

Traces of explosive residues were found in the scientist's SUV wreckage.

Patrick and the president exchanged glances. "We should keep this to ourselves for now." Patrick said.

The president nodded. "It's the opening shot . . . a direct attack on America." Rufus sighed and raised his tone, "I will not tolerate it!" He shared a glance with Alvin and Patrick and said with a forceful tone as if the Russians could hear him, "Work it out all of you, without opening the missile silo doors, I don't want to get into the muddy fields of war in Europe."

Alvin could not help himself and butt in, "Expect cyber-attacks soon, sir!"

"If you remember Alvin, the Russians hacked Lockheed Martin and copied all our original hypersonic missile designs and—" Patrick stopped.

Alvin aggressively cut him off thinking that Patrick was attacking his defense department and replied, "That was not under my watch."

"That's not my point, Secretary Alvin." Patrick was polite, and at the same time sent a signal to the president. "I want to bring up that the original design had flaws and many snags that the Russian scientists overcame and resolved quickly to my amazement. Their top missile scientist, a Jewish man named Oleg Beerzinkov, originally from Ukraine, changed his Jewish name of Belinkoff to show solidarity with the Soviet Union regime at that time. He was promoted to run the MKB Fakel/Grushin Lab and developed the Russian hypersonic missile; he resolved all the snags in our stolen design. He is the man responsible for giving the Russians a two-year advantage ahead of us. Therefore, my recommendation a couple years ago, was to develop the Hypersonic Interceptor at the same time, which means we also need to invest in new age defenses!"

"We had no budget then to tackle new developments." Alvin jumped in like a cobra ready to strike. "We know of your recommendations and implemented them in this year's budget."

"John Gregory was working on that program too, and he was murdered. Someone leaked the info to our enemy!" said Patrick gloomily.

"I see you connected the dots, Patrick," said the president sadly. "They slowed us but can't stop us! How we go forward from here is up to you!" he raged and growled, frustrated, and looked for a quick fix. "Pay attention to hacking!"

"We do, but the hacking origin is not conclusive, sir. Could be from any computer on Earth or could be a mole in our system!" replied Patrick dramatically. "The North Koreans and Chinese have huge cyber-attack departments and that's all they do!"

"So, we need to secure all the software gaps, put an eye on our scientists' lives, and stop the data leaks! It's pathetic, Patrick!"

"True, we need to refund the Jedi program and have our defense developers start working, sir. We also need to upgrade all our military hardware computers and secure our data," said Cody with a serious tone and look.

"Where have you been? This is what we talked about the last meeting!" scolded the president. "Alvin got the go ahead! It's not like a hocus-pocus and boom, it's done; it's a five-year program." The president looked at General John Duke in the corner of the room who concurred by nodding silently.

Patrick ignored the little temper outburst and referred to the president's first unanswered question.

"I have a plan to stop the flow of information from us to our adversaries, but it will take time. Perhaps it won't help us in Europe's current war, but it will lay the foundation to avoid a Russian invasion into Europe, sir."

"Are you sure, Patrick? Do you really think Primankov is eyeing Europe? This is very serious. Cody might be right; sorry I snapped at you!" The president apologized to his Secretary of State who seemed to lose a little steam.

"Yes, I know how Primankov thinks. We have his full profile and philosophies," replied Patrick.

"He wants to bring Russia back to its USSR glory," Marcus Barbour blasted out from his seat. The NSA director was working closely with Patrick on data breaching and leaks of information to foreign agents. "He demands Russia stole land once owned by his ancestors. He won't stop, his administration is backing him up; the public not so much," said Marcus calmly. "He is a dangerous messianic person!" he added dramatically shaking his head lightly.

The president was puzzled. A sudden headache made the room seem smaller and smaller, pressing on his brain, crunching him like a ten-ton hammer, extracting the oxygen from his lungs with an awful feeling of anxiety.

"Mr. President, drink water please; you look pale," said Alvin ready to take a sarcastic punch resulting from his call.

The president took the glass offered to him, then stood to walk around the table, taking a break. Then he turned around back to his seat. "Thank you, Alvin; sometimes I don't know when to stop. What else gentleman?"

Marcus Barbour intervened and apologized to Patrick, then replied from the NSA perspective. He spoke in a calm tone. "We have no proper response to the hypersonic missile now." Marcus directed the statement to the president. "This missile can endanger our six fleet operations in the Mediterranean Sea if it's involved in the war in Ukraine–"

"Yes!" Alvin yelled. "It could wipe out our navy in one deadly attack if they chose too, so I concur with Marcus!"

The president didn't like to hear the consequences. "Damn! This is serious. I am handcuffed from responding to aggression. Get me out of this, fellows!" thundered the president and held his head again. "We are in this together, and we damn well will get out of this together," he said loudly, and hitting the table with a thud again. There was anxiety in his voice. "All I need is proof that we are under attack, before I order a dusting of our nuke silos, understood?"

All nodded their heads and leaned on the NSA and CIA to keep the Russian horses in the stable as long as they could, until they turned the corner, using all the tricks and schticks available.

"Do I get the green light to act gentleman?" Patrick shot back the question.

Cody jumped back onto the hot seat asking the president about a diplomatic solution with the Russians. The President shook his head and said, "Would you consider heavy sanctions first, sir?"

"Hell NO!" Rufus was quick to respond, raising his voice. "They never worked. Primakov has almost a trillion dollars in his national reserve, another good reason for him to fulfill the greater Russian dream and start a full-scale war. He does business with Iran and China and the sanctions will not be effective in the long run. We need a better plan."

"The HHS secretary asked me to bring this up sir; should we prepare to raise the DEFCON in the event of a radioactive emergencies?"

"Where? Here? Absolutely not, what radiation? Scaring our citizens is the last resort. This also would send the wrong message to our enemy as if we accept the situation and are ready to start a nuclear war. Like we are saying, '*Hey, you see we are ready when you are*,'" he scoffed. "Pathetic!" Then the president waggled his finger at Patrick fondly. "You have my full support to get them Patrick!"

Patrick smiled mischievously. He had a plan already brewing in his head and it was getting better by the minute. Some details, he called "moving parts" were well-aligned like a Swiss clock. Step-by-step, he listed a few objectives he wanted to accomplish to keep his country safe.

"Thank you, Mr. President, you won't be sorry!"

"I am sorry already, Patrick," Rufus scoffed and dropped his head on the table.

CHAPTER FOUR

March 15, 10:01 a.m.

The Northrop B-2 Spirit, named *Kitty Hawk*, serial number 31086, took off on runway 21, southwest, from Naval air station NAS Point Mugu near Los Angeles to an undisclosed destination climbing fast in the same direction as the runway. At 5,000 feet, the bomber banked to the left thirty degrees heading south and continued climbing. Two crew members wore the newly developed oxygen masks as they crunched themselves into the compact cockpit following their flight plan, flying outbound using stealth technology to navigate at 50,000 feet, above commercial flight patterns.

The bomber took off in full view of enthusiastic spectators who were using their special phone app to announce events to watch, and exchange information. They always gathered at that same point on the Pacific Coast Highway taking photos and videos to share with their social media fans. Some knew each other and shared information about their interests or participated in small talk about everything. Others were bloggers, or magazine article writers, and not ruling out, perhaps foreign spying eyes.

Under its right wing, tucked on an external pod was an experimental Lockheed Martin hypersonic missile AGM 183A experimental prototype, a rapid response weapon. On its left wing were two different hanging pods with two long, black, mysterious missile prototypes attached; new missiles never seen before, marked with the same flight mission code name in big white letters 'Polar Protocol'.

Reaching its cruising altitude on schedule heading south toward Antarctica, the captain activated its stealth technology systems and the plane vanished from the radar to the disappointment of the fans who watched the internet for its flight plan. The crew kept code silence.

They were not the only ones watching. Foreign covert intelligence agencies were watching too. "They love free stuff," Patrick Stevenson had said chuckling once when they wanted to show strength for deterrence. "Sometimes you have to throw them a bone to get the rest of the wolf pack exposed." He always recited that mantra.

The communication system hissed and broke its silence.

"*At T-minus fifteen minutes.*" Declared the mission control room, calm and focused.

"Roger!" exclaimed the copilot, Lieutenant Dina Gabish, the youngest crew member in the bomb wing squadron, monitoring her glass cockpit intensely, flying precisely over the green navigation beacon on her screen.

"All looking good," Major Dicker said from the control room, keeping his calm and relaxed tone.

"Roger that," replied the captain, Major Clark Abshille, pilot in command. He lifted two toggle switches up and switched their position forward from off to on. Two tiny red lights turned on, meaning the missile system received the electronic signal and were armed and ready for launch.

"Target coordination location locked," confirmed the copilot with her peaceful voice on the intercom which was also heard in the control room.

The exact target point and target were kept confidential. The control room commander at Vandenberg Space Force Base, Major Remi Dicker dramatically announced, "All systems GO for launch!"

It's been three long hours since the B-2 bomber's departure, flying high above the Pacific Ocean heading to the Southern Ocean close to the frozen Antarctic continent. Still unseen by radar and ready to deploy the hypersonic missile and its Interceptor in a single test.

"Captain, we lost our stealth shield," said the copilot and switched a toggle switch back and forth to reactivate the shield. "Might be a computer glitch; check it out!"

"Control? Are we monitored via satellite?" asked the captain.

"Yes, you are viewed on satellite. Turn on the transponder and proceed with the mission, Captain!" General John Duke, nicknamed Dor, the mission commander, intervened with authority.

"Roger sir!" the captain responded.

"T-minus one minute. Are we GO for launch?" asked the copilot confirming for the last time.

"Affirmative!" exclaimed the general and tapped Major Dicker's shoulder for reinforcement.

"AGM launched and on course southbound; reporting good status," said Major Dicker monotonously watching his screen flickering with a red dot on a straight green line, the missile path.

"Thanks," commented the general, then went to the back of the control room joining the Pentagon representative reporting directly to Secretary of Defense Alvin Nelson who looked like an undefeated wrestler champion.

"AGM locked on the target," added the copilot with a slight excitement in her voice.

"Roger," replied Major Dicker and glued his hazel eyes on the monitors. He looked back at General Duke and the Pentagon representative giving them two thumbs up.

The missile launched showing Weddell Sea on its path, flying straight into Filchner-Ronne Ice Shelf in Antarctica toward Palmer Station, exactly as planned.

Dicker exchanged another glance with General Duke looking for affirmation, he nodded his head and then Dicker stated confidently, "Roger. Go for Interceptor number 1 launch, counting . . . 3 . . . 2 . . . 1 . . . fire!"

"Interceptor number 1 launched, heading the opposite direction of the hypersonic missile. It will attempt to hunt it down by circling the planet to intercept the hypersonic missile!" Major Dicker continued in his low tone, "and search frequencies at the speed of light to lock onto its target."

"The hypersonic missile will lock on its target as planned and the Interceptor will lock onto the hypersonic missile. It's a dual test," explained General Duke to the Pentagon representative next to him, the only civilian in the room. He wore sunglasses and a gray business suit with a yellow tie.

"They fly opposite directions circling the planet?" the Pentagon rep asked curiously.

"Yes," replied General Duke, eager to explain. "The Interceptor is acting as a ballistic missile, twice as fast as the hypersonic missile!"

"So, what's the second Interceptor on the bomber wing pod for?" the rep asked.

"The second Interceptor has a dual mission. First, in case of the first one's failure, and second for computer testing of which attack path is more effective," answered the general, then he paused. "The second Interceptor will fly the same direction and the same path as the hypersonic missile, which flies the opposite direction of the first interceptor!" General Duke chuckled seeing the Pentagon rep's eyes roll in confusion and perplexed expression.

"I'm out," the rep mumbled and shook his head with an embarrassed smile.

"Second Interceptor launched!" declared the B-2 bomber captain and all eyes locked on its route.

The B-2 cockpit conversation was heard over the loudspeakers for guests in the room. The rest of the Air-Force control center technicians and software engineers listened via their headsets, intense and focused.

"Interceptor released successfully, all reading green, heading back to base," announced the bomber captain as his mission at this point of the test was over. "Now it's all under the control of the Air Space Force engineers," explained General Duke and the rep nodded.

The technician and engineers gazed at the monitors. The missile sensors registered every move, speed, height, temperature, and direction of the missile and its interceptors, both flew in different directions around the globe with the intention of meeting before the target was destroyed by the hypersonic missile at the South Pole.

"Control, I have a stabilizing control problem!" reported the captain trying to stay composed.

"What's your emergency, Captain?" asked Major Dicker and moved his head closer to his microphone.

"I can't stabilize the yaw controls after the second Interceptor launched. I'm losing control of the airplane."

"Is it flyable?" asked General Duke concerned.

"We can't . . . it's locked. We are going down!" the copilot breathed hard while trying to stabilize the heavy plane. She murmured aloud, "All computer systems . . . total shut down!

"No way to recover!" the captain hollered. "Mayday!"

"Mark location!" ordered Major Dicker to the technician next to him who seemed to already be on alert.

"Mayday, mayday," the captain declared loudly and started the emergency sequence operation protocols.

"Captain, can you ditch?" yelled General Duke stepping down from the observation platform toward Dicker's post.

"Controls . . . the controls aren't responding. I can't ditch, we are ejecting!" he replied, starting pre-ejection preparations.

"Eject!" cried Major Dicker. "Eject!"

"Good luck, Captain," replied General Duke, ending the communication with the bomber. The communication frequency went down. Silence.

A deadly silence spread a heavy, somber ambiance in the control room. They all looked at each other perhaps for answers or perhaps for console. The plane cameras recorded the ejection and as the entire plane disintegrated into pieces plunging into the Pacific Ocean it left a trail of fireballs.

"Major malfunction," announced Major Dicker in total shock and wiped an invisible tear. "Did we miss anything?" he asked softly.

The Pentagon rep was stunned. He could not figure it out. *Was the crash tied to the missile testing somewhere?* he asked himself. He did not expect an answer from anyone. Everyone was busy figuring out what happened.

Just a few minutes ago the technicians and scientists were cheering and in a great mood now they sat motionless in front of their monitors with horrified faces, open mouths, speechless.

"Major, please declare emergency to rescue the crew!" ordered General Duke.

"Sea and air rescue teams are on the way sir!" Major Dicker reported. "We lost a billion-dollar plane!"

"Worry about the crew, Major," hollered General Duke, disgusted by Dicker's comment.

The red alert light began to flash in the room and the computer monitors flickered.

A technician yelled, "It's the Interceptor, we have a signal, sir!"

"I see," replied Major Dicker.

"It's flying erratically. Not locking," he mumbled more but it was unclear.

"Which one?" yelled Major Dicker back.

"Number one!" replied the technician, excited and almost hyperventilating at his post.

"What about number 2 Interceptor?" asked the major as General Duke watched the drama in tense silence with the Pentagon rep's wide-open eyes staring in disbelief.

"Apparently the missiles are operating!" screamed the technician with joy.

"Doesn't look good for number one!" exclaimed General Duke watching the path of the hypersonic Interceptor on the screen, unlocking from its target and diving into the South Pole below.

"Shall we keep the number 2 Interceptor on course, sir?" asked Dicker, his face inches away from Duke's face. Both locking their eyes on the computer screen as Duke announced aloud, "It's gliding down toward the Palmer Research Station."

"Yes!" shot General Duke. "We need at least one of the Interceptors to succeed on this mission!" he whispered loudly enough so everyone heard him despite the humming of the computers.

"Keep the landing site of the first Interceptor confidential Major Dicker," he ordered. Then he joined the Pentagon rep with explanation of what just happened and said, "After the hypersonic missile is launched, its nose cone is separated in two sections, and activates an automatic navigation glide system toward its target at hypersonic speed. It follows the shallow atmospheric flight path with an extreme degree of maneuverability that can erratically change course making it extremely difficult to destroy it. There was an electronic disconnect between the two frequencies we suppose."

"I lost you!" scoffed the rep.

"The Interceptor and the hypersonic missile transmit frequencies. They need to lock on the same frequency to have a successful kill!" General Duke was patient like a professor.

"So, why was it impossible to lock frequencies? Was it a glitch?" the rep asked.

"One of the challenging reasons it's impossible to kill a hypersonic missile is that it changes its frequency a thousand times a second!"

Time flew by monitoring the test. The B-2 bomber emergency now was under another team's responsibility and Major Dicker needed to concentrate on the success of their mission with all the pain associated with the loss of the bomber. He hoped the crew would survive.

Another alarm sounded and General Duke tensed a second time. Major Dicker raised both his hands and gave a thumbs up.

"The second hypersonic missile Interceptor locked successfully and destroyed its target. A dual success!" Major Dicker declared loudly and shrugged.

"Target destroyed," repeated a technician, satisfied.

"The Interceptor killed the hypersonic missile!" Duke explained to the Pentagon rep who understood the complicated mission.

"Did you record the second Interceptor launching?" General Duke softly asked the technician who last monitored the Interceptor.

"Perhaps there was an electronic malfunction, a glitch with the hanging pod. The captain triggered the emergency release system and the rack plunged into the ocean," answered the technician, worried, and puzzled with disbelief.

"Can we pinpoint where the first Interceptor landed, lieutenant?" General Duke asked the officer monitoring the missile's trajectory.

"Not accurately sir, looks like you were right. It's close to our ice station. If it continued on the same path¬—given the speed, weight, and weather—I assume the first assumption is correct, somewhere on the Filchner-Ronne Ice Shelf," he detailed the data that could affect the landing site location.

The transmissions and communications abruptly ended, and the computer went silent.

"What's that?" asked Major Dicker and arched his shoulders.

"Hacking, sir!" replied the technician. "Our test was hacked and perhaps controlled by a foreign force!" he assumed aloud.

"Dicker, what is he saying? Someone caused the Bomber ditch and the missiles to act radically?"

"My first thought, General, is that the Russian foreign intelligence services SVR and FSB counterintelligence services sometimes collaborate on overseas missions, could have something to do with that," Major Dicker said gravely.

CHAPTER FIVE

Same day, right after takeoff, 9:32 A.M.
Los Angeles

Among the spectators watching the takeoff of the B-2 bomber that day, seated comfortably on top of his van roof, wearing ripped jeans and his favorite MLS soccer team T-Shirt, and using a powerful camera to shoot photos, was Ronald Hill, a military magazine blogger and photographer who worked for *Today's Military World*, a military monthly magazine based in Los Angeles where he lived.

Ron, thirty-seven years old, tall, and slender with slightly arched shoulders, held a double major in communication and computer science engineering from California State University. Diplomas hung in his office a few miles away from where he was now seated.

After graduation he met his first wife, got his green card through this marriage, and then his full citizenship. He divorced later with no children and stayed single since then.

He published articles about everything in the military world emphasizing on aviation, space, new developments, and new weapons. He had thousands of followers on social media from all over the world, most were enthusiastic military fans. The flight he just witnessed was the third, after two previous hypersonic missile tests conducted by the Air Force. He blogged about the first one miserably failing a few months ago and the second a few weeks ago.

Dan Schmidt, the director of the FBI was one of his readers and especially interested in making sure no top-secret information was leaked to the adversaries across the pond.

"Hope to find out where you landed buddy," Ron said to himself out loud for the success of recording the missile testing success. Ron periodically hit this place watching the activities and reporting to his fans who followed him, and this was the third time watching the missile testing. He asked himself what the Bomber was carrying under its wings. It was a completely different and unfamiliar set of missiles than the previous tests. Something new.

One hypersonic missile and two unrecognizable black cylindrical missiles. "Surprise!" he mumbled softly.

The B-52H bomber was previously testing those missiles, and now the B-2 took over that task, thought Ron, *something had to change, sounds stealthy.* He decided to investigate the details later and write his monthly article about it. He turned his Los Angeles Dodger baseball hat around the other way, so he could get his telescopic camera lens to shoot photos.

"Hey," a spectator with cool aviator sunglasses standing close to his van called to him and said, "nice camera you got there!" He smiled with an invitation to start a conversation and asked further, "Nikon?" He pulled his shoulders back and smiled to expose a line of perfectly white teeth. *Another foreigner,* thought Ron hearing the man's slight accent.

Ron was sure he met the guy once somewhere; the voice was familiar. Perhaps his elongated face, blue eyes, and short dirty blond hair crossed his mind; it's a face he couldn't forget. The man was dressed better than the usual nerdy computer engineer would. He probably had thousands of dollars budgeted for nice clothing, accessories, and gadgets, but under his expensive Hugo Boss suit he was wearing a $10 T-shirt you buy on Amazon or AliExpress.

Nah! He pushed that thought away. He remembered him as just an upscale nerd who was easy to connect to events. No one he knew before.

"Yeah, thanks buddy!" he replied laconically turning his camera to the man's face. The man covered his face with his palm.

This man, in his early forties, with an athletic proportional body, had a leather cowboy hat appropriate for this type of event. He smiled broadly and radiated a strong social appearance.

Seems pushy, thought Ron.

"Did you take a photo of the U-2 that passed by a half an hour ago?" the stranger continued and got closer to the van, leaning on its side with one arm.

"NO, that was a B-52," Ron scoffed and tried not to sound too arrogant.

"Oh yeah, the B-52," the man chuckled with embarrassment. "I need more education," he cracked a self-deprecating joke. "Really love that stuff, huh!"

"Ha-ha, me too, that's why I am here!"

"Don't the B-52s fly ahead of any testing, especially new weapon testing?" asked the man and Ron was skeptical of showing off his 'expertise' in military hardware; at least not before he knew who this man was and his objective.

"I don't know," replied Ron and clicked his tongue.

The man stood up straight and raised his chin, "Oh, I am sure, that is what it is!" He tried to hide his accent.

"I am puzzled too; it was a B-2 this time, interesting!" said Ron adjusting his sunglasses to examine the man more carefully.

"Yeah, I noticed the missiles, what are they? All experimental?" he asked, full of charm. "It was too far away to see well!" he exclaimed apologetically.

"This is why I bring my telephoto camera lens!"

"Smart. Is that your hobby? I mean, sniffing around military bases?"

"Sort off, more like something I am paid to do," Ron chuckled. "A paid hobby you could say!"

The man stretched out his hand and said, "Peter, my name is Peter!"

"Nice to meet you Peter. I am Ron. Never seen you here before. Where you from?"

Peter had wide muscular shoulders, a huge, inflated chest, and a large round clean-shaven face. He was charming and social, chatting and talking so fast he gasped for air time-to-time, which sounded funny with his heavy accent. His words sometimes sounded like a mix of blurry sounds, then he said, "We need to grab lunch together sometime soon."

"Sure. By the way, where is your accent from, if may I ask?" Ron tried to ask the question subtly.

Peter chuckled, "Oh you noticed my English? Is it that bad? I thought I sounded American already."

Both chuckled and Peter continued, "I am from Sweden, up north by the way."

"That explains your good English and your accent," Ron chuckled back.

"Do you have a card?" asked Peter.

"No, not with me. You?"

"OK!" Peter waved his hand goodbye without answering back, walked away a few feet then turned around to see if Ron was watching him, and he was. "Strange," Ron murmured softly. Peter entered a rented white Honda Civic on the side of the road and drove away. Then Ron noticed with a slight delay after that another black SUV followed Peter.

"*Sayonara*," Ron waved after the cars.

* * *

Ron drove first to his magazine corporate offices close to Gilbert Lindsay Plaza in LA, picked up what he needed to work from home, and after some socializing with his co-workers he went home which was only a few blocks away on South Hill Street. Peter's face flashed in his mind. *Why do I think I have seen him before?*

Ron could not resist the idea that the FBI approached him a few days ago with a serious offer to watch suspicious spectators who might work for foreign agencies. He was given a ton of materials to read and went for a crash course on how to identify someone, select them as a target, and then report to the FBI who would take it from there.

The FBI agent never exposed his identity. He called himself "J" and after a couple of calls, they met in the downtown FBI offices, and he gave him his business card. *J. Block - used car dealer* with a local LA phone number probably linked to the local FBI office.

Ron wondered if he missed Peter's intentions and per-haps, he was supposed to report him to J. His imagination drifted, asking himself questions about any connection to the test flight itself and his monitoring of spectators from basic training. *The FBI could assign an experienced expert agent, why me? But J's explanation was what got me hooked,* Ron thought. He was a well-known celebrity military blog-ger, and no one would suspect him of fishing for foreign spies and turning them in.

"It's a serious national security issue and I can elabo-rate," said J and that intrigued Ron enough to think he should take the shot and collaborate. *It was probably his expertise in aviation and military hardware predictions that got someone's attention,* Ron thought. As a writer he learned that his articles should be authentic and accurate, that is what gravitated his readers to subscribe to his magazine and log on to his blogger website.

Ron's mind analyzed the moving parts. It looked like the FBI was after something big, perhaps after Peter himself. Perhaps they wanted to keep him loose to monitor his moves.

His cellphone rang and he answered. "Speak of the devil," he mumbled noticing it was already close to midnight, time flies.

"Ron here," he answered laconically. The phone number was discrete and read "*unknown*", typical of a spam call.

"Hi, Ron. We suspect the man you talked to is a Russian intelligence agent," J went straight to business.

"Oh really? Nice. Why are you telling me this?" Ron asked, somewhat uptight.

"No worries. You are safe. We wanted to observe his activities!"

"Well, good to hear. How safe?" Ron sounded sarcastic. "You just told me I spoke to a Russian agent, and I should feel safe?" Ron paused and waited for a response, then he burst out loudly, "He was probably armed! Why didn't you arrest him? Strange. At least you could tell me more what this game is all about?" Ron shrugged, annoyed.

"Calm down. Ask not what the country can do for you—"

"And what you can do for your country, right? Which country?" Ron completed the famous statement from JFK's inauguration ceremony, but then said, "Spare me this bullshit crap J, how many people in this country really care for the country?"

J was not in a mood to joke or go into a political discussion he may lose and said dead-seriously, "We need to know Peter's objectives, there was some sniffing around our hypersonic missile test; I want to know what he knows. Is he getting any valuable information from your blogs?"

"My blogs are censored J!"

"We suspect that there is an entire network in the USA, this is why we just monitor looking to catch the big fish, understand?"

"Go on, I am listening."

J got to business. "Why do you think we chose you? This is more important than you think. We want to intercept the SVR disinformation about the test of the Poseidon in North Sea and see if there is anything about the test you witnessed today. I am sure you know that most adversaries' intelligence agencies follow your blog!"

Silence. *Is this a trap?* Ron asked himself.

Ron could hear J breathing hard on the phone. He wondered if the FBI suspected him of collaborating with a foreign agency. He needed to do what the FBI agent asked to show his loyalty, after all he was considered a naturalized citizen, expert in defense military information, and his ideology was never put to a test. *This is it, it's a test!* He smiled.

"J listen, I don't think I am competent enough for this. I have no expertise in espionage or tracking people. The two hours in your office didn't make me James Bond!" Ron replied and then lightly scoffed, "I can't do what you ask!"

The phone line hissed.

"Look!" J exclaimed. "The Russians intercepted a message. It's about the missile mission test today. I would like to use your blog to confirm the test as a failure. Your followers will join a talk in the comments. You have many fake followers who are cyber agents sitting in offices around the world sending false messages to create chaos. We don't want anyone to know the test was a total success."

Ron was very surprised to get this kind or any kind of info from J. It started to become clear that there was something tricky going on with the third US hypersonic missile test. No one was sure what the test result was, especially broadcasting that the B-2 was lost in the middle of the Pacific Ocean. *So, the FBI wants to use his blog for disinformation?* he asked himself.

"What was the purpose of the black missile on the other pods under the B-2 wing," asked Ron.

"That is top-secret Ron. It's a combination of failure and success, you understand?"

"NO!" Ron was decisive. *If the US failed the test, it would put the country's military in a panic? Or did they want to sabotage a full success, but why?* Ron asked himself.

That was an answer he needed to confirm for his blog anyway. The speculations would soon hit the media and he didn't want to lose the opportunity to gain more popularity by being in the middle of it all.

J continued his momentum.

"We also know that the test flight control room was hacked and the SVR was listening to the entire test live. Peter might know something about it," J continued. "We knew that Peter would take the bait, and now it's show time," he explained. Ron listened peacefully. "He was after you!"

Ron gasped and looked through his open home office window for fresh air. "In other words, I am your Guinea Pig. How should I defend mysel—"

"We watched you all the time Ron! We followed Peter after he left you this morning from the observation deck. Trust me!"

"You don't leave me much of a choice, J. Should I trust the 9mm Barrera you gave me?" He chuckled.

"Do what you need to do, Ron!"

"Peter was the most polite foreign agent," Ron grinned. "Totally excited and curious to see a B-2 bomber taking off for the first time, like most of the spectators there. It's an impressive scene, by all means."

J cleared his throat and didn't rush to ask for more questions. Then after a short silence on the line he cleared his throat again saying, "As a well-known military reporter, you were his subject of interest. Sorry we used you as bait, he could not resist," J emphasized the last few words.

"It's a puzzle, J, perhaps you don't know everything," Ron sighed. "All I know in your world, yes is no, no is yes and maybe is never!"

"Yes, that sounds right, and we all are just small piece of the puzzle!" J inhaled deeply and Ron exhaled softly. His mind raced for answers he could not find. *It's only getting interesting and more dangerous,* he thought.

J paused thinking for a couple of seconds before Ron proceeded. "Yeah, it seems strange to me, it's like we purposely advertised the test flight to everyone asking all foreign intelligence spies to come and watch. Then invited them to a news conference to answer all their questions. Is it a failure or success and which part is what?" Ron grinned and stretched his stiff neck.

"Right, it seems strange to you Ron, I know!" J exclaimed. "It's an advertising deterrent."

"Not sure I want to be in your shoes J, all I am getting from you is very confusing and contradicting information. You basically want me to put sense to it and advertise it on my blog!"

"It's a confidential puzzle, Ron! We already said that one day it will be very clear to you and me, promise. So, you have my card, call me if you need!"

J hung up the phone before Ron had the opportunity to respond. He muttered to himself, "Weird guy." J did not put Ron at ease, but before he forgot the episode, Ron went back on his computer to write the article when the info was still fresh in his mind.

He turned off all the apartment lights on the fourth floor of the small residential building. The cool breeze from the window kept him awake and he started clicking the keyboard as the computer screen gleamed a faint light that reflected on Ron's face. In the corner of his room his Smart TV was on CNN news, showing the military test.

* * *

At 11:12 p.m. CNN station flashed with big red "BREAKING NEWS" letters tab at the bottom of the screen.

Ron turned up the volume. The anchor with a very serious dramatic expression on her face moved her head from left to right, and announced:

I am Pamela Graham with a special report: A military B-2 stealth bomber on a special secret assignment vanished over the Pacific Ocean. The military spokesman declined any further details on the disappearance and confirmed it was a routine mission which they had done many times before. The incident was under investigation as Navy rescue vessels and search and rescue aircrafts were rushed to the scene where the aircraft was last reported. Our military contributor, General (ret.) Heath Roland is here with us. General what can you tell us about the incident?

"Huh well, I am very sad for the families of the aviators. It's a big loss."

"But General, we interviewed a couple of spectators who said it was a new military missile experiment!"

"Yes, without shedding any further details, it was a very successful b—"

"The Air Force lost one experimental missile!"

Ron turned off the TV. They added more confusion, he thought. He figured that it was the same bomber he watched earlier taking off with the experimental hypersonic missile. "It's a total disaster, missile failure and now the plane is gone?" he whispered.

My FBI involvement started to take a turn for the worse in its very first step. Might be a connection between the bad news, the FBI inquiry, and Peter showing up in the scene, Ron thought.

A clanking noise from his entrance doorknob put him on alert. Someone at the door was twisting the doorknob, trying to open the door silently. "Damn, crazy." Ron tensed and his skin bristled. All his senses sharpened, and he opened the desk drawer and pulled out his 9mm Beretta handgun and adjusted its silencer. He could not be happier to be one of the supporters of the second amendment, even though J gave him this gun with a temporary license.

He carefully approached his front door in the dark, on his toes and with his back against the wall. Then, as the knob was still twisting, he moved to the shadowed wall across from the door to face the intruder.

"They are looking for you!" The voice of J echoed in his ears. "I'll crack his skull," he whispered to cheer himself up. *It's Peter,* the thought crossed his mind like rolling thunder. *My polite friendly spy.*

"Drop your gun, Ron!" The low voice sounded like thunder and came from his side entry near his computer room. The accent was familiar.

Ron had been so ready to greet the person at the front door he neglected to watch the hallway from the office, allowing someone to climb the fire-escape and enter through a slightly open window. *Smart plot,* Ron thought. He bet the person behind the door already left. Ron nervously froze and raised his hands.

Ron stood shrouded, waiting for the man's next step. His first instinct was to fire, but he was at a disadvantage not being trained for a situation like this. *Better to follow his instructions,* Ron thought.

"Turn on the light, Ron!"

"Peter?" Ron asked spontaneously. "You sound like Peter!"

The man's voice had an accent that sounded fresh in Ron's mind, the same unforgettable European mix of Russian and German.

"Turn on the light, Ron, now!"

Ron slowly turned on the foyer light and Peter opened the front door a crack, "Thanks Carlos, I'll take it from here!" He dismissed his temporary helper, a homeless man.

Peter wore the same cloths from earlier that morning at the spectator's deck, he still wore those leather cowboy boots.

"Long day, Peter? Isn't a shame to ruin an expensive suit climbing emergency steps?" Ron called out with disbelief that he had the courage to provoke Peter who had his handgun pointed at him. Ron shrugged it off as a way to ease his initial shock.

"Pieter! My name is Pieter to you Ron. Nice apartment, who pays for it? The SVR? The SSU, Ukraine must be desperate for intel these days," Pieter replied with a tone of sarcasm without revealing his objectives.

"What do you want? Who do you work for?" Ron responded.

"First, drop your gun."

Ron obeyed and the handgun dropped onto the floor with a loud metal thud.

"I am sure you figured out who am I at this point, right Ron?" Pieter's icy tone was chilling, and his eyes watched Ron's every move.

"No, not really, I haven't. I'm not sure how you could follow me to my apartment. What do you want?" Ron's chest pounded. *I was right. He was followed by the Russian SVR agent.* A tsunami of adrenalin put additional pressure on his chest, it became hard to breathe, and the room began spinning around him.

"From your van license plate, free internet domain information, a military expert Ronald Hill. We need people like you," scoffed Pieter. "Stealing identity and marketing it for profit, Ron?"

"Who is *we*, people like *you*?" Ron asked and a chill went down his spine. "How did you get into the building?"

"I called a homeless locksmith," Pieter chuckled. "We have friends everywhere," he said arrogantly. "I need all the information you have about your hypersonic missile development and its Interceptor plans!"

Ron let out a short nervous laugh. "What plans? I am not working for Lockheed Martin!"

"Stop Ron, I mean the Russian plans, the ones you stole from Lockheed Martin and transferred to the SVR!" he raised his tone and made sure the gun's nozzle was aimed at Ron's chest. "You being a disguised FBI agent is a big achievement, and we seem to think you know more then you want to admit. I want everything about the Interceptor, the CAD plans, specifications, everything you got and sold to the world!" He spat the words fast and directed Ron back to his office's glowing computer while the cold silencer nozzle poked Ron's neck.

"What are you saying? I am marketing the complete development plans to foreign agencies?"

"Turn on your computer!"

"It's on. What do you want to see?"

"Your password," the nozzle urged Ron to comply. "Click it!"

Ron clicked the keyboard, and the screen came on with all his apps, in a very organized matter.

"Here we go!" said Pieter. "The design drawings!"

Ron looked at his screen and saw very detailed information about the missile program and its Interceptor and was in shock. *Who planted it on his computer?*

"Someone hacked my computer!" Ron's head was spinning. "This is not my doing!"

"Sure, that's what they all say, 'It's not me!'" Pieter chuckled.

"Move to the corner, slowly! Over there, sit down on the floor, and stop playing with me Ron. You have all this info, and we want to make sure it goes to the right place," Pieter scoffed.

"What's the file password? It's encrypted!"

"I don't know, someone transferred those plans files to my computer, I swear!" Ron sighed. "Let me see, can I?"

"Slowly," Pieter aimed his gun at Ron who moved slowly and glanced at the screen.

"Yeah, I don't recognize those files. Someone hacked me."

"I don't have much time. I want to see your Outlook, where those filed were transferred to."

"I..."

"Don't move Ron, go back to your corner slowly!"

Ron sat back in the same corner, confused as he watched Pieter going through all his files. He tried to distract Pieter. "Pieter, I don't know who you work for, as far as I know Russia already deployed the hypersonic missiles on submarines, what else are you looking for?" asked Ron and released a short snort. "I am a reporter–"

"Shut up Ron!" Pieter thundered.

"We all know the Russians will not allow any government to have the hypersonic Interceptor, not before all the military goals are achieved in Europe!" Pieter said without disclosing who sent him and which agency is behind him.

"What goals? Conquer Ukraine, Poland?"

"No Ron, conquer fucking Europe. If you are an FBI agent, which I know you are, your government and NATO created a strong alliance to protect Europe, and the Russian leaders thought it was the right time to start a linear war after the success in Crimea."

"Oh, I guess you work for the SVR then."

"Does it matter? If your government wasn't tangled in the stupid Iranian nuclear agreement and hadn't left the door open to Primankov to announce victory and retreat, all this crap wouldn't have happened!"

Ron was not sure which agency was confronting him, felt that Pieter could be unpredictable, and this could go in any direction with bad results. Not sure why the SVR would turn to him, he selected his words carefully. Perhaps there was an identity mix-and-match error, perhaps the agent mixed him with someone else, but that didn't change the reality of a Walther PPK pointed to his head. It was way after midnight, and he felt his body caving to exhaustion.

"This is a brilliant cover Ron, an FBI agent specializing in military hardware, disguised engineer as a magazine re- porter." Pieter licked his lips while continuing to type on the computer keyboard with one eye watching Ron as he sat on the floor.

"Transferring files to my contacts now," Pieter said. "Wow, two hours and fifty-one minutes, I better take the desktop with me. So, which ideology are you loyal to, Ron?"

"It's all public domain, didn't you hear the news? The bomber plane vanished over the Pacific Ocean, the test failed, and the crew is missing." He sounded threatened and impatient, his Beretta was too far away on the floor and that made him feel vulnerable.

"I know all this. I want to know where the Interceptor landed. I thought you might know."

Ron scoffed. "How do you know it landed? The airplane crashed!"

"Yes, from that perspective the mission was a failure, but one Interceptor hit the target and the other one landed I believed in Antarctica."

"Then you know more than me," Ron declared and wondered what Pieter would do next. Would he kill him? Ron didn't doubt he could do that. The info Pieter shared was a game changer. If it's true, every agency in the world would love to put their hands on that piece of technology. With the Interceptor deployed, it would send the hypersonic missile neutralized back to storage.

Ron looked tiredly for ways to get the upper hand on Pieter. He needed to initiate a move to save his life, otherwise he could count the remaining minutes before his last breath. He passed the need to resolve any identity error and despite his anxiety, he slowly gained the courage to act.

His heavy Nikon camera was still on his desk next to Pieter who pushed it to the edge of the table to have more room to use the keyboard.

"Pieter, CNN or Fox will tell you more than my computer!" Ron tried to distract. His mouth felt dry, and his voice cracked harshly.

"Where is the file of the Interceptor and the B-2 bomber test?" Pieter snorted.

"Let me show you. May I approach?"

"Easy, slowly, no tricks or I'll shoot you, Ron."

Ron made a slow step forward, approaching his desk.

"The file name is 'Polar Protocol'. That's the name of the mission," Ron whispered. He was tensed and his muscles felt like tight springs ready to explode. He couldn't let Pieter get away with this even though the article didn't shed much light on the top secret, confidential information about the mission. He tried imagining how he could take Pieter down and he needed to find the courage to make the first step. He hesitated and Pieter noticed.

Ron went through his files which required another set of passwords and Pieter cried, "Got it!"

Pieter was distracted for a second going through the file photos, notes with explanations, and detailed specifications. The complex draft article was not planned for his readers. Ron stood closer blocking Pieter's view of the heavy camera on his desk. In a split-second decision, he grabbed the camera strap quickly, swung it around, and slammed Pieter on the back of the head with full force.

Pieter was surprised and shocked. His intuition didn't help him this time. The camera slammed into the computer screen while he groaned still holding his cocked gun tight. Ron tried to reach his gun on the floor while Pieter was paralyzed trying to clear his vision. Pieter was quick to recover from the sharp pain inflicted on the back of his head and neck knowing that his life was on the line.

Ron jumped on the floor and stretched out his hands to grab the gun while trying to twist his torso for an accurate shot. But Pieter was faster, and his silencer released the flop sound and the bullet hit Ron. He groaned as his body dropped back onto the flat floor slammed lifeless in a trail of thick red blood. His eyes were still open wide glaring at Pieter while he choked and spewed blood from his open mouth. Then he closed his eyes.

The computer chimed with a new email notification addressed to Ron and Pieter clicked on the link and read it twice.

Confidential. Erase after reading. This message is not to be used in your circles.

The Interceptor *was a big success, however, one of two* Interceptors *had a glitch and landed in Antarctica somewhere on Filchner-Ronne Ice Shelf. Searching for it now before the wrong eyes find it, take care.*

The source of the email was unknown.
Pieter replied with an email:
Your agent is down; he is no use for us anymore!

Then he typed an email message to his contact:
Agent neutralized; his desktop will be delivered via our regular diplomatic channels. Worth seeing.

Then Pieter vanished down the dark alley as the light wind blew drizzle from the west making him feel fresh and alive.

His phone vibrated. An encrypted cell phone message:
Good Job. Dispatch yourself to Hilton Wembley London. Meet the coach.

CHAPTER 6

March 16, 2022, 6 a.m.
White House Situation Room
Emergency development meeting

It was early Wednesday morning, and the president was grumpy. His grim face displayed his mood. Three hours earlier, Ron had been attacked in his home by a foreign agent. It was still dark and a brisk 38 degrees outside, sunrise was at 7:18 a.m.

The weatherman promised another mild day to warm up the Capitol which was preparing for the Easter Holidays. The White House prepared its annual holiday festivities projecting to the public that all was calm.

The situation room was warm and comfortable with a light odor of furniture polish. However, it was hard to cover up the tension in the room. No refreshment was offered yet, and the Security Cabinet impatiently waited for the president who was the last to enter the room, like a storm. His presence was noticed, and so were his eyes which showed the signs of a restless sleep. He wore his slippers and the casual training outfit he slept in.

"Good morning, gentleman. Sit down!" he growled. "What the hell is this?" He started the meeting with a snort, lifting a few newspapers' headlines from the table. "C'mon, hit me. What can you tell me?" The president's agitation escalated. "I thought we had a year, maybe two, tops!" He shrugged and slammed the conference table, his usual attention-getting act. "Did anyone know about this?"

Rufus Barker, the President of the United States, who was known for his calm nature and rational leadership, snapped at his Security and Defense Cabinet. They had all assembled in the situation room after an emergency invite upon hearing the "breaking news" on CNN and reading the headlines on the morning newspapers. He was agitated. He frowned and stared at his cabinet members one by one looking for answers. Their silence let him vent first. They knew how serious this was since his fuming was out of character.

The global tensions simmering in Europe and Asia were concerning for the US military and Defense forces and the Cabinet knew what the meeting would be about. One thing was for sure, it would be ugly as hell, and some of them were not sure what the president was hoping to accomplish. Was he searching for someone to blame before finding a solution? Or would he concentrate on diffusing tensions around the world? The red phone line between the Kremlin and the White House established after the Cuban Missile Crisis was silent for sixty years and Rufus did not expect the Russians to use it first.

"Patrick, what does the CIA have to say?" Rufus pointed at the early morning newspapers spread on the conference table, the headlines circled in red marker to emphasize the subjects. Rufus never felt so close to a nuclear war and wanted to keep Russia, China, North Korea, and Iran who were muscled up, at bay. Rufus locked eyes with the head of the spy agency for response.

Having been with the CIA, serving four presidents in various positions in the agency, he knew each one of them like he knew the palm of his hand. Patrick ran complex global missions last year and was promoted a couple of years ago to run the spy agency after successfully handling a series of high-profile incidents. Several of the most notorious cases were the assassination attempt on the president during his inauguration ceremony, and the "Doomsday Alley" incident with the Russian navy, sparked by the threat of a deadly epidemic.

Patrick cleared his throat and kept his face stern. He pursed his lips, then looked at Marcus Barbour, the director of the NSA who sat next to him. Marcus was his previous boss, not counting the short period someone else took the helm and quit. Patrick hoped he wouldn't be the first one to talk in this emergency meeting. He had cursed the Chief of Staff, who woke him up at 12:02 a.m. ordering him to join the mandatory meeting without any prior preparation. "Lack of sleep" was his middle name now.

"Well, Mr. President." He paused as all eyes were on him. Patrick hoped to send them back to their regular days soon. "All I can tell you is that we already know that the Russians and the Chinese have operational hypersonic missiles. General John Duke can shed light on that matter from the technical point of view. We are behind on our development here at home and only a couple of weeks ago it was tested. The defense contractor engineers at Lockheed Martin evaluated its data. As far as the stealth bomber which vanished–" Patrick searched his colleagues' faces before he continued, staring back at the president. "It's the secret plan we talked about in our last meeting. With your approval, I can go on."

Alvin, the defense secretary, raised his chin and chimed in. "We should keep the plan confidential and low-profile, sir. We don't want to show panic, Mr. President!" He inhaled deeply to cover a yawn.

Patrick proceeded. "People are tracking airplanes with free applications and others are simulating flights on computer simulators as a hobby, then downloading it on Twitter, Facebook, and Instagram and it looks real. This is creating a disinformation chain of chaos. Intelligence agencies have seen tons of videos about that missing B-2 bomber and its mission's purpose since it disappeared from the radar yesterday. People posting speculations that the bomber landed in Area 51 or in Diego Garcia and this is all bluff. For your information we have the situation under control, sir."

"That's all I want to hear; I will not ask you any more questions." Rufus was amazed when he heard the rest of Patrick's plan and nodded his head time to time. "I hope this will work," Rufus mumbled. "Or you all can leave your office keys on my desk!"

Marcus, the NSA director, reinforced Alvin saying, "It's part of our big plan to give the defense contractors the time they need to resolve the design glitches and fix the bugs on the final development."

The president was not at ease; however, he had no choice. He needed to trust all the minds in the room. He felt the burden of running a complex country and navigating it through a military disadvantage crisis again. Then he barked as if he forgot all that was discussed before, "Why is that, that we are never prepared? What happened to our national wisdom, national ingenuity, and world class innovation?" He waggled his finger and squinted. "Yes, I agree that our adversaries, scrutinizing every piece of information with a magnifying glass, whether true or false, is not good for us. If we don't have the Interceptor operational, it means the Russians and Chinese will not hesitate in executing their plans to expand. That leaves me with the dilemma of how to respond. So, where are we standing today? We must cut short the technological gap with an upper hand."

They all agreed that the situation was unbearable, and he hated to act in response to failures and deal with the escalating cost of new hardware developments. To shift defense funding to the hypersonic missile, and its Interceptor, it was decided to turn off the cash flow to the F-22 Raptor future production. They would also put on hold the development of the new sixth generation jet fighter and its new avionics systems, so they can invest funding, for a limited time, to cover the burning issues.

"DARPA put a lot of pressure on the contractors to show progress," Alvin said as it was under his Defense Department's responsibility to manage the "Defense Advance and Research Project Agency."

"Bottom line, gentleman, the gravity of the situation is that it doesn't matter how you dress the issue up, without a proper deterrent like having the Interceptor operational, we lose the ex-Soviet bloc alliance a second time. Do I make myself *clear*?" the president emphasized the last word. "Not on my watch. Now get me the fucking hypersonic Interceptor operational in three months, not six! Meanwhile, what aid do you recommend sending to Ukraine, Alvin?"

"We asked them for a list of military equipment that we can ship from Ramstein, but I would wait to see how the war develops!" replied Alvin who shook his head slightly defying the military aid request politely. He knew that his mighty navy was vulnerable without defending themselves against the enemy's hypersonic missiles. "So we come in first," he said when meeting with his top brass. Alvin inhaled.

Marcus Barbour added his thoughts from the NSA point of view. "We cannot get involved early in the conflict, sir. The hypersonic missile impact could destroy a Navy carrier with no defense. See how they shred Ukraine with these missiles and vessels in one launch and threaten its military power as now they are cutting Ukraine to pieces. With that situation we cannot respond effectively or deter dictators from challenging us, and Alvin thought it was best to wait for a better time and I agree. We should not provoke Primankov any further, otherwise he could be pushed to use unconventional mass destruction weapons, tactical nukes."

The president listened with full focus, then said with a somber tone, "It is scary times and I understand the state the country is in." *Where is JFK when we need him?* passed through his thoughts. Then he replied to Patrick, "I don't get it Patrick. You lost me there saying, 'We have a plan' and explained it. Is this the only CIA option?" The president frowned waiting for an answer. He wiped an unseen cold sweat from his forehead with his handkerchief looking grim.

Under the confidentiality in this forum, Patrick disclosed his plan in further detail looking for support and approval. The Cabinet and the president nodded tensely and gave Patrick a serious glance that questioned his inner soul and twisted mind.

"That could work Patrick. I can see this plan as *part* of the efforts but not in lieu!" the president exclaimed hoping for a better answer in the future. "I am glad their Poseidon test failed," Rufus murmured and started a small chatter that quickly subsided.

"The CIA's plan will give us time to complete our design development sir, but I'm not sure three months is a realistic time schedule!" intervened General John Duke, seated all the way back on the other side of the table; he moved uncomfortably in his chair.

"CNN is dispatched to help," Patrick disclosed, almost in a whisper as if someone was listening to their conversation using advanced listening devises across the street from the White House.

"I am concerned about President Primankov proudly announcing in his 'state of the empire' speech in front the entire world, '*We will use nukes*'. Basically, taunting us. I want to make sure we do not go belly-up, gentlemen, and we do not jeopardize our national security status!" The president made it clear to his Cabinet that the military must step up and respond to the adversary's military advancements. "I can't tolerate it!" he growled with frustration.

"It is the previous administration's fault that the missiles are not deployed yet!" exclaimed Marcus. "They stopped the development, called it a *'low priority'* even though Patrick, the CIA agency, and my department, warned them on every opportunity that it would haunt us in the end."

"It's mixed information. Primankov announced he deployed his hypersonic missiles on every Russian navy boat and submarine, and all the strategic heavy bombers, if we should attack them." replied Alvin.

"It could be a bluff, like Reagan's 'Star Wars' plans. We should not make a stupid move, but we should prepare for war!" the president said softly.

How much can we absorb, thought Patrick, *we get it.* Then Patrick took the helm to lead the conversation with an analogy, perhaps to allow them all to go back to work. "Last year the Russian missile failed miserably exploding and resulting in a nuclear mushroom. Did they resolve all the bugs? We don't know. Then there's the second catastrophic failure in the Doomsday Alley event, exploding a Russian nuclear submarine with a second mushroom cloud. Do you think we should operate under the premise that we don't have any evidence of the Russian hypersonic missile with a nuke warhead will be used? Is it true? Perhaps they are bluffing?"

"We need to take their deployment seriously!" mumbled Marcus as he looked at Patrick.

"Assume they will," said the president.

"But we also have China which is backing the Russians by announcing the successful testing of its own!" Alvin responded.

"That upsets me. Look at the headlines!" Rufus spat looking again at the latest editions of morning newspapers. "Look!" the president exclaimed and immediately recited aloud, almost slurring, "CNN! Quote: 'A nuclear capable hypersonic missile successfully operated on Kiev', *The Guardian*: 'Second successful test as China nears passing the US hypersonic missile development race', *New York Times*: 'Successful attacks using the hypersonic missiles, echo the sputnik surprise launch that woke us up. Wake up America', *The Washington Morning Star*: 'As always, we are the last to know, embarrassing'. Should I go on and on and on? It's agitating! What will the *people* think?"

Marcus responded with caution, trying not to step on any landmines; volunteering to take the president's next punches if he chose to scold him. "We are quite aware of the situation. We will prevail guys. Don't we always prevail?" He sounded cheery, trying to erase the gloomy ambiance in the room.

"Thank you, Marcus, for your optimistic approach. I expected more. Alvin, any comment?" Rufus gazed at his secretary of defense who was silently drifting into his own thoughts for a moment.

"I think the Russians and Chinese collaborated, creating a unified front against us," said Alvin.

"We know that, Alvin!" snapped the president and waggled his finger.

The barrage of legitimate questions put pressure on the Cabinet, especially on Alvin Nelson. The ex-marine, highly decorated general, was born and raised in Harlem, fought all his life against all odds to excel at West Point, and graduated at the top of his class. He was the tallest presidential Cabinet member, with a wrestler's body reminiscent of André the Giant, the professional wrestler from years ago. He took the post as the top US military soldier with anticipation of a calm global environment. He looked back at the president, curled his lips and with a tense look, shook his head lightly.

"Honestly sir, it's ugly and we all know it. We got caught with our pants down. I get it. We thought we had another six months to a year to get up to speed with the Russians and Chinese military hardware. We don't have any measures or capabilities to intercept any aggression of this kind yet, but it–" Alvin was cut off by the president. He lowered his head and shrugged.

"Alvin, that's exactly my point!" The president could not hold his temper. "Not being prepared! It's like we committed treason . . . all of us!"

Then in a rage, he aggressively swiped all the newspapers from the table with his right hand, scattering them on the situation room carpet. He gulped his coffee before slamming the mug forcefully on the table. "Get me out of this gentleman!" he thundered.

CHAPTER 7

March 16, 2022, 10:12 a.m.
Langley VA, CIA Headquarters

From the situation room it took Patrick about an hour in morning traffic to get back to his office. Light rain mixed with snow and gentle wind, made the wipers squeak with every swipe.

"When did you check those wipers last?" he asked his driver while going over emails on his iPhone.

"They are new!" snapped the driver watching the road.

The emails on his phone piled up after the meeting with the president.

What's up Alvin? Patrick replied to an email.

The president didn't officially permit the navy submarine to start the hide-and-seek games with the Russians navy fleet. Alvin emailed.

I don't understand. What is he waiting for? The first shot? Patrick replied.

You do what you need to do, and I will do what I need to do!! replied Alvin with two exclamation marks. *Do what the CIA does best!* Alvin sent another email without waiting on a reply.

Patrick's mind started to roll through his plans. He totally agreed with Alvin to get the ball rolling and prepare his agency to do what they do best: direct his agents on the ground, collect data, hack anything that could shed light on how the Russians resolved the stolen plane, with all its glitches had a Lockheed Martin hypersonic missile that their design team didn't control yet.

Part of his plan was to steal the planes back from the Russian MKB Fakel known as "Grushin, Machine Building Design Bureau" and create a profile on its lead engineers: learn everything about their habits, political orientation, family, friends, marital affairs, anything that can lead to an extortion, kidnaping, elimination or lead to new top-secret info. He directed his department to target and profile Oleg Beerzinkov especially, the lead on the hypersonic missile development team. If the president wants to cut the plan from six months to three, Patrick needed Oleg to overcome the glitches faster than his overseas American scientist colleagues.

Patrick already knew Oleg lived a mysterious life. He left his wife when she was pregnant in Ukraine to join a special closed scientist cult in Soviet Russia. A science ghetto to develop futuristic new Russian weapons, working nonstop to challenge and race the American development which threatened to control the world.

He was a pure communist, socialist, idealistic, a pure loyal groupie of the communist regime. After the collapse of the Soviet Union, he joined Primankov's party and supported his tough policies against the western world which he saw as demonic, as did most Russian scientists his age.

When he returned home a year later for a short visit in Kiev, his wife's new boyfriend opened the front door. Shortly after, they got divorced and she remarried while their daughter, Inna, was a toddler who knew only her step father. When she started to form a pro-western ideology at college in Moscow, she opposed and confronted her father for helping the Russian military machine kill innocent people in Ukraine.

Inna was not thrilled to find out what her father did for a living. She especially opposed his communist political ideology and his long career in the military science labs. She despised the old regime with its old-fashioned doctrines of the "Greater Russia" and slogans that the west was the "evil empire". She ridiculed the old animosity and tough line toward the west, even though the west was not perfect itself however, she accepted its flaws. She supported peace and young people mingling and interacting with the world through social media. One part she agreed with after the fall of the Soviet Union, though she was born long after that event, was the effect of open markets on the economic side improving the life of Russian citizens and its ex-bloc countries.

Across the pond at the same time, Lucy, Patrick's most experienced and most daring CIA agent in his arsenal, walked into his top floor office in Langley, skipped knocking on his open office door, entered, and then closed the door behind her. Victoria acknowledged her with a fake smile and let her pass through without any drama. "He is expecting you." She sounded bored and went back to her phone conversation.

Patrick, with his back to the door, stood in front of the bulletproof glass window blocking the sun with his tall body and wide shoulders. His white hair lit by the sun looked like he was exposed to electrified air during a lightning storm.

His earbud was attached to his right ear, apparently, he was talking to someone. He turned around to face his "stray cat" agent whose bold red lips accented her smile.

"Hello stranger," she whispered knowing that he was capable of listening to two conversations at the same time. She giggled.

She sat confidently on the leather armchair without invitation. She wore a soft black cotton jumpsuit that hugged her slender toned body and low-heeled pointy red shoes which she considered her secret weapon when the Beretta was holstered. A red silky scarf hung around her long smooth neck, imitating the exotic look of a foreign airline stewardess. In addition, a large red leather belt cinched her waist into a curvy hourglass form around her hips. All accessories matched her shoes. "My Chanel girl," Patrick used to call her from time-to-time and chuckled. He knew how much those outfits cost at Nordstrom. Patrick wore a boring navy-blue business suit, white shirt, and red tie, something you would find at Macy's, like most of the agents in the office.

Still on the phone after she sat down, Patrick put his iPhone on speaker and signaled her to listen with lips sealed. She carefully paid attention to the conversation.

"How do you know we have a mole and where?" Alvin asked, sitting in his Pentagon office watching the planes taking off from Reagan National Airport.

"Oh yeah, Alvin. Our cyber department intercepted an encrypted 'killer' email which was attached and said that a few 'hypersonic missile' design files were transferred to an unknown address in Russia. I presume probably to the SVR headquarters in Moscow. We are tracking the transaction from where and whom it was sent to."

"Do you mean they stole our design? What would they do with our design if we don't have the equipment operational yet?" Alvin was skeptical and challenged Patrick.

Lucy nodded quietly but was not surprised to hear that. She thought the country was full of spies and double agents roaming the neighborhoods and information was more valuable than oil or gold.

A quick knock on the door made them tense especially with his request to hold anyone from entering his office.

When Patrick identified the agent, he allowed him in. The sullen-faced desk duty agent walked in without his blazer or tie, took a quick look at Lucy as courtesy, and handed a short briefing note just sent by his cyber department, then closed the door behind him.

"He looked pale," mumbled Patrick. "Hold on Alvin, I got an interesting briefing just now," he said and recited the note: "*A Russian nuclear sub was spotted testing the hypersonic missiles one hundred miles from the coast of Virginia.* Damn, when it rains, it pours!" Patrick reacted abruptly. "Our deterrent is eroding badly; that also means a signal to us that they deployed their subs with those missiles and it's not a bluff."

Alvin sighed, inhaled deeply, and said, "Patrick, you still didn't answer my question, how come the Russians are operational with our stolen incomplete design while we are still struggling with bugs?"

"It's simple Alvin, they had the same bugs during test flights, but their engineers fixed them faster than we did. Besides we are perfectionists; they can shoot hundreds of missiles, if only one can hit the target for them it's a success."

"Pathetic Patrick, I don't believe it!" Alvin was deeply offended.

"I'll prove this to you; I collaborated with Dan, the head of the FBI, to have Russian spies intercept another piece of information and see if it surfaces in one of their weapon designs."

"What information, for example?" Alvin was curious.

"It's part of the plan we discussed in the situation room!" Patrick exclaimed and gasped softly looking at Lucy who was listening quietly, figuring out the mess that Patrick was about to dispatch her into for her next mission.

Alvin reacted with caution and refused to lower himself with a dire reaction. The burden of keeping the American people safe had a cost and the next steps would determine its price.

"Got it Patrick, I know what you mean. 'Let them see,' is your motto isn't it, Patrick?"

"Yes, you make adversaries see what they want to see!" exclaimed Patrick and Lucy nodded her head again in support and rubbed her hands together as a symbol of being ready for the extra dose of adrenalin she needed that this mission would give her.

"Reports from South Korea say that NoKo announced a successful test of a hypersonic missile as well."

"Shoot me, Alvin. I guess it's all fake news in order to get us scrambled; pure provocation," replied Patrick.

"It would be especially embarrassing to us if that's the truth."

"Alvin, you keep pushing DARPA and its director, Elizabeth Harding, and General John Duke. They have the key to get the hypersonic missile Interceptor operational. It's the key."

"This is shit, Patrick," Lucy whispered getting the picture of the unfolding situation and how she would fit in.

Patrick *shushed* Lucy to stay quiet during the call. She frowned but nodded softly.

"Unfortunately, it is what it is Patrick, the defense contractors did everything they could to bring us up to par, but they needed more time; that is something that only your agency can do. *Time!* In this case, time is our only safe haven: time to complete our test flights, time to deploy the weapon, time to diffuse the Russian's eagerness to fight us," Alvin tried not to sound too dramatic by throwing a life jacket at the CIA which the country needed. "You heard

Duke say we need at least six to twelve months, that brings us to October as the best-case scenario!"

Lucy was restless and signaled to Patrick, then without permission whispered, "They are putting all the pressure on you!"

"I'll keep their horses in the stable while we approach and pass that bridge, and I'll keep the enormous pressure from the White House under control," Patrick replied.

"By the way, about your briefing message, we knew of the Russian sub's presence on the Virginia coast, Patrick," said Alvin loudly and continued, "Ilya Primankov is not playing games. He was very proud announcing the new hypersonic missile confidently to the world. Now he is proving it, using it to kill innocent civilians in Ukraine. Basically, he reported to the world that the glitch during the 'Doomsday Alley' crisis last year was a thing of the past and resolved."

"This was the best Easter present he could give to his people. This gave the Russians a sense of national pride raising their chins up, but not without protestors calling a stop to developing expensive weapons to destroy the world a few times over. They can be as proud as they want while the Ruble is collapsing," said Alvin coldly.

Patrick could not take the flimsy excuse. Many times, America rose above its adversaries after a short military disadvantage, like the race to land on the moon or after the attack on Pearl Harbor. The only difference was that Marcus, who was leading the NSA, was worried about the threats of conquering other democratic countries after Ukraine and Taiwan, would suck America into a global war again. He knew that without deterrence it will be hard to keep the blood thirsty greyhounds in the cage. "Let me put Elizabeth on the call," said Alvin. A few seconds later DARPA Director Elizabeth Harding was online, and Patrick made his thoughts heard.

"It's all about a self-pronounced threat; the Russians and Chinese will put all their military eggs in the same basket now or later and take the opportunity to unify their threats on us with all their combined military might. The test of the hypersonic missiles deployed on the Russian sub close to our shores was a strong signal that they built up their defiance and escalated the pressure while we had no solution how to intercept such a weapon if attacked–" Patrick's loud analysis was cut off by the director of DARPA.

"Patrick, we know all this!" thundered Elizabeth. "It's not changing the fact that we need more time; we are doing our best, but the targeting of our scientists by foreign agents is frightening," she snapped. "All we ask you to do is to make sure that our adversaries are taking their fingers off the triggers. We will prevail eventually and build up our deteriorated deterrence, w–"

"Keep calm and off the trigger," Alvin repeated sounding like the president.

"I'll get you the time you guys need until October. The president backed me with the support of the military departments with full cooperation of my plans!" Patrick replied without letting them drill him for explanation.

CHAPTER 8

Same day early afternoon
White House emergency meeting

Alvin and the rest of the room had déjà vu. The president did not stop pressing the subject and they had no breakfast or lunch yet other than the fresh coffee that was served.

"Damn," Marcus cursed.

Alvin prepared to reply to POTUS. He wet his lips and said, "From our intelligence agency sources, the missile is capable of being launched from a mobile platform launcher as well–a submarine or even from space–approaching its target at a speed of six or seven times the speed of sound, and capable of changing its set directional course using an advanced built-in AI technology. This makes it hard to predict its route, spot it, track it, or kill it."

"Again Alvin, all intelligence sources might be fake. We are on it!" chimed in Patrick as he inhaled slowly.

"We need to hear from Lockheed Martin. I hope at least, they are positive!" exclaimed the president. "How's the investigation of John Gregory's murder moving along?" He changed the subject.

"According to Dan, the FBI has a few leads," Patrick replied. "We are in communication!"

Alvin replied to the president's first question, "Mr. President, DARPA explained that we need to successfully complete the testing of the hypersonic missile first, understand how it works, then develop the technology needed for a hypersonic missile Interceptor. DARPA Director Elisabeth Harding guaranteed we will be first to deploy the Interceptor, dissolving the Russian and Chinese advantage. Mr. President, General Duke will keep them aggressively on course and focused." Alvin found himself in the hot seat again trying to shift some of the weight to the others.

"I hoped for better news," the president scolded. "After all the money they keep asking for!"

General Duke piped up softly from the same corner seat of the long table, "In order to intercept the Russians or the Chinese, we also need to hack their missile AI technology and frequencies which they use. Knowing how they communicate with the satellites or control centers will speed up the process, otherwise it will take longer to figure out how to develop an AI that can intercept millions of frequencies in a second. Unfortunately, it's time consuming!" exclaimed General Duke who was directly involved with the defense contractors and DARPA.

"Thank you, general." The president calmed down and got back to his authoritative demeanor. *More sarcasm will not solve the situation and will act as a boomerang,* he thought before saying, "When you have white hair, you know how to handle crises. Let's keep the pressure on!"

General Duke, the liaison between the government agencies, the defense contractors, and DARPA, reported directly to the president and Alvin was present due to his request. Duke didn't elaborate further and held a frozen expression and was motionless. His white hair the president referred to had been uncut for six months and curled on his head. He wore round glasses and looked more like a computer science professor than a general.

"Meanwhile sir, we need to show a strong presence on all fronts, sir!" Alvin said. They all nodded in support waiting for the next barrage of questions from the president. They all waited anxiously for the meeting to end.

The president stayed calm despite the gloomy ambiance and wondered again what JFK would do next. Then he said, "We need a superior mindset!"

"We added some new specifications which caused the delay," said General Duke sitting tensely.

"We should test an upgraded prototype in six months," added Marcus and yawned. "Sorry," he whispered.

"We drafted the best minds from Microsoft and Google to develop the artificial intelligence software capable of predicting the adversary's missile frequency and change its course by selecting an alternative target back in enemy territory," General Duke said hoping he sounded rational after the long meeting.

"I want a full report from Director Harding on the hardware development status EOD!" commanded the president and General Duke nodded his head.

There was a knock on the door and the Chief of Staff walked in with the White House chef behind him along with two butlers carrying the brunch buffet trays which they laid on the credenza.

Outside, the sun shone brightly, giving everyone hope, changing the grim look on their faces. As the president saw it, it would be a global military chess game with casualties and death.

As soon as the chef left, the doors were closed again. Patrick continued where Duke and Alvin left off. "The danger, in other words, is even if we could intercept one or two in a military conflict in the future, if they launched hundreds, it takes only one to penetrate through our defense shield network. Losing a missile would be catastrophic." Patrick thought aloud while grabbing an everything bagel, cream cheese, and Nova Lox made by the president's favorite place in Brooklyn. Patrick smiled since he knew who introduced the lox shop to the president, his fellow Mossad agent.

"Take this all under consideration, General Duke," said the president. "We also need to develop a shield network. Discuss this with the Israelis. They have that tech installed in their tanks and armored vehicles, and now have added it on the rest of their equipment. We might be able to adapt this technology on our Navy ships. Keep this out of the public eye!"

Duke nodded. "We are well ahead of you, sir. We contacted the Israelis already. They are OK with that but want something in return!" General Duke scoffed.

"It's Middle East squabbling, General, nothing more!" said the president fiddling with his pen and waving his hand to stop the general from continuing.

Alvin lifted his chin up toward the general, sat up straight as he grabbed his coffee mug and said, "We considered this in our revised scope requests, is what John is trying to say, sir!"

General Duke smiled and exchanged a quick glance with the Defense Secretary, nodding slightly, hoping that Alvin had not undermined him.

"Go ahead, General," encouraged the president. He ignored Alvin's reinforcement statement as small talk and tried to stay focused on the main issue. He understood perfectly what the general meant without explanation. "Why don't you sit closer, General?"

General Duke moved from his shadowed corner and sat next to Patrick in a spare chair.

"The specification we added to the scope was to develop a new platform that could control multiple missile paths at the same time and intercept them all." The general was encouraged by the president's support and added, "It's a shield technology like a magnetic field umbrella, similar to what the Israelis developed for their tanks, called 'Wind Coat' and the 'Iron Dome'. It covers the sky with multiple missiles with multiple sites scenarios!" His answer was delivered dryly and monotone; he humbly shrugged his shoulders. His mind ran faster than his words could come out causing him to sound like he was mumbling a few of times.

Rufus cut him off, "Well, that's what I am talking about!" He snarled, "And you estimate a year or two to develop?"

"Eventually, sooner or later, we will test one successfully. This will put us ahead of everyone for years to come and keep us dominant. We also need to implement a clean space agreement policy from military weapons. But in the meantime, I recommend the CIA investigate the Russian and Chinese technologies, hack their design programs, tap into its frequencies, and see how the entire system communicates! We want to intercept their hypersonic missile signals, destroy it, or direct it back to where it came from. Boomerang!" John inhaled heavily and exhaled slowly letting the weight of his words sink in. He felt intense déjà vu. His nerdy look helped them trust that he knew what he was talking about. "It's a new concept for weapon developments."

The president scoffed, which started a low chatter in the room that subsidized with a wave of his hand.

"We got most of it on paper, sir!" General Duke didn't stop or lose his focus. "We are also developing a satellite control system for all tis–"

"We are covering a few different fronts. We can always declare that our missile test was successful. They bluff, so we can bluff too!" Marcus blurted out, not sure the president would like that idea knowing how Patrick's mind worked.

The president shook his head as Patrick jumped in quickly and said, "I have plans Marcus!" Then he turned to the president and stated, "Let me stay calm and float this out there. Let the CIA take the lead on espionage. Duke needs six months; I give him a year to complete his work!" Patrick sneered with a sardonic smile.

Alvin was not sure where Patrick was going with his last statement, especially when his facial expression appeared to be hiding something. Instead, he jumped out of his chair with optimism and said, "We all know that we are at a slight technological disadvantage currently, and it's not the first-time gentleman, I trust our defense contractors will astound the world when we take the lead."

"Nice and patriotic, Alvin!" the president said. "We are behind and that's what pisses me off!"

"Thank you, sir. I understand, we will manage the crisis. It's not like we are starting a war tomorrow!" Alvin exclaimed, "The Russians and the Chinese know our retaliatory capability and we will keep them at bay, sir!"

The president sighed and went to the credenza to dig in on the food plates. He then turned around to answer Alvin, "We are at war in Ukraine, Alvin. The fact we are not fully involved is that we lost our deterrent. It's Patrick's war for now: hack, disinformation, deception, espionage, and sabotage!" he mumbled. "That is our war now!"

"We have done this before!" Patrick scoffed. "We can do it again!"

"I bet you can, meanwhile until your plans are solidified, lower the level of our national anxiety. We need to calm the American people with a joint statement. Have your spokesperson draft a statement and let me look at it." The president directed this at Alvin, who felt relief that the meeting was over so they could concentrate on the food.

"Turn up the volume!" demanded the president as CNN came back on with its "Breaking News" flashing graphics.

"We just received a report from a press conference just minutes ago presented by our military contributor Air Force Chief of Staff, General Heath Roland."

The screen shifted to the General in his Pentagon headquarters. He was seated on his chair with the American and the Air Force flags in the background.

"General Roland, what was the secret mission?" asked one reporter.

"General, has the crew been rescued?" asked another.

"What kind of a secret weapons were tested, General?"

General Heath scoffed at the tsunami of questions. All were related and in response to the social media explosion from the download of the B-2 airplane taking off. *"My statement is brief. I'll try to cover all your questions and concerns. First the crew. We are searching the area for them and have a massive rescue operation in place. The weather is not cooperating right now. We have tropical storm Mina which might develop into a hurricane in the next few days. Next? Mitch?"*

Mitch, a hippie with a big nose and large reading glasses that hung loosely on the bridge of his nose, wore a gray beret that covered his long, shoulder-length hair. A Fox News press badge hung over his black Nike hoodie sweatshirt. He made a strange face and asked, *"Did the crew call, 'Mayday?' Did they eject? And if yes, where? You should know that by now!"* He smiled as if he was saying: You can't fool me for too long.

"As I said, we are searching, and the weather is very stormy, making any rescue very challenging and dangerous."

"My question, if you didn't understand was, is there is anything to rescue, General?" Mitch insisted and yelled above the rest.

"*We hope so!*" the general replied laconically and raised his eyebrows.

"*Come on, General!*" screamed another.

"*Nancy!*" called the general, pointing his finger at his favorite CNN reporter.

Nancy, a young field reporter, simply tried to compete with the media wolves. "*What went wrong? Is it true that the Air Force lost contact with the bomber during a test of an experimental weapon prototype of some kind?*"

"*Yes, it's true!*" The general threw a bone in the room to nibble on and started a massive speculation on social media.

"*So, the test failed?*" shot one reporter angrily.

"*We will circle back to you when we have more information, but I don't think so!*" The general's mysterious smile seemed to hide a secret and the reporters picked up on it immediately.

"*What were we doing at the South Pole?*" asked Nancy waving her pen in the general's direction.

"*The experiment required navigation over the South Pole. Sorry I can't give you more information folks!*" The general kept his cards close to his chest and his face was icy cold.

The reporters were frustrated by not getting the "breaking news" they expected to hear.

"*It sounds all the same, a major cover up,*" reported Nancy on CNN News that evening, with an outfit that made many men forget the news.

Mitch from Fox News reported that evening that, "It's all one big crazy puzzle that needs to be resolved." He ended his report with, "*The sloppy Air Force lost a secret prototype missile that probably will require an expedition to the South Pole to retrieve it before it falls into an adversary's hands and reveals our secrets. It's not the first time we lost a nuclear bomb.*" He referred to the 1958 midair collision losing a Mark 15 nuclear bomb near Tybee Island.

* * *

"Does Mitch from Fox News know something I don't?" Rufus' question echoed back like a hammer pounding into Alvin's head. The president didn't get his answer, but he didn't dig further. The Chief of Staff urged the president to attend his next meeting with Cody, his Secretary of State and NATO top brass.

* * *

Alvin called Patrick from the limousine on his secure line and coughed lightly. "Are we going to tell Hulk your entire plan?"

"Nope! What plan?" asked Patrick laughing. "You want him to have a heart attack? He is a politician not a soldier, so keep this on a need-to-know basis. We will find a way to tell him when it's all over if I don't fuck up!" Patrick mumbled watching to make sure his driver took the fastest way to his Langley office.

"I am puzzled why he didn't say anything when listening to the press conference on CNN," Alvin pressed, even he didn't know Patrick's entire plan, but he trusted the CIA.

"I guess he didn't pick up the plot entirely Alvin, Mitch and the Fox Network played the part well which was part of my plan. I hope when all this settles in history, he won't be fired from Fox News for assisting us," Patrick chuckled and looked from the limo window to see an American Airlines 737-Max climbing above them retracting its gear. "Mitch is a hippie but a true American patriot," Patrick said after the jet was out of earshot. He took a deep breath of fresh air.

CHAPTER 9

March 16

Patrick gazed at Lucy while contemplating the next steps. He took a few minutes of silence to change gears back to counter-intelligence productivity and directed Lucy on her new mission: deception.

Victoria, Patrick's administrative assistant, walked in and asked in her British accent, if they needed anything before she left for lunch. Twenty minutes later she showed up with two freshly brewed coffee carafes on a tray with a continental breakfast for both. During this time Patrick disclosed his plans for Lucy and encouraged her to think alike. Once she was on the street, she would be on her own.

"Nice woman," said Lucy even though she thought Victoria was cold to her when she walked in. "Check for bugs under your coffee mug," Lucy chuckled, and Patrick frowned.

"Oh yeah. Victoria? It's been four or five years already; her husband died a couple of years ago," he gossiped. "He could have been our next president."

"Oh," Lucy moaned. "That's a shame, any children?"

"No, she married a divorced B-2 pilot, who had grown children from his first marriage."

"How did she get to be your admin here?"

"I inherited her. Her husband was Senator Harper!"

"Senator Harper? Wow, I didn't know she was his wife. Everything is a secret here!"

"She was in the car accident, too, and survived!"

"Wow, I remember the incident but never followed up on the details. Was she hurt?"

"Not a scratch! Where are you going with that, Lucy?"

"I don't know Pat. I don't trust anyone, including you sometimes," she scoffed. Patrick laughed aloud shaking his head.

"So, they met when she was in her twenties? Went out probably a couple of years . . ."

"They got married right after his deployment in London expired, anyway, look at this, she wants to be a junior agent; she thinks she can contribute to the agency."

"Who? Victoria?" Lucy was stunned.

Patrick changed the subject. He showed Lucy a bunch of profiles of mostly men, with information they needed to collect about them.

"Here you go!" she said watching Patrick rip apart each man and the profiles she needed to memorize.

"Who are they and what is their connection to the mission?" she asked.

"They all were at the Lockheed Martin conference in Denver. We suspect that one of them works for a foreign agency!"

"A mole?"

"Yes, a ruthless mole, one of them must be involved in killing our lead scientist!" Patrick inhaled and exhaled slowly trying to weigh if Lucy got it.

"Interesting, but it could be someone who only invited them, and is not on the list here," she said analyzing what Patrick laid on the table.

Patrick nodded and turned around to show her a few more characters.

"Well, it's true; that's for you to find out. You heard the phone conversation with Alvin," Patrick sipped from his black Pike Place coffee while Lucy added cream and sugar to hers.

"Huh, yes." She nodded scrunching up her face. "Is my buddy, Evan Harris, involved in this mission?"

"He will be on standby. This is all connected, we might have a network of spies or a single individual among us, who knows? There will be a lot of disinformation and cyber-attacks on our communication systems in the days ahead," he said. "Your mission is to find out who the mole is, and if he is working alone." He sounded serious. His thoughts drifted to find the thread Lucy would need to start pulling.

He looked outside from his office window to clear his head, preparing for a fresh thought when he saw the early blooming Forsythias' bright yellow flowers outside near his window. "Spring, the time of rejuvenation," he mumbled then heard Lucy's sharp tone.

"Don't tie her to me. I work alone!" Lucy pushed back any joint venture. "I am sure I am the first to get this intel to avoid any hurdles on my mission."

"No worries, Lucy. As always, we will be ready to support you. Meanwhile, NoKo just released a State Media Statement touting its leader personally oversaw the successful launch of their own hypersonic missile, adding this to their *deterrent arsenal*. This heightens the pressure on our military," Patrick added soberly, when he saw the briefing on his computer screen.

He rolled his head and with wide eyes, moved slowly to his desk. With no explanation, he blurted out, "This is going to be bad! We are all furious!"

"Wow!" Lucy was astounded. "That leaves us as the only superpower without a proper response to the same weapon!" Lucy groaned, her face tense.

"Yes, we are chewing on this with Hulk like crazy! I'm sure he will go berserk in the Oval Office when he gets the briefing about NoKo today. I am glad we are not there now; I can hear him screaming out loud, *'Patrick, stick sticks in their damn wheels.'*" He scoffed nervously mimicking the president's voice.

Lucy lifted her eyes and looked intently at her boss. They had worked together for a long time, and she had never seen him so deeply concerned. "Not sure what retaliation measures POTUS has? Sanctions? They don't really help!" She asked, then answered her own questions.

"That's what Secretary of State Cody is pushing. Honestly Lucy, the way I see it is, yes, he will respond with heavy individual sanctions, plus move troops to aid NATO and then deliver more logistic weapons to South Korea. We need to show fire power in the area," Patrick read aloud from his political map and the threats the nation faced in the event of a global war which were never more real.

Lucy's political views saw it differently, that the president's strongest sanctions response would not adequately suffice to stop a war. Russia, NoKo, and China as a team would find a new economical avenue and create a new Asian Economic Initiative Alliance just like NAFTA. As a matter of fact, they did better financially now than before when the sanctions were applied to fuel any war they want.

"POTUS will respond hard on NoKo but will ignore the other invasions if escalated!" she stated after a long silence of listening to her thoughts.

"Concurred. How do you feel otherwise? Ready to take on the mission?" he asked his agent moving the conversation in a different direction.

"I feel fine. It was the Omicron variant, nothing serious. Just severe headaches and trouble sleeping for a couple days. I'm well now and YES, I am ready!" she exclaimed. "You know? This tension simmering spread fast like a wildfire. The tiniest spark anywhere in the world could blow up the planet," she said and inhaled slowly.

They continued noshing on the pastries and coffee while Lucy asked herself, *What exactly is Patrick's final objective? What would his twisted distorted mind come up with? What will he come up with next? How is he going to hold the tanks and the soldiers from marching on Ukraine and Taiwan?*

He rounded out his defense forum with their arsenal in his possession to assist the plans, meaning the Navy, the Air-Force, and their resources. It was a huge liability showing Lucy that this mission was not like any others before. This time the entire country's defense system was involved, and she would be at the helm.

"Precisely Lucy, we need to navigate carefully not to step on a mine field. I believe we must pretend that what we don't have, we *do* have. It's painful, like a secret weapon never existed. I believe that if the Russians and the Chinese are sure the USA has a proper defense against their new weapon, they will postpone any military provocations that would cross the line. If I'm wrong, we could be on the brink of a catastrophe."

"That's a damn realistic fiction, sir," said Lucy grimly with a nervous smile. She changed the subject. "The goal-scorer sent a signal to an MI-6 contact; he wants to meet and confirm his intentions to work with us," she whispered like keeping a big secret from the walls. "This man is in London now for a few days for his soccer tournament, the MI-6 agent confirmed."

"Yes, I know. There is more to it, but for now you don't need to know all the details." His mischievous smile was short-lived. "Anything else?" Patrick didn't want to miss the tiniest bit of intel.

"He wants only to talk to us directly but uses the MI-6 contact as a conduit, B said. Perhaps we should negotiate a better and more comfortable deal. He wants to work with us. I need to meet him, but I don't really know, Patrick," Lucy replied and moved her chair closer, a cat-like move. She declined more coffee when Patrick offered it saying, "Fourth cup makes me hyper."

Patrick chuckled. "Is the goalscorer personally in touch with him or did he use a proxy?" Patrick asked eyeing the whisky bottle on the counter bar, delaying the drink for later for a good reason to celebrate.

"This message came from the goalscorer himself. I don't know if he was in your plan since he mentioned it had something to do with the escalation of the war in Ukraine and the country military buildup along ex-Soviet bloc countries. They are confident that the hypersonic missile they have is a winning formula!" she exclaimed and focused on Patrick's facial expression which didn't reveal much.

"I agree that you need to meet him. You need to confirm all the info he wants to share, face-to-face. Lucy, I just started pulling this thread. We need to control this development and bring it to fruition. I trust the MI-6 contact but the fewer people delivering messages the better. I understand why he couldn't contact us directly. I want to make sure that he doesn't change his mind if he truly has an offer we can't refuse!" Patrick sounded enthusiastic.

Lucy hesitated. *Perhaps it's the first clue of the mission ahead of her. He plans on going to get it started on the right foot,* she thought.

"Is Scorpion involved with that? Is she still operating in Russia?" she asked suddenly and took Patrick by surprise making him lean out of his seat.

"She has her mission. We are all on the same page, why?"

"I haven't heard from her for a long time . . . wondering if she could be utilized. Anyway, the soccer match is on schedule in a couple days and that gives us a short window and doesn't leave much time to operate. I forgot about the British time zone. The goalscorer will stay in London with his team until after the game is–"

"I know Lucy, you are all set to fly tonight as planned. I have all the info at my level," Patrick interrupted and gazed at her respectfully. "Once you have confirmed and closed the deal with the goalscorer, pay him the down payment and plan our South Pole expedition to protect the Interceptor that landed there intact." He was starting to believe his own lies.

She listened, calmly nibbling on what was left on the food tray. "So I should not unpack my suitcase when I come back?" A smile melted across her face.

"You will be part of the expedition when you come back from London. Please no international incidents!"

"Oh my gosh, Patrick, South Pole? My brain doesn't work below 50 degrees! You know that. That's why I love Florida." She giggled exposing her perfect white teeth.

"You will be fine. Florida can wait. Just be careful, the SVR is watching every step we make, especially now. They will connect you with the CIA's next step and follow you wherever you go, including looking for our scientist," Patrick said and pulled out a few photos and handed them to her.

"Who is that?" She examined the photos taken from every angle and distance from a hidden spot. Perhaps someone followed the subject, and these were taken without their consent. "Who cares? Let's move on," she mumbled under her breath.

"We know him as Pieter, he used to work for us. We see him on and off in the Russian consulate in New York City, a Russian SVR agent. I want to recruit him back with us; he is a hybrid product of a Russian father and Swedish mother; looks German if you ask me." He emphasized his next words. "He was on the list of agents the state department wanted to expel last year, but I asked to keep him here to see what the SVR was up to and expose their network of spies!"

"This is the first time I've seen you show mercy on spies. What else can you tell me about him?" she shot back, more interested about the agent's abilities rather than who his father was.

"All you need to know is that if it comes up at all, he shot Ron Hill, who was our FBI recruit obtaining information about the Interceptor testing mission and B-2 bomber LA mission. This is what the Russians are concerned about, perhaps a mistaken identity," Patrick exhaled, ignoring her comment.

"OK. Connecting the dots, Patrick. So, the Russians are interested in our Interceptor program which already an–"

"Yes, more than likely you will meet Pieter along the way, Lucy. He is a dangerous, ice-cold killer. We hope to tame him or have him join us; be gentle."

"They all are," she muttered. "Is the FBI agent dead?" She was a bit puzzled, but Patrick shook his head.

"Ron went through emergency surgery to save his life and was in critical but stable condition after the surgery and will survive. We are keeping this confidential for now; let them think he was killed. His neighbor reported 911 about a noise and was saved by the paramedics on the scene."

"Tough luck!" She shook her head lightly.

"We are keeping Pieter alive to serve as a conduit to deliver disinformation and spread conflicting news to confuse Russian Intelligence. One of the things we want the Russians to believe is that we started mass production and they are being deployed. That was the task of Ron Hill; we all thought his background as a military reporter was authentic and would grab the attention of Intelligence agencies."

"Bait . . . and he almost died!" scoffed Lucy, her face showing disappointment that Pieter was not caught.

"Collateral damage Lucy. It's a compelling argument any-way you look at it; that's how we need to operate some-times, and many times things drift away!"

"Well, getting on a new assignment is exciting. On the other hand, when I meet Pieter, I'll make sure that he tells us which side he is on, otherwise, he will be collateral dam-age too, Patrick."

"Wait, not before your mission is completed Lucy; then you can do whatever you want with him. For now, we need him alive."

"Not sure how long you can use him as a conduit." Lucy challenged Patrick to think. Like Patrick, she knew that in the espionage world, no one is loyal to anyone. Time is the best witness to remove them. Many times, agents switched sides and annexed new ideologies. Sometimes enticed by money, other times succumbing to a beautiful woman as a trap.

"He took Ron's CPU which we can track: Trojan horse. They think Ron is dead and they have a short window to use his CPU for information we send through it," Patrick explained.

"It's a short window for us too. It's possible that he wants to sell the CPU for profit to a third party, like China or Iran."

"True, meanwhile we will continue with our plans," Pat-rick smiled mysteriously and didn't elaborate.

"And that is where the *goalscorer* and MI-6 get in the pic-ture, isn't it?" She emphasized the word *goalscorer* slowly to hint that she would have to find her role in this plan by herself and it didn't feel comfortable.

"Yes," Patrick snapped. "It's not just about the Russian ex-pedition, it's about whom we want them to send to the South Pole. That's the point and that's why I want Pieter on our side."

"Really, do you want Pieter to send you a list to choose from?" She laughed. "Patrick be transparent with me, af-ter all, you are sending me to Daniel's lions' den. Should

I know why Antarctica?" Lucy snapped at her boss with a "what the hell?" expression.

"We will send you info on the go, Lucy. We will take precautions in case an agency captures you!"

"So, for now all I need to do is to legitimize the goalscorer's serious intentions and his connection to your plans?" she replied with a question.

"Yes!" Patrick locked eyes with Lucy and stretched, arching his back insinuating there was more.

"OK, got it. I am one of your pawns," she scoffed, upset. She knew Patrick would not like her comment, but she kept her look dead serious.

"Yes. You will know who and how." Patrick started to show exasperation. It was a short and stressful night for him after a long day with a tight schedule ahead. He still needed additional details for his plan to shorten the design time of Lockheed Martin's schedule on top of a secondary plan using the *Arctic Star* for the mission he kept confidential. "Too many moving parts," he murmured.

"Wow!" she exclaimed. "Sounds like a movie you recently watched Patrick!" She cracked up with a loud laugh and continued, "Sorry Patrick, how should I beg Pieter to cooperate with us? Mummify him and put him in a sarcophagus?"

Patrick didn't like that remark and scolded her, "Stop your sarcasm; we will continue and keep our eyes open to events as they emerge. I will notify you piece by piece. After the London excursion, you will join the *Arctic Star* from Santiago, Chile. A transport plane will bring you back home, I expect many characters will show up to examine our Interceptor, Lucy."

"You plan to see the Russians there? Do you expect a full military force?"

"Yes, the whole nine yards. All we need now is to chat with the goalscorer and cinch the corners up. That's a different type of a mission than you are accustomed to," noted Patrick. "In London you need to connect the dots, the only question left to answer is to confirm it's not an SVR trap; they would love to kill you!"

"I have nine lives, Pat!" She paused waiting for reaction, but Patrick sank into his thoughts again. "That's a $10M question," Lucy scoffed.

"It's worth every penny. We will pay him the first $1M installment, transferred to his account once you confirm it's all legit. We need proof. If needed, threaten him that if he is sabotaging us, he is a dead man walking!"

"Roger, I know how to threaten; it's my specialty!"

"Also ask him why he chose to approach the MI-6 first and not us directly. Was it a caution?"

"That's a good question, Patrick!"

Her eyes sparkled and she was excited, as was the case every time she went on a mission. Adrenaline was her drug, like insulin was for a diabetic, a drug needed for life.

Her new background story was that she was an English freelance reporter working mainly for the English desk of an Arabic news agency named *Global News Network,* based in London.

She had a few hours to get to Reagan National Airport to catch an American Airlines flight to JFK for a connection to London on British Airways. Within thirteen hours, Lucy was in her Waldorf Hilton Hotel in Aldwych, London. She loved that section of town, feeling the long and rich history, the house of Windsor monarchy always attracted her.

She ignored her jet lag and prepared to meet B, the mysterious MI-6 agent, and then hopefully, meet the goal-scorer. She'd grab a couple of hours of sleep in between her meetups.

CHAPTER 10

5:12 p.m.
Virtual video meeting
Russian president office, Moscow

President Primankov liked the idea of stealing the Interceptor and avenging Russia for the CIA secretly plucking his soviet era submarine from the bottom of the ocean when he was a young KGB recruit. It was humiliating and he wanted to make sure that this time his country would not get the short end of the stick.

He sat behind his maple executive desk with its removable T-shaped extension. At the end of the T, stood an eighty-four-inch Smart TV screen projecting a virtual meeting with all his security and defense cabinet members. They were discussing their love/hate relationship with the Americans while seeing if the plan his top brass proposed was doable.

On another note, he was not happy that the Americans closed the advantage gap so quickly. As everyone was seated comfortably in their chairs, he thundered, "Short-lived was our advantage comrades." There was macabre sarcasm in his tone and uneasiness in his team. "Only a few weeks ago, I announced our hypersonic missile was operational, and we started mass production. I announced that we deployed our new missiles, then I get a report from our intelligence agents who intercepted a communication from an American control room in Vandenberg Space Force Base about a successful launch of a hypersonic missile killer, the Interceptor? Do you know how this made us look?" he snorted and frowned angrily. "And the worst part is, with all the money we spend on our agents, we didn't even know about it!" he yelled.

"We knew they are trying to develop the hypersonic missile and failed three separate times. Now under deployment tests, what we didn't know was that they designed an Interceptor at the same time! It's a record," stated the FSB agency director in charge of the counterintelligence and counterterrorism. "We successfully smuggled the plans from a local agent, and it is being analyzed as we speak," his round red face flushed as his chest full of medals deflated.

Primankov shot criticism toward his FSB director and said, "I can NOT see our efforts and financial expenditures go down the drain. Where is the Russian ingenuity? We were first in space. First, damn it!" he snapped at his team, losing his temper. "What will it take to find the Interceptor they clumsily lost in Antarctica? What means will it take to bring this victory to Mother Russia?" he scolded and rallied them at the same time, gnashing his teeth, looking for a response.

"They tested two Interceptors on the flight. The first one failed and landed on Ronne Ice Shelf somewhere in Antarctica, the second apparently hit the target successfully. That's what it sounded like from the control room recordings we intercepted," the SVR director said, thinking he should get some credit for that, but the contrary happened, panic.

"Yes Anatoly, the SVR is doing a great job; they have been on top of the American development. The frustration began during the development of the hypersonic missile when agents found that the Americans were also in the final stages of developing an Interceptor. That was the clever and unpredictable part. We should have thought of that too;

they cannot outsmart us, comrades!" the president scolded. "I need an audacious plan, fast!"

Anatoly, the head of the SVR, was seen on video sitting in his headquarters' office in the Yesenevo District of Moscow. A grunt of a man with a grumpy long face, he looked composed and confident with thinning white hair, and large oversized reading glasses which sat tight on his face. Like all the generals, he was proud of his military service, showing off his medals in defiance of his president's attack.

"Is it retrievable?" the defense minister asked, keeping the focus aimed in Anatoly's direction.

Anatoly replied calmly, "Everything is possible. Our agents reported that the Americans disclosed that one Interceptor landed intact about 100 kilometers from our floating research platform at the South Pole, declaring it operational."

"*Admiral Karlinsky*, a research boat, is docking there now, but how dangerous is it to retrieve it intact without starting a conflict? I am sure the Americans will not sit silently and watch us steal it," Primankov scolded as he scratched his temple.

"It landed close to our claimed territory. We are preparing to send an expedition; our agents are working on it!" Anatoly sounded satisfied and hoped someone else in the cabinet would take the heat this time.

"We claimed the property, but it doesn't mean we own it. An expedition should be OK if it is done properly!" the president said. "Antarctica has no owners; they can claim it too. What's the point of discussing that at all?"

"The *Admiral Karlinsky* research boat can break the ice up to a point which is close to the landing site, then we need to cover fifty kilometers with our DT-30 Vityaz carriers. They fit eight people fully-geared and comfortable for—"

"The ice there is a few hundred feet thick, so forget about using the research platform. But you can use the *Admiral Karlinsky* research boat instead."

"To sabotage the Americans, we need to land near our ice camp." Anatoly threw out this idea.

"It's 3,000 miles to the Interceptor. Holy Mother of God. How will you cover that?" asked Primankov. "I do like the sabotage part though!" he added.

"Submarines as a backup, to be honest–" Anatoly added to his plan.

"Armament?" the president cut him off.

"Machine guns, shoulder SAM missiles, just in case," Anatoly replied.

"You can't land with that kind of weaponry and expect the vigilant Americans not to notice!" the FSB director stated with a slur and scoffed, the rest chuckled and started a low chatter.

"We can load it on the research platform ahead of time. Let's steal it comrades!" declared Primankov.

The spread of the new Covid variant virus forced the virtual meeting of the security cabinet and reminded Primankov of the Doomsday incident when the military took upon itself to prepare for a preemptive strike on the West in a miscalculated step. They learned their lesson when the Delta SAR-2 virus caused vulnerability in the military to defend the country. Primankov learned his lesson, and it made him more comfortable as an ex-KGB Agent managing the ongoing events by himself and keeping the military brass out of this conflict.

On the other hand, even if they weren't able to ask provocative questions or say anything crazy, they believed that stupidity could not be replaced with optimism. They trusted President Primankov's sharp judgement even at the cost of his charismatic approach to become the

"Greater Russia" again and the possibility to bring back the old Soviet Union bloc under his command. It was assumed they knew what they needed to know, and the expedition was a full GO.

Primankov shot point blank at his cabinet without considering the dangers. "Figure it out!" he thundered.

They nodded and made sure to say what the president wanted to hear with confidence and no hiccups.

"The Israelis stole the entire Iranian nuclear library right from under their noses and brought it to Israel, so don't tell me they are smarter than you are?" Primankov scoffed, disdained by the Iranians even though he had no shame in asking them to assist with attack drones and missiles since the Russian arsenal was depleting fast.

"Our labs have photos. They interpolated and compared the bomber size with the Interceptor attached under its wing, sir," said Anatoly helping his embarrassed defense minister. He added, "We also diverted our spy satellite to comb Antarctica's grid. Meanwhile, we hope our agents on the ground will find the exact coordinates of the landing site!" Anatoly defended his theory as he was eager to get this piece of technology.

Anatoly was rough and didn't take prisoners in combat. He had the same bad table manners as his colleagues and didn't defer to the Russian president to promote him as he always used to say, "brilliant minds think alike." His brilliant analytical brain worked fast, and this explained his undeniable courage, though his opponents attributed this to stupidity, sometimes it was a thin line between both. He figured out his entire expedition plan as they were still chanting patriotic propaganda.

Anatoly knew Primankov since they both served at the KGB together. Under their belts were many daring missions in the European theater, poisoning spies and double agents, neutralizing networks of spies that threatened their country policies and keeping Primankov in power. Especially notable was one assassination attempt that was leaked after an important president's political opponent was poisoned and died in an Italian hospital. From then on, Anatoly's way to the top agency rose meteorically. He'd blacklisted the president's political opponents who rioted in the streets and sent them to meet Saint Peter at the pearly gates.

Primankov knew Anatoly had ruthless agent capabilities. If he asked him to bring in the Iranian nuclear library like the Israelis did, it would be in Primankov's office the next day. So, to bring in the failed American Interceptor was low-hanging fruit. Anatoly would bring it back as promised.

"Check what kind of help we can get from the team of scientists in Vostok Research Station if we land there first!" suggested the defense minister in his baritone voice. "They have only two trackable snow cruiser vehicles and six jet skis fully operational."

"Good thinking, Rubi; whatever you need," said the president calling his defense minister by his nickname for Rubishenko. Anatoly chuckled at the defense minister's last remark. He would never trust what machines worked and what didn't at Vostok Station. For him it was an expensive junkyard contributing practically nothing. He disclosed, "I have two agents there!" Then added, "The rest are sixteen scientists and one chef who is a woman." Anatoly exhaled loudly.

"It's normal to increase the team at the station in the summer, so no one will suspect that we are sending troops in!" said Rubi, determined to get deep into the mission.

"It's the end of the summer, comrade!" Anatoly jumped in again. "The weather in Antarctica is relatively warm. Good timing to land there first, regroup, get the coordinates and shoot–" Anatoly was cut off. He frowned and shot a look of disdain toward Rubi.

"Do not clash comrades!" scolded the president. "We have enough enemies, don't waste your time with hate toward each other! We should keep the Americans in the dark and surprise them. It is what we are good at."

"Work in mysterious ways. Got it. We should be there first." Army General Vitali Grudenshko, who ran the FSS (Federal Security Services) tried to plant his own seed in the chatter.

The president coughed loudly and reached for a glass of water on his table. "Vitali, find it first!"

"Yes, we are all working on it. As I said, we shifted all our satellites into the area, and are sending recon planes. We are checking inventory within the research ice stations for tools and equipment we need, except Vostok station; it can't help, but I'll confirm!" Vitali exclaimed. "Our SVR agent, Pieter, sent us an upload of new information to analyze the B-2 Bomber flight plan and Interceptor specifications to help us calculate the landing location." Vitali sounded confident and had a mischievous smile like he held a secret. "Our lead missile scientist from MKB Fakel, Oleg Berzinskov, is checking the data."

"OK, keep this all confidential. It's a shame his daughter Inna is against us!" The Russian president looked disturbed. He was feeling even more pressure since the war in Ukraine was not going the way it was planned. He also felt the political pressure on his administration to resign if he failed in the Ukraine invasion. *At least he could come out victorious when he brings the* Interceptor *home*, he thought.

"I wonder what President Chong is doing about this. I'm sure they know," concluded Rubi, his baritone voice resounded with seriousness.

"No, we need to be on our own here. The Chinese and Americans should know nothing about our expedition!" Primankov advised his team with an intense look. He was just short of blaming himself for the fiasco he got the world into.

Vitali volunteered to head the expedition in Antarctica with Vladimir, his lieutenant, and Pieter would represent his SVR agency. This team would select the Arctic Commando troopers; they knew it would not be a fun place to end a summer vacation. "It's warmer than Moscow," Rubi mumbled.

"Just before we go, note that our scientists are concerned about the ice sheet shelf cracking up and separating from the main Ronne Ice Shelf," Anatoly gasped just talking about it. "It's the size of Crimea!"

The president nodded and drifted back to his thoughts. Most of his time as president had been silencing his political opponents and the underground opponent's media. There was little time left for other matters.

"I wonder why the Americans don't just bomb the Interceptor!" Rubi whispered not sure his statement was lost in the chatter.

Anatoly took the helm and answered abruptly, "Yeah, let's bomb it and announce, 'We found it, we bomb it.' Then run to the US and file a complaint for using weaponry in Antarctica." He laughed. Vitali reignited the president's attention.

Primankov drifted to another issue to diffuse the tensions. "I am pleased with the American's reaction to our missile testing submarine off the coast of Virginia. Is the sub back?" He shifted his glance to his defense minister who started to wonder if the expedition was worth the risk at all.

"Yes, Mr. President, the test outside of the territorial waters of the east coast of the state of Virginia stunned the American Navy," Rubi stated nodding his head. "We heard no complaints from them at all!"

"That's what worries me. No American response means they are up to something. It's strange." Primankov sounded skeptical.

"No, they don't feel the need to monitor us anymore. They even didn't know we were there," Rubi scoffed. "So, we made sure they spotted us as you directed, deterring them from getting involved in the muddy war in Ukraine."

"Yes, it was a direct threat not to mess with us."

"They got the message," Rubi replied. "All is calm!"

"Once a fearful giant adversary; today rusty junk yard," scoffed Anatoly in disdain. He did not take seriously the American threats. "They love to talk the talk!" He chuckled.

Primankov's assistant knocked and walked into his office with a printed message and read it aloud shaking his head lightly.

North Korea announced its second hypersonic superior gliding system technology as full success, hitting its target in the Pacific Ocean about 670 miles away.

"Bravo, Bravo, Shin Il Sheng!" Primankov congratulated his unlikely ally.

"That leaves the Americans as the only superpower without a successful hypersonic missile operational and deployed," scoffed Rubi and started more chatter.

"Calm down Rubi, don't forget what Yamamoto said after the Pearl Harbor attack, 'I feel all I have done was awaken a sleeping giant'. Be respectful of your enemy since they have the power to turn their rusty junk into a massive armada with nuclear power in a short time. They might not have the hypersonic missile now, but they developed the Interceptor; it's a killer!" the president thundered loudly with a stern message. His disdain for the US was evident but they also had his full of respect.

CHAPTER 11

March 17, 5:30 p.m.
London

Lucy tipped the Waldorf Hilton Hotel's bellhop who brought her suitcase to her room and left. Immediately she searched the room for cameras, microphones, and other monitoring devices and checked the window positions and views of Aldwych Street down below. The street was busy and cheerful, decorated for Spring.

It was already dark at 5:30 p.m. and very cold and damp outside. Despite the thick fog she could see the people shopping for last-minute Easter presents with kids trailing behind on the sidewalks. She refrained using the hotel room phone in case it was bugged, then plugged her cell phone in to charge for a few minutes. She could not resist the minibar and made herself a Bloody Mary although she was craving a "French 77" cocktail but was too lazy to call for room service and wait an hour for it.

The jet lag made her a little lightheaded. *It's about noon in Washington DC, I haven't slept enough*, she drifted in thought. Picking up her cell phone, she put in her earbuds and pushed the letter "B" from her encrypted contact list which required a password.

"Spider!" she shot laconically into the speaker. Her voice was decisive and firm.

"Welcome to our misty capital. Ten minutes? Say 5:45?" the voice on other end of the line replied sounding cheery and confident with a heavy Shakespearean British accent.

"Roger that," Lucy replied and hung up. She quickly freshened up her make-up and changed her clothes into a more appropriate elite Easter tourist. She wore a neon green silk dress with a leg slit on the right side all the way up to her hip, showing her statuesque leg that could kill an opponent with one kick to his face with a pointy metal heel. Her second-best weapon after her handgun.

B's room was on the fourth floor, a floor above hers which was arranged that way by the MI-6 special travel agent; a subtle message that the MI-6 is always above the CIA. She knocked three times, quick, and three times, slow. The door opened a sliver which was held by a chain and a tall skeletal man in a dark oversized suit stood with an expressionless face looking at her up and down. After a short password and identity confirmation, the man opened the door wide and peeped into the corridor both ways to ensure that no curious eyes were recording or listening before he locked the door behind them. He examined Lucy's femininity out of the corner of his eye.

"Did they send a beauty queen or a CIA agent?" he mumbled, and Lucy ignored the demeaning comment.

Routinely Lucy checked the room for bugs as B watched amusedly. Then he said sarcastically, "We rent the same rooms all the time; you should trust my agency."

"It's a habit!" she said ignoring him and continuing to comb the room, lifting pillows, and checking behind mirrors and artwork on the walls. While Lucy was busy, he poured two glasses of scotch and offered one to Lucy and motioned for her to sit. A black leather bag was on the wooden coffee table, and she noticed he took a quick glance at it and then stared at her. His body language suggested to her that this bag had contents attached to her mission. She figured it should be her 9 mm Glock handgun, transferred via diplomatic bags to her security department at the embassy.

In a soft and friendly tone, he said, "A holiday gift from your embassy; needs a sign out when you're done." He pursed his lips up in a serious manner.

Lucy chuckled. Usually, Lucy liked the dry sarcastic sense of humor the British were known for. *Another day and better time*, she thought. The jet lag had a schedule of its own, forcing her to soon find a nice clean pillow and a soft comforter to cover her tired body. "Sign out?" she repeated the words with slight disdain and chuckled.

B ignored the belittling comment and continued with the subject. "The soccer match is the day after tomorrow," he stated and threw the drink down his throat in one shot "like a man" and snorted hard. He added, "The Russian soccer team is staying at the Hilton London next to Wembley Stadium."

"Makes sense. Right next to the stadium for security purposes. When can we meet and talk to him?"

Lucy reviewed the photos of the goalscorer on the coffee table between sips of Scotch on the rocks.

"Twenty-one professional soccer players, the pride of the Russian soccer fans," B said.

"If you have the photos, you have the name, right?" she replied.

"Yes. Nikita. They play Liverpool FC. The match is the second leg of the Euro quarter-final championship. Tomorrow the team has half a day off after morning training and many restrictions. The SVR agents are guarding and watching every move they make; no phones, no cameras, and always escorted by undercover agents. Tomorrow they will have the last training session before the game. Not sure we can meet him then."

Lucy's mind worked differently, more like a Lamborghini on a racetrack. "This can't wait," she mumbled to herself. "If Muhammad can't go to the mountain, the mountain goes to Muhammad," she recited the famous phrase. "So how do you suppose we rendezvous with him? Make an appointment?" She giggled. "Or are we allowed to crash into his hotel room, Byron?" She laughed and looked at him with her penetrating stare and lifted her eyebrows knowing he wasn't accustomed to hearing his name anymore.

"It's not funny!" Byron scolded. "Keep your voice down please; you are not in the Bronx!" He snarled and shot back, offended. "We are professionals and I want to keep it that way," he criticized Lucy with a continued serious look. "Got the signal from him only three days ago and since then we followed his team via social media and his registered fan website. In addition, it took us some time to authenticate the request and forward it to your boss, Patrick, in DC. The goalscorer wants to talk to the CIA, without further explanation, something about your lost missile and perhaps an expedition to the South Pole."

"Wow, news travels fast," Lucy mumbled. *Must be Patrick's hand steering it,* she thought. "We know; we are ready to transfer his first $1M installment," Lucy revealed to encourage him to say more. "Must be sincere intent from him to put himself in danger. Must be more than money." Lucy frowned. "So, what better deal would he want?"

"Both agencies hope the information he has is worth the money asked for!" Byron said seriously. Then Byron tightened his lips and ran his fingers along his thick mustache, the pride of his manhood. "The monetary request is for one purpose and the other purpose is that he is engaged. His fiancé is in danger of disappearing in the depths of hell with the help of the FSB. She was involved in political activities which demanded Primankov's resignation, so he wants to include his fiancé in the deal to save her. She is underground in Moscow now."

"What's his fiancé got to do with the deal?"

"She is the daughter of Oleg Beerzinskov, the scientist who developed the Russian hypersonic missile. She grew up with her mother in Ukraine when her father disappeared while looking for a job in Russia, and then ended up working in MKB Fakel after his graduation from his university.

"Asylum in America," Lucy completed his sentence.

"The fiancé, yes; the father, no! He is a hard-core communist and not interested in defecting or seeking asylum, even though he was born in Ukraine!" Byron inhaled and exhaled slowly waiting for her response.

"And she? What is her name? What is her interest in this?"

"Inna, Inna Berzinsikova, a freedom feminist fighting against the Russian invasion of Ukraine which is destroying her homeland and her city of Kiev." He added, "She came into the spotlight after a few killing attempts, a few of her comrades were killed."

"And her father doesn't give a shit?"

"She looked for him all her life, and when she found out what he was doing, she blamed him for the destruction of his own childhood neighborhood; the barrage of hypersonic missiles that landed on his family and friends were his own design." Byron raised his glass in a sarcastic salute and said in Russian, "*Na Zdorovie!*"

"He must bring more value to this deal Byron. We are not a career smuggling band or an immigration agency. We do help people to defect if it's in our nation's interest. So where is the beef?" Lucy kept her focus and raised her chin up wondering what else he knows? Perhaps nothing.

"We should ask him when we meet then," Byron said and raised his eyebrows, eyes wide.

"Perhaps the fiancé's father is the one who has the value and Nikita is just cashing in on it?" Lucy asked.

"You might be right; we didn't think of that!" Byron stated and sat beside her on the couch.

"He might want to bring his fiancé and her father with him, so the Russians don't suspect their intentions to defect?"

"Simple, join the Antarctic expedition as volunteers. They have a good reason to," Byron said.

"Easier said than done." Lucy was skeptical hoping her trip was not in vain.

"Nikita mentioned he has SVR connections helping him join the expedition and 'voila'!" Byron sounded optimistic.

"Sounds like a trap to me!" responded Lucy. "Abducting her father and bringing her in on American soil, huh!" Lucy shook her head trying to figure out what a soccer player, his fiancé, and her father could bring to the table for her agency? She trusted Patrick and his judgement and she knew that she didn't see the entire picture yet. Perhaps all he wanted was to confirm with Nikita his serious intent to defect with his fiancé and her father and bring more details later.

Lucy left the answers for later as well since the MI-6 agent seemed to be in the dark as to the informant's intentions. *I need to drive this forward from here,* she thought.

"This is what might happen: his fiancé is not interested in leaving Russia, she wants to fight to stop the attacks on Ukraine, she wants her father to quit his job. Nikita fears for her life, but once defected, he wants to have enough money to live on and pay those who helped him their share. Does that sound better?" Byron asked.

"We pay him to bring the scientist to the USA!" Lucy exclaimed her simple logic. "This is the appropriate value!"

"We only hope he can join the Russian expedition and get them out of there."

Lucy's mind began piecing together the puzzle of the events during the last few days. The B-2 test flight, missing missile, Nikita, and Inna's father, all mixed into the one big picture, but there was still something missing in her thoughts. Lucy was sure that wasn't all Patrick was trying to achieve.

It's something internal and Patrick will not talk about it, Lucy thought, *I'm sure that's the case.*

"The left block in Russia is opposing the money Primankov is spending on his war machine to attack Ukraine while his own people are in a deep economic despair," Byron said. "Hard to see the connection between the war and Nikita's plans, it's confusing."

"Opening question for the goalscorer," Lucy quickly responded making a devilish face. "Trust me, I have a good sixth sense!"

"Perhaps you are right, Lucy," Byron mused. "When he briefly told me that an SVR agent, his good friend, asked him to volunteer for a possible expedition to the South Pole, perhaps it's actually the opposite. Perhaps it was Nikita who asked his friend to find a way to join the expedition using his fame for propaganda. How did Nikita know about the expedition that was marked as a top-secret mission? This needs to be answered. In return, Nikita would help with the internal SVR propaganda upon a successful mission using his celeb status when bringing the Interceptor home from Antarctica. You can see the breaking news headline on Pravda and TASS agency, *'Our hero soccer player retrieved the lost secret American Interceptor,'*" Byron said dramatically.

"I am sure the Russians will bring their alpine commando soldiers on the expedition, specially trained to operate in the arctic. There is valuable information, perhaps worth the $10M he requested, we need to unlock Nikita's mind. If the CIA agreed to it, it means Patrick already knows," Lucy said and poured herself another glass of scotch from the nearly empty bottle. "Let the MI-6 pay for the drinks," she mumbled and chuckled to herself.

"And if the CIA knows, the MI-6 knows!" Byron tried to level his agency on par with the CIA and Lucy chuckled softly again. After a short pause he added, "So why you here Lucy, what is your objective?"

"To confirm everything that you and the MI-6 know! And if that's how Nikita came up with his plan, it's smart *and* profitable! Perhaps it's all a hoax, a trap but if not? He knew we would take his deal!" she inhaled heavily, wondering, and throwing out all she had. She knew she would have to answer all her questions, as she decided right at that moment that the MI-6's role in her mission ended now. *She was good at working alone*, she thought.

"Perhaps Anatoly, the head of the SVR, is assuming the goalscorer team will lose," he chuckled and pulled a cigarette from his fancy silver box. "May I?" he asked politely. She nodded.

"Not sure what you mean Byron?"

Apparently, Byron was on a different frequency and changed subjects. "I expect street fights like always between the two teams' fans when they play each other, hulk gangs you know?" he joked and laughed. "The British don't like the Russians and the Russian fans don't like the British, and the beer will make sure we have a lot of drama. It will be fun to watch!"

"So, you suggest making contact with Nikita as soon as possible before the start of a street fight?" She laughed hardily.

"Oh no!" He laughed and replied, "We have covert field agents following the soccer team tomorrow and contacting us when they think there is an opportunity of a secure place to exchange a few quick words with him. Seeing the whites of his eyes, we don't want to burn him, and this has to be performed very professionally?" Byron stood looking down at her while she was still seated on the couch, his tone a bit condescending. "I am sure he expects us to contact him when it's all clear. Remember he will be very nervous and hard to approach."

Lucy didn't like to be patronized but contained the insult by biting her lips. "Well, I am sure if the MI-6 agency is running the first contact mission for us, I'm pretty confident you will do it very professionally, not like our sloppy aging CIA agents," Lucy scoffed and shook her head in disbelief.

Byron inhaled the cigarette smoke and exhaled in Lucy's direction with defiance due to her sarcastic tone of voice.

She had enough. She got inches from his face. "See you tomorrow, Byron, keep your pants on!" she snapped and grabbed the gun bag. She left the room immediately, without any formalities or polite salutations.

It was her turn to act, and she decided that the best way was to do exactly the opposite of what was expected. "Better alone and unexpected," she murmured to herself on the way out. But not before emptying her drink and wiping her mouth with her back of her hand in defiance of proper British table manners.

"I'll call you!" Byron managed to spit out before she closed the door behind her, agitated. She went to her room and pulled out a gold sweater to accent the green of her dress, and a Zara olive-colored trench coat with a built-in handgun holster. She checked the gun, cocked, and locked it. Now she felt secure and ready to get her questions answered.

"Damn you, English chauvinist," she mumbled and left her room, exiting the hotel from the back door into the drizzling rain and growing fog. The mist penetrated straight to her bones.

She hailed a cab and three cars stopped one after the other competing for her fare. Her agent instinct skills never failed. She chose the second cab while the first cab driver waved his hands and yelled. The warm interior was comforting and relaxing, and she snuggled into the black leather seat thinking of what was ahead. *Who knows?* A stray cat never knows what is ahead; they just manage.

"Hilton Wembley," she laconically directed the driver who glanced at her from his mirror.

Traffic was heavy due to the thick fog and low visibility and the fifteen-minute drive took about half-an-hour. The driver apologized and blamed the Easter tourists that swarmed the city by the thousands. *But he never complained about the weather, a true English gentleman,* she thought smiling.

The cab screeched to a stop in front of the grand hotel's entry façade, and a porter greeted Lucy by helping her out of the car. She walked into the large open lobby with its magnificent brown marble floors and forty-foot-high ceiling. Above her was the full splendor of luxurious chandeliers hanging low on thin metal cables. Lucy immediately tried to figure out where the soccer team might be hanging out. She didn't plan to be there all night.

She knew all three hotel hang-out joints in the same building. The Sky Bar 9 provided space heaters on the outside balcony which was empty. *Who wants to hang out on the cold terrace?* she thought. Then she tried the second spot; Icon Bar, Grill & Terrace was full of cheery guests, most of them ready to leave with gastronomical satisfaction. She combed the crowd but could not identify a soccer team among them. The last place was the restaurant. The Association Restaurant was a glamorous and inviting place full of people dining as well, but no sign of a soccer team in their jerseys or unified training outfit with their logos on sport coats due to dress code.

Oh well, Lucy remembered she hadn't eaten anything since she purchased a sandwich meal on her British Airlines flight and went back to the Icon Bar, Grill & Terrace and sat on a bar stool. The small menu offered was exactly what she craved, a double cheeseburger and hand-cut French fries. The bartender recommended the "Mango Citra" soda from a local brewer called "Cloud Water Brewing Company".

"It's a safe order," she mumbled to herself and started with a full mug of coffee to keep her focus.

If the soccer team did not show up by the time she was done with her meal, she always had Plan B tomorrow with Byron. *Even though she preferred to contact Nik alone, tonight* she thought as she scanned the room.

"Say, was the Russian soccer team here tonight?" she asked when the server brought her meal.

He scoffed and shook his head hiding a smile. "They are very discrete; I saw them earlier in the second-floor conference room preparing their strategy for the match." He sounded friendly and ready to talk soccer with anyone, anytime, if you dared show you knew more than him. "Are you a fan? Which team?" he asked and bent over the counter murmuring softly. "Liverpool will eat them alive dude," he clicked his tongue. "Five to zero," he made a five sign with his fingers.

"Oh, I am sure, I can't wait to waste those bastards!" She giggled like sharing a secret and both chuckled like old friends.

"Are you visiting?"

"Yeah, I wanted to watch the match," she said and almost choked on her cheeseburger which was as big as the lie she just told.

She decided to stick around for a short while since she had already gambled on finding Nik, and patience was always her best friend. She felt a little better after she ate and ordered a drink that resembled a non-alcoholic IPA.

"No Mango Citra soda?" He smiled and exposed his perfect white teeth. "It's on sale . . . oh, here is your team." His face radiated suddenly, and the server whispered excitedly, "Your team!"

Lucy turned around and noticed that most of the tables in the restaurant were empty and had been cleaned. A new sign posted at the entry to the restaurant said: *Closed for a private event.* The team walked in; The restaurant manager directed them to a section of tables arranged close together.

They were chatting in Russian, relaxed and cheery, wearing matching navy-blue casual team hoodies with the large team insignia, and white athletic pants with long blue lines along the sides.

She realized she was the only female in the restaurant and naturally they all paid attention to her presence. Sitting alone at the bar, Lucy didn't like to be the center of attention. "My job is to blend in not to stand out," she mumbled.

She almost immediately recognized the goalscorer from the photos Byron showed her in his hotel room. Five-feet nine-inches of tight muscle and a slender athletic body. His face was young, resembling the late actor, James Dean, who died in a car accident more than half a century ago, lady-killer looks with dirty blond hair hanging down to his shoulders and covering both sides of his face. His deep blue eyes looked around as if searching for something.

Time passed and Lucy locked her eyes with the goalscorer for a brief second. He reciprocated with another glance, and she didn't miss it this time, locking eyes again while casually sipping her drink. Lucy decided to make her move and nodded her head almost unnoticeably. He nodded back the same way, but it was good enough for Lucy to understand that contact was made. *He is reciprocating and he is handsome as hell,* she thought.

She paid in cash and asked casually in a normal voice where the restrooms were. It was loud enough that Nikita could hear but not too loud to draw anyone else's attention.

She left for the open lobby area toward the second-floor restrooms via the curved set of marble stairs, holding her coat loosely on her shoulder. Her sixth sense sent chills down her back. *He is watching me going up,* she felt.

The ladies' room was empty; she checked the stalls and made sure they were vacant. Then she waited; holding her breath, her heart racing while she caressed her gun in the holster. *Five minutes is too long. Didn't he get the message?* she thought and pushed the door to exit.

To her surprise, the door pushed back with the force of a hurricane. She wanted to draw her gun, but her trench coat was loose and in her way. She almost lost her balance but held onto the metal stall which prevented her fall. The hurricane who entered was Nikita, the famous "goalscorer". He immediately grabbed her arm, twisted it around her back and drew his face close to hers. She was trapped with her arm twisted with unimaginable force on the bathroom wall and she grunted aloud, "What the hell is wrong with *you?*" She snorted trying to free herself from his tight, twisted maneuver.

Pressing her tighter against the wall, he tried to lift her silk dress with the high cut slit and aggressively take her panties off. She threw the trench-coat to the floor and managed to lock her foot behind his foot, swiveled the same direction, causing him to land on his back. She stood firmly on the floor and planted a back kick directly to his genitals when he turned around, quickly hitting him on the back of his head with a round-off kick, Lucy's specialty. He fell to the floor groaning with pain.

"You will survive to lose another game. Not sure you will be fit for the soccer match or bedding any woman soon, NIKITA," she whispered in his ear. "Think of Inna, you son of a bitch!"

He blinked his eyes and opened them slowly looking at her face while on the floor groaning.

A thin layer of tears covered his face. She continued, "Send my regards to your fiancé and tell her I am not a whore, mister!" she hoarsely whispered. "I am here for your fucked up message to save you and your fiancé, for God's sake!" She helped him stand up and held her gun firmly now.

"Who are you?" he groaned holding the back of his head and the other hand holding his genitals.

"I was sent to meet you regarding defecting. So here I am. Be very serious if you want to play another game of soccer!"

"Are you with Patrick, the CIA?"

"Yes, I am! With warm regards from Washington! Do you know anyone else who can kick you like this?" she whispered loudly watching for anyone who might join the party from his side.

Nikita was stunned and his response was numb, trying to gather his thoughts. Then realized his hormonal reaction was a misunderstanding of Lucy's flirting signals. He tried to crack an apologetic smile, "Sorry I thought you were flirting with me out there." His heavy accent continued to turn her off.

"You are a stupid son of a bitch, perhaps in another life. I understand you are engaged, your poor little fiancé!" she whispered sarcastically in his ear, then licked his ear with her wet tongue and bit it with her teeth. He groaned.

"Can we do business now? We don't have much time; they will be looking for me," he whispered back and looked around the bathroom, which was empty. He became tense and nervous.

"What's the deal then? First, how are you connected with the MI-6? Quick!"

"It's Patrick. I have a friend connected with the MI-6 and he helped me connect with Patrick. I wanted to make sure he was serious and accepted my deal and wouldn't double-cross me. Marcia contacted Inna, my fiancé, and she agreed. The scientist agreed as well, with a twist. It was all set up; we will be on an expedition to Antarctica and from there defect to the USA. Pieter is here with us, and he is my friend, too, and will arrange everything. You should know that the SVR intercepted your Vandenberg Space Force Base 'Polar Protocol' mission, they know all about it . . . everything. They decided to steal the failed Interceptor and bring it to Russia. I conveyed my idea to Pieter to bring along Oleg, Inna's father, who is our hypersonic missile engineer, to inspect the Interceptor and figure out its design," he gasped for air and exhaled in relief.

"Well, we know all this. What's the catch?" Lucy inhaled deeply and arranged her thoughts. Patrick, Inna, Marcia, the names he mixed were a tossed salad without connection on who and why they were defecting. Names that Patrick didn't disclose to her. *Patrick needs to know, or perhaps he already knows,* she thought.

"If we bring the engineer, you know what you must do, right? Regarding my fiancé, she must leave Russia or die in a gulag, as for me? I'm very famous in Russia. I offered to use my name for propaganda," he said and touched his hurting genitals and groaned again.

"Don't worry, your genitals will survive. I hope I didn't hurt you too badly. Confirm your full name."

"Oh," he grunted "Nikita, Nikita Goretzki. They call me Nik."

"Sorry Nik let's get back to business. So, you expect to rendezvous in Antarctica with an American expedition, have a little commotion, exchange punches and 'poof' you are in America with your fiancé with the Russian scientist engineer. Is that your plan? Look into my eyes!"

"Yes, you need to figure this out yourself from what I just said. The engineer is your price, $10M. One million dollars now with a promise of full American citizenship, for all of us!" he grunted again.

"The engineer too? I understand he is a hardcore communist even though he is originally from Ukraine."

"No, the engineer thinks he is joining the expedition to check out your lost Interceptor. You might need to abduct him!"

Lucy got that side of the picture. It was a simple offer to assist a Russian scientist abduction for a fee of $10M. *But there was something else, there is always something else,* she thought.

"OK Nik, if this goes wrong, know we will find you. You know the CIA's reputation I hope?"

He nodded his head.

The loud calls from the corridors froze them in place.

"Nik . . . Nik!" The voices came from the corridor.

SVR paranoia at its best, she thought and tried to vanish from the powder room.

"Damn!" Nik slurred and left the ladies room quickly into the open corridor.

"Oh, there you are! What took you so long?" Pieter asked concerned and examined Nik's wounded neck. "What the hell happened to you?" he sounded both concerned and puzzled.

"I slipped!" Nik said calmly and touched his wounded area. Pieter escorted him back to the restaurant down on the first floor. His teammate and agent intercepted a signal from Pieter to check the surrounding areas while he went to the men's room, leaving after a couple of seconds when he found it empty.

Then he saw a drop of blood next to the ladies' room marble floor. He opened the door slowly and saw Lucy fixing her make-up in front of the mirror. She saw him from the back mirror image and reacted calmly. The Russian agent continued to look at the floors and saw a couple more blood drops on the floor and figured out there had been a struggle and connected it to Lucy and Nikita.

The SVR agent cautiously pulled his gun from his blazer and just before he could aim it at Lucy, she went from calm mode to killing-machine mode in less than a second. Turning around quickly with a double martial arts swivel kick that landed her fatal metal shoe heel to his temple, that was it. He fell on the floor with a loud *thud* slamming his face straight onto the hard marble floor. Lucy didn't waste any more valuable time to check on the limp body. She knew her strength while he was lying down, vulnerable. His gun slipped away a safe distance from her, she looked at him motionless, then stomped directly on his sternum with her heel hearing his ribcage bones crack. He stopped breathing.

She didn't check his status; she knew he wouldn't survive her deadly maneuver. Many times, she practiced that kick and was able to crack a solid cement block. The results were always the same. *"When your opponent is on the floor, finish the job,"* she heard her martial arts coach echo in her mind. Fixing her cotton gloves, she picked up her coat from the floor and put in on. She left the bathroom toward the open curved staircase leading down to the lobby and outside to the street.

Although she knew it would be very difficult to deceive the experts who retrieved the videos from the hotel security camera system. "Crap," she growled hoping she didn't jeopardize her mission. *Now Nik will have to explain why and how his escorting agent was killed and by who?* she thought. It's his problem now!

Two Russian agents rushed from the restaurant where the soccer team was sitting facing her with threatening eyes and tough looking faces. They blocked her way to the street and route to safety and freedom. The only way out now was to jump from the second floor down to the lobby and die. They started to move up the circular stairs closer and closer to where she was standing.

They pulled their guns inches from her body and tried to grab her. She leaned backward over the second-floor rail and jumped over at the last moment. From the ledge, she extended her jump by grabbing the metal cables holding up the chandeliers, slipped down to the lower floor, but lost her coat on the way. Looking back to see if she was clear, she thanked her luck for wearing the gloves. She could have injured her hands and dropped dead without them as they helped her hold onto the metal cables. She went back a couple of steps and quickly grabbed her coat from the floor and ran out to the street.

The two agents ran down the stairs only to see Lucy disappear into the sea of passersby.

She grabbed the second cab at the taxi stand down the street from the hotel and urged the driver to drive quickly out of the area. "Trafalgar Square," she barked in an excited tone. The driver nodded his head and stepped on the gas.

The show must go on! she thought and then remembered that Nik said, "Marcia." She heard that name for the first time but didn't ask due to time constraints. *What had he meant and who was this woman? Weird. She needed to flush this out soon with Patrick,* she thought and looked back to see if anyone was following her cab.

CHAPTER 12

March 17, 8:40 p.m.
Hilton Wembley, London

Pieter escorted Nik back to his seat and interrogated him about the wound. It didn't look good; his instinct told him something was up.

"It looks like a strike Nik. What the hell really happened?"

"It's OK. Don't be worried; I can still play soccer!"

"Stop playing with me Nik; who did it? Who is this ninja woman who just escaped our agents out on the street?"

"Some stranger. She attacked me when I went to the men's room, asking for a photograph and when I refused, she grabbed me into the ladies' room, struck me in the face and when I resisted, she kicked me in my genitals."

"A woman did this to you. Are you serious? Is that the one that slipped away?"

"She was an English soccer hooligan, drunk!" Nik tried to convince Pieter.

"We saw her in the bar earlier and her performance escaping the hotel, she is definitely a professional agent. Glad she didn't kill you. Why didn't you just send us a sign?" yelled Pieter frustrated this happened on his watch.

"I hate English soccer hooligans, she flirted with me from the bar and lured me to the bathroom, understand?" Nik yelled back. "I thought she wanted to flirt with me Pieter!"

"You are a damn horny son of a bitch; how can I convince my superior to add you to the expedition? You could jeopardize our plans!" Pieter snorted.

"Sorry it's the last time Pieter. Sorry to put you in this position. It won't happened again, promise!" Nik blubbered.

Pieter looked at the restaurant entrance and asked the two returning agents who were visibly out of breath.

"She ran away!" they said disappointedly.

"Andre check for Vasily? He is probably still in the bathroom!" Pieter sounded concerned and didn't mind if they came back empty-handed after chasing Lucy.

"Stay here with Nik, I'll be right back!" Pieter commanded as he left to find out where his colleague, Vasily had gone. He went back to the men's room and checked it out. No people, no hooligans, and it was clean as a whistle. Then he opened the ladies' room door checking to see if it was vacant, he immediately saw his agent lying on the floor face down, motionless.

"Vasily!" he screamed as he checked for a pulse. He looked around, seeing blood spots on the floor and figured they were from his agent's struggle.

"Damn hooligans," Pieter yelled at the walls. He called the rest of the agents who had joined the soccer team and asked them to search the floors thoroughly for any other collaborators who may have assisted her. He could not believe one woman could have created such havoc working alone. He took Vasily's gun from the floor and tucked it in his jacket; it was loaded, perhaps he saw something and was not ready until he was struck. He checked Vasily's wounds, "A professional killer, that's not a hooligan job," he mumbled, his head spinning with a splitting headache.

* * *

Pieter was nervous. His boss, President Primankov, was frustrated and agitated when he heard the news.

"It's a London police issue; they needed to protect our team," Rubi said. "It's not a hooligan who did this. They are trying to cover up the event."

Pieter, on the encrypted phone with his boss and the defense minister, discussed the killing. "I know the difference between a hooligan killing and a covert agent killing. I took a piece of Vasily's shirt and checked where he was hit. Looks like a metal object–"

"I am missing the big picture," the defense minister responded.

"It was a foreign agent, probably a CIA, and it was not planned. My question is who are they after? And why?" Pieter asked. "I had never seen a performance like this, minister; she was very acrobatic, a–"

"And Nik survived a ninja?" Rubi was sarcastic.

"Probably a coincidence; perhaps an accident."

"I am not convinced, Pieter! Why would a foreign agent try to contact Nik? That is my question."

"We'll get to the bottom of this, but right now, we should quietly accept the hooligan explanation theory, so the police will release our team to play. At home after the game, we will interrogate everyone," advised Pieter.

They hung up and Pieter went back to his team. The police arrived quickly and took reports from everyone. The hotel security officer added his own theory based on his surveillance recordings.

Pieter went to Nik and asked about the attacker while checking his wound carefully; he asked compassionately if he was OK. Nik nodded his head, running the events in his mind like game playback, it had all happened so fast.

"Why you, though? She was a hooligan, right, Nik?"

"Who else would attack me?" he shot back angrily.

The wound was treated by a paramedic who told him he needed stitches since it was not a clean cut, in order to avoid a future scar. "You need to go to the hospital for that," said the paramedic.

The hotel security officer led Pieter and Nik to his room full of screens that recorded the hotel from every angle and every corner. "This is the video from the second floor during the time the team left the conference room to the restaurant. In this one you all entered the restaurant as one lady dined at the bar. She left after paying in cash and, by the way, the police interrogated the bartender and he said she was a soccer fan. She was not a guest of the hotel–"

"That's a detail to remember," jumped in Pieter. "What was she doing there then?"

The security officer continued in his monotone voice which could put any insomniac to sleep, "And here she went to the ladies' room–" announced the security officer.

"Hold on, go back to the bar. Do you have a close up of her face?"

The camera focused and showed Lucy searching the team and then a slight nod. "Wait, what is this, who is she signaling to?" Pieter struck like a snake.

"We don't have a camera angle on that." The security officer gasped and inhaled deep. "Here he's leaving the restaurant and–"

"I was going to the men's room," Nik explained, exasperated looking for a life vest in this stormy mess he got himself into.

"Did you respond to her signal Nik? The truth!" Pieter said loudly.

"It will sound embarrassing to you, Pieter, I thought she was a prostitute. I told you that!"

Pieter scoffed and hit Nik on his shoulder. "Yeah, you told me that!" He shook his head and could not come up with words. Then erupted with anger. "For God's sake, Nikita, what the hell were you thinking? Is that why you lied and said it was a hooligan?"

"Perhaps she was a hooligan prostitute!" exclaimed the security officer who surprisingly backed up Nik. "Many high-dollar call girls come and sit at the bar hunting high-roller soccer fans who come from all over the world to watch our premier league," the security officer said moving the conversation in a new direction about the biggest sport in the British soccer empire.

"Or perhaps she wanted to hurt our team," Pieter interrupted the security officer's emotional explanation.

The video examination was done, the rest would be done by the police. In the meantime, every agent, police officer and security personnel in London got a pic of Lucy's face and the hunt was on.

"No, this is not a coincidence, more likely a foreign agent was sniffing around," Pieter spoke in Russian and shared his thoughts with Nik.

"I want to kill her!" Nik reacted emotionally in an Oscar-worthy performance.

"You play soccer and let the SVR handle it."

"Help me join the SVR, kill her, and get back to soccer. I can do both at the same time."

CHAPTER 13

Same day, late night

L ucy needed confirmation from Nik that the plan was still intact and decided that she must talk to him face-to-face one more time before he returned to Russia and then communication with him would shut down. Perhaps Patrick knows more than he tells me, perhaps Marcia is his contact person, she thought. The words Nik said, "It's Patrick," echoed in her mind from when they spoke in the hotel's bathroom.

Was there another contact with Patrick and Nik before?" she would have to find this out, she thought.

The commotion took a turn for the worst when the hotel security got involved, checking security cameras. Paramedics showed up at the scene. The Metropolitan Police Service of London (the former Scotland Yard) were happy to investigate since the Russian soccer team managers blamed an English soccer hooligan for the killing, without disclosing that a foreign agent might have been responsible for the killing. Lucy knew she was trapped.

She paid the driver extra in cash to get out of there fast. Lucy ducked into The National Café across from the Square but not before she heard the taxi driver say, "Was nice driving you, Miss Marple." He laughed. She knew from her training to break up her escape route to as many legs as possible. She always paid in cash to lose any financial tracking and erase the connection she ever visited Hilton Wembley. But her bright green dress could be used to track her down and disclose her. She gave her coat to a homeless person who was feeding breadcrumbs to hundreds of pigeons while sitting on the cold stone sidewalk. He thanked God for the gesture.

Lucy hung out in the restaurant for ten minutes to warm up and got a cup of coffee and a pastry. She sat at an empty table she was lucky to get since the place was crowded. Intent on spending as little time as possible there, acting naturally, she left looking for a small boutique to change her clothes. She decided to walk north along Whitcomb Street toward the Z Hotel Piccadilly, the opposite direction from police headquarters. She was a little chilly but not terrible and hoped to find what she was looking for. Then she changed her mind, swallowed her ego, and called Byron on her encrypted line. *Would he pick up the call?* she wondered.

The line opened and Byron barked, "Yes!"

"Can you pick me up?" she asked without giving any explanation.

"Where are you?" he snorted, infuriated. "The entire world is looking for you, goddammit!"

"I'll explain," she replied shortly. "I am on my way to Z Hotel on Orange Street. Bring a new coat for me please, I'm freezing."

As she walked into an empty alley, a Mercedes Benz driving very slowly, as if searching for something, stopped by her side. Two men emerged and jumped out from both sides of the car, threatening to shoot. The closest one, the driver, called out in Russian, "It's her!" and aimed his gun at her. The other man was slower reacting than his colleague. "Yes, that is her, the same one I saw at the hotel," he yelled, rushing his colleague driver to react.

"Stop!" the driver screamed at Lucy as they tried to seize her from both sides of the sidewalk. She backed up a few steps closer to the hotel's entrance in order to protect herself from the back. Pulling her gun quickly as well, ignoring she was not the first, she shot the driver who hesitated. His gun fell on the ground near his body. He was dead, falling like a sack of Idaho potatoes, blood pouring from his wounded chest. The other man did not expect such a quick and brutal reaction from Lucy and was confused.

"Don't pull your gun," she called in Russian. "Or I'll kill you, too!" she sneered, and the other man froze. He didn't want to end up dead like his colleague. Lucy's gun barrel to his head convinced him to put his gun back in its holster and he raised his hands, surrendering. "Get in the car," she commanded and sat beside him. "Drive!" They heard paramedics and police hollering at cars in the distance.

The gun fight in the middle of the narrow London street caused many of the hotel guests to scatter chaotically looking for cover while the concierge pressed the panic button to call the police.

"Stop at the next corner," she ordered with the barrel still pressed to his skull. "I do not need prisoners," she added with a cold expression. Then she squeezed the trigger, shot the driver dead in cold blood. "I don't need a witness either," she mumbled, and quickly got out of the idling car.

A white Vauxhall Astra screeched to a stop in front of her. "Get in!" he yelled as police cars sped all around. She jumped into the car.

Byron, despite his sleepy appearance grasped the situation immediately seeing the dead driver in the Mercedes' front seat with the engine on and diplomatic license plate; he understood the gravity of the situation Lucy was in. The Vauxhall made a turn into a narrow alley as police cars set up roadblocks, investigating drivers. From a safe distance, they saw police checking the Mercedes with its dead Russian agent inside. Both sighed loudly.

"Thank goodness," he stated and threw a coat her direction. "Get warm, there is a lot of explaining you need to do!" His disdain was evident for being sucked into this deadly situation. "This is why we lock wild cats like you in cages," he stormed. "You could have created an international diplomatic incident! Where have you been?" he yelled angrily.

"Watch the road!" Lucy replied calmly. "The Russians didn't buy the hooligan killing story and as of right now, they are all after me!"

Byron sighed and said, "We realized your actions in the Hilton Hotel dear! He paused "So, we asked the hotel security officer to block the videos from being publicized on the web and media," responded Byron.

Lucy was impressed how fast "sleepy" Byron could connect the dots between the event in the hotel and her last hour's activities. "Crazy!" he yelled and snapped her back to his reality.

"We'll see if blocking the video helped!" Lucy snapped back. "The Russians paid the security guy for the videos showing my full face and quickly distributed it to their agents at large." She kept the same angry tone.

"How does an experienced CIA agent get caught on camera? Can you explain this to me?" He gasped, driving into historic London's notoriously narrow alleys with their dim streetlights trying to avoid main street exposure while he thought through their next move.

"We'll see how this ends up," he said calmly. Lucy watched for followers and was eager to get back to her safe hotel room and a hot bath.

"Say Byron, something doesn't add up," Lucy replied sharing her disturbing thoughts. "Either I am being used as a pawn, or there is a bigger game being played!"

"What game?" He frowned and kept his voice calm for the benefit of them both.

"Who did the goalscorer contact first? The CIA or MI-6?" she asked, even though Nik explained that to her. "This piece of information is missing for me!"

Byron made a circle around their destination before finally entering the hotel driveway. Their conversation was as confidential as it could be inside the car. "I am not sure about your question Lucy; this assignment was simply to contact the goalscorer, not sure what your objectives were. I was told to help and assist you. Why is this important to know at this stage of the game?" Byron tried to convince himself more than trying to convince Lucy.

Stopped finally at their hotel, they went straight to Byron's room on the fourth floor. The hotel was busy. Many people walked in and out but it was hard not to be seen. She put her coat over her head and checked her gun, feeling safer when touching it. Byron, on the other hand, was more comfortable with the surroundings and felt at home. Not Lucy.

"What's your point? Who cares whom the goalscorer contacted first?" he asked, shutting the hotel room door.

"Because I think someone from the MI-6 turned me in!"

"Rubbish, you are out of your mind!" Byron snapped.

Byron went straight to the bar to pour himself a drink. It was probably his tenth drink since Lucy met him; but who's counting? she thought. He settled for scotch on the rocks again making sure not to leave any unused bottles in the minibar before his assignment was over.

He raised his glass as if to ask if Lucy wanted a drink; she denied. *There was enough alcohol in her blood mixing with adrenaline,* she thought.

"Someone wants me dead, perhaps because I didn't play by the rules and changed their game?" She laughed nervously. "Another thing that puzzles me is that Nik mentioned Patrick which means Patrick knew about Nik before I did. I thought

I was making the first contact. Patrick did not disclose to me that he established contact with Nik and not the MI-6; understand?" she inhaled deeply and exhaled slowly thinking perhaps Byron might be able help. Then she realized even if he knew, he would not share with her more than what she already knew.

"The name Nik came from you; I didn't know the goal-scorer's name when I arrived. My agency only gave me the photos. Why is it important?" he asked, puzzled.

"It is important since I need to know if I met my objectives, and the purpose of my mission."

Byron's cell phone rang, and Lucy regretted not having him make her a drink. She took this opportunity to make one. Taking a sip, she made a face. "Yuck."

"B here," Byron greeted the caller laconically. He listened politely and then put his cell on speaker. "Police are investigating a Russian soccer team member's murder at Hilton Wembley and the–" Byron hung up the phone call abruptly.

Lucy rolled her eyes. *The objective was met,* she thought.

CHAPTER 14

March 18, 2:10 a.m.

Six hours later, safe and back in her hotel room, Lucy was still full of adrenaline, her chest pounding. She left Byron on his own to fume. On the ride back to the hotel, she had her fill of his criticism over her escalation of the commotion in London just before the important world soccer match at Wembley Stadium.

The global soccer fandom ranted on social media that the game must go on and put politics aside.

The media competed amongst themselves with bombastic headline coverage like *BBC*'s A Murder in Hilton Wembley, or the *London Evening Standard*'s Killer on the loose! Where is Agatha Christie When We Need Her? or *FIFA*, The Game Must Go On! was nonstop around the clock from evening into morning. They showed Lucy's blurry images as a suspect for questioning. How they obtained the security videos was another compelling argument no one asked, especially MI-6 who tried to minimize the collateral damage.

MI-6 stopped the frenzy by releasing a statement through the London police stating they were investigating a sole hooligan responsible for the killing.

Lucy turned off the television in her room and called Patrick. It was 11 a.m. in DC and Patrick was on his way back to Langley from a political breakfast event. He was in a good mood as he watched the flurries landing gently on the windshield of the Chevy SUV.

Before he had a chance to greet his agent, Lucy spoke first on the line and sounded like a greyhound growling at a cat. "Who is Marcia, Patrick?" Lucy asked. "Nik mentioned her name briefly. We could not talk much. It was chaos there."

"Why couldn't you work with the MI-6 agent to interview Nik tomorrow; I mean today, your time?" Patrick scolded. "Why did you go rogue, Lucy? This was a bad move. Even though I backed you up, you could have obtained more information from Nik if you would have waited as planned."

Lucy didn't like the feeling of being put in a corner, like a child. "Byron rubbed me the wrong way Patrick. He was arrogant and I have the experience to make my own judgment in the field. You taught me that!" she gasped as the phone line hissed for a second, a sign that the encryption call was working. "I thought Byron would be a burden and an obstacle; no help at all. He looked and sounded bored plus he defiantly blew smoke in my face. I can't work with someone who thinks he is better than me!" she shot back trying to hold her temper by lowering her voice out of respect but needing to make her point heard. "The soccer team is very shielded by the SVR agents, Patrick. I thought my spontaneous step would yield more productive results and save ti–"

Patrick took over the conversation. "Did you think through this plan thoroughly, Lucy? First, did you clear the plan with Nik? Second, was his fiancé on board with the plan? Her father? If all that was clear, then yes, you could make a step forward!"

A car horn sounded loudly in the background and the windshield wipers screeched as the flurries grew into a sudden snowstorm which made it hard for Patrick to hear.

"Well, yes!" she snapped, agitated yet still composed. "You wanted to push the Russian expedition. Nik said they are on board with that. He knows about the Interceptor and their plans to retrieve it. So yes, he mentioned he was working that angle. Pieter will include him on the expedition. Isn't that the main valuable and critical information you needed?" she asked awaiting further instructions.

Patrick thought quietly while directing the driver of a short cut to avoid the traffic. He always gave his agents a free hand in the field. It was important to improvise and bring forth the results regardless of the means and methods used; even a small action could keep information flowing. Patrick knew Lucy was under more pressure due to the media exposure and the entire soccer world speculating who she was.

Lucy reminded Patrick of his own field agent doctrine which was, every time they were sent to a mission, they were in charge. "You are in Patrick's shoes and as Patrick, the director of the CIA in the field, I'll back you up with whatever you do."

Patrick always kept some details of the plan to himself until the proper time, to move his agents onto the next step like in a chess game. Step-by-step he played with the world intelligence agencies as the master of the game. No one should know too much at a time.

"Yes, that's a good point," he mumbled.

"What kind of a deal did you make with Nik that's worth $10M?" she asked and wondered why she hadn't asked that earlier.

"Marcia helped Nik and Inna to contact her estranged father. Especially important since Inna was in the underground and Marcia was the conduit among all three of them. She convinced her father to ask to join the expedition and Pieter thought it was a good idea and presented it to his boss, Anatoly." Patrick kept a few cards up his sleeve and knew it would all come out sooner than later.

Lucy figured that Patrick did this for her own safety, as well as keeping the full plan out of reach of the SVR in case she somehow was caught by their adversary agents. Her head was spinning; jet lag hit her like a hammer, and she could not crack what was churning in Patrick's head.

"Nik's on board, sounds like his fiancé is in too. Who else is on the expedition list, no surprises?" Lucy tried using another fishing strategy on Patrick.

"In time you will know. We need to get you back here tomorrow, today I mean."

They both chuckled and Patrick was glad he had calmed his agent down. So, Marcia was a CIA collaborator, probably the only one who survived the SVR elimination of her network.

"Patrick, the media is reporting that the Pacific fleet was dispatched from Pearl Harbor and started maneuvers near the Polar coast. Is this related to our mission, your plan?" Lucy asked changing the subject, "I predic–"

"Yes, we are sending logistic and rescue support operations to our polar expedition to protect the Interceptor from falling into foreign hands," he said quickly and called his driver to watch a semi driving erratically.

"The entire fleet for one Interceptor?" Lucy laughed loudly in disbelief.

"It was scheduled anyway, I just changed the plan a little, yes!" Patrick's resolve was obvious with the shortness of his reply. He wanted to end the conversation since he was near his destination. The snowfall tapered but it was still difficult to hear with the squeak of the wipers. He tried to lead Lucy to her next move.

"The *Arctic Star* icebreaker is heading to the South Pole and currently on the high seas. When you get back to US soil, prepare to join them!"

"Really? Sick world, sick minds!" she coughed as she opened a Pellegrino from the minibar, making sure to empty the hotel room minibar paid for by the good English taxpayers. She grabbed an apple from the fruit tray and one of those little, tiny chocolate bars housekeeping leaves on the pillow after service–under different circumstances, those things would never meet her mouth. "I need sugar!" she chuckled.

"Stay focused Lucy. You're booked on the next UA flight 919 to Dulles Airport. A nonstop departing at 12:05 p.m., Byron will escort and board with you onto the plane via the back door," Patrick disclosed looking at his watch.

Lucy understood what that meant: no regular check-in, no security process, no going through the terminal, no long, congested lines at the boarding gates. She passionately hated all those things anyway. The back door entrance was used frequently for safety and ease, by heads of state or dignitaries with prior approval.

Lucy's reassignment to the icebreaker surprised her. Another reason why she thought Patrick was the best director at his post. "Logistics and rescue mission," she mumbled and smiled. She would never be able to read his mind, but his quote could be tattooed on her forehead. She laughed at the thought.

Now Nik was on her mind. She needed to find out how to communicate with his fiancé and him in the future. *Patrick should make the contact, but he won't*, she thought. Seems like Patrick may be scheduling a rendezvous in Antarctica with all of them; *interesting*.

The *Arctic Star* icebreaker, scheduled to sail from its home base in Seattle, Washington a few days ago, prepared to greet Hurricane Mina, classified as a Cat 2 and increasing quickly to Cat 3. The Coast Guard vessel was already enroute to the McMurdo research station, ready to break ten feet of ice on its way, but now Mina was on the radar ahead with destructive hurricane winds gusting to 110 miles per hour and growing. Mina was being fed by the warm Pacific Ocean water which surprised the scouting mission that sailed in late March. Global Warming became suspect for the cause.

"Don't leave more messes like in London," Patrick said. "I know you would never waste a good fight, Lucy, but chill!"

"So, Patrick, was my mission accomplished? My objective?"

"Of course, by all means. Small steps lead to a big one. The Russians know what we wanted them to know, and they will plan an expedition to Antarctica. Now we just wait."

"They know about Nik?" Lucy asked.

"Sure, they know. That's why they sent Pieter straight from LA to watch him; they wanted to make sure no one defects or works for us!"

"I hope Antarctica will not turn into a graveyard!"

CHAPTER 15

March 21, Morning
Moscow

The soccer match's final score with Liverpool was a tie, which ended Nik's soccer team's quest to seek their first European championship trophy. But for the Russians it was a big victory to tie with one of the top soccer teams in the world. This elevated Nik's celebrity, by scoring the tieing goal, big news in Russia. "It was the best loss ever won," *Pravda* announced in the morning paper, and the soccer club fan page went ballistic.

The Domodedovo airport was full of soccer fans waiting to greet the returning team. Nik was the center of the attention with interviews and photos covering newspapers and the internet boosting his prestige as a hero, exactly how the SVR wanted him to come back–internationally famous.

The little scar and stitches on his face were attributed to a soccer hooligan attack in the hotel and the media knew how to turn it into another heroic event in which Nik prevailed.

Pieter knew the truth and went along with the story and knew that Vladimir would keep his eye on the odd civilian group joining the Russian expedition. Vladimir trusted Pieter who put together that ensemble.

In London, the British police granted the request to bury the case in the archives and blame hooligans. Byron went back to his boring administrative desk work since he lost

Lucy under his watch. They all knew she was responsible for the diplomatic incident.

Russian Defense Minister Rubi, with a nod from his president, started the virtual meeting to discuss the international incidents and develop strategic new plans to keep their military's advantage. The expedition logistics and objectives were important, even though the navy had already dispatched three Akula nuclear class submarines to surround the frozen continent, protect the future expedition, and deter anyone whose plans interfered with their secret assignment—the pilfering of the Interceptor.

"Yes, it's confirmed!" exclaimed Rubi. "All three loaded subs left their bases and are enroute."

During the encrypted virtual conference meeting, Rubi coordinated with FSS Director Vitali, Anatoly the head of the SVR, and his senior agent, Pieter; also attending was the director of the FSB, Counterintelligence Director Lenny Kratzki (a civilian position) a tough ex-general with the army, and the head of the Russian Arctic Special Commando Forces. The topic of discussion was to solidify the expedition's needs and requirements and they report directly to Primankov.

Rubi asked to keep the mission confidential. "It's not an open call for volunteers; it's a military action and keep it that way," he stated, knowing time was of the essence.

"Long debates would not serve the confidentiality needed for the success of this type of mission. We already know and saw signs that the Americans have no intention of losing their Interceptor a second time. That shows it's not a trap; we see some 'out of the ordinary activities' at the South Pole. The American South Pacific fleet is preparing to set sail south from Pearl Harbor," Rubi said and waited for a response before continuing. No one said a word. He continued, "The fleet can't cross the 60-latitude south line with its military forces according to the mutually signed international agreement from back in the '50s. The agreement states that no military personnel, equipment, or mission is permissible in order to keep Antarctica neutral, therefore confidentiality is needed."

"Our satellites confirmed clearly that the Pearl Harbor fleet was preparing for a long-haul mission. They have stocked the fleet to full capacity in the last couple of days," Anatoly reinforced his minister's statement.

"They also announced it on the news," the president said. "The media over there can't shut up." He detested the American media commentators who chatted freely on morning news.

"We are lucky the Americans always tell us their plans ahead of time," Rubi mused. "Makes our counterintelligences' lives easier. It's evident the US Navy is still on autopilot," continued Rubi.

Primankov was in listening mode. "American naval crews have fewer training excursions. They seem to be tired, handling their activities with no specific global threats anymore. The Cold War is over for them, that's good a–" Vitali stopped.

Pieter tried to get him back to reality and abruptly said, "Not for us, The Cold War was never over, perhaps for the old generation, but not for the young Russians. It's not over ye–"

Vladimir cut Pieter off, "The young generation does not want to fight. Only people associated with the Army want to fight."

"We used awareness engineering to put the Americans in sleep mode for thirty years while we built the massive and mightiest Navy in the world. The US gave up on monitoring our submarines around the world, scrapping most of their navy equipment in junk yards. It's not the strong navy we confronted once upon a time," Primankov stated adding Russian might for persuasion.

"That is a good sign, but you never know what they have in their arsenal confidentially," said Anatoly. "We don't want to be surprised in Antarctica!"

"They did not discover our Akula sub in Virginia as we planned though we deliberately gave them a signal," Rubi chuckled. "We wanted the US to know our resolve and keep out of our affairs in Ukraine."

Within the Russian military, soldiers and old timers had never forgiven or forgotten the humiliation after the collapse of the Soviet Union. It was the same military, only the past lieutenants were now generals and admirals, who were eager to retaliate and fully confident they would win. However, when the media confirmed Pacific fleet maneuvers close to Antarctica, they lost some of their steam and snapped back to reality. They couldn't deny or ignore the American's strength.

"Look, perhaps the fact the Americans do not show any sign of provocation and are not monitoring us does not necessarily mean they are sleeping. Perhaps they are keeping their resources for something else; or it means they are not taking us *seriously,* nor do they fear us. So what if we conducted a test in Virginia? It means we are assholes in their minds. If we attacked them 100 miles from their home, they would hit us with their nuclear missiles from Poland, with less than five minutes notice. We would be demolished too." President Primankov stressed his point to the overly confident team, watching their inflated egos deflate. "We should focus on our mission and our mission only—the Interceptor. Otherwise, our hypersonic missile advantage could be wiped out and set us back ten years." Primankov inhaled deeply. "So, if you recommend an expedition, I want to make sure we are not going to war and do what we need to. Do you understand?" Primankov asked.

"We know the Americans will fight to keep their Interceptor from falling into our possession. We are not going to Antarctica for vacation, Mr. President but to fight a 'linear war', dressed in civilian clothing, disguised weaponry, and protecting ourselves in case of emergency only. This way no one knows who is whom, or why. So Vlad, when selecting your team, be cautious, include the best elite Arctic commando troopers who can use their bare hands as weapons," Rubi advised.

"That's the plan, a 'linear war'. Understood!" Vladimir responded right away since these were the same war tactics he conducted in Crimea.

"You see why I want Nik to join the expedition?" asked Pieter. "I thought it was good to have a civilian celebrity for our future propaganda purposes," he said without disclosing any more of his personal thoughts.

"Good idea, but we should keep this confidential in case of a failure; then no one knows," Anatoly agreed and thought it was a good idea to use Nik for propaganda purposes.

"Yes, it makes sense," agreed the defense minister, composed. "Once we bring the Interceptor home, we can explode it in a grand ceremony and make Nik the new Gagarin," he said exhaling.

"There is one condition. Nik requested his fiancé in the deal along with her father a–" Pieter stopped.

"No!" growled Rubi. "She is a member of LFD (Liberty, Freedom, and Democracy) movement, against our president. It's like asking a Trojan horse to enter our stable."

"Well, perhaps it could work for the best. If I may say, from lemons comes lemonade," said Primankov using his analytical mind to quickly calculate the data in his head. "Perhaps she won't survive the harsh expedition conditions,

Antarctica is not an inviting continent." He clicked his tongue and kept his icy expression.

The eerie silence after that statement served well for Pieter. This was the silent approval to kill her when the mission was over. They all digested what the president meant and looked at Pieter as he made a gesture like shooting himself in the head while tightening his lips. "Execution," Pieter murmured.

After a short silence, inhaling loudly, Rubi was the first to speak. "Yes, yes, but it's still a compelling question to ask why Nik wants her to join? Does she know what that means? She knows how hard it is to trek the Antarctic tundra, right?" Rubi asked.

"I think it will work great for us, killing two birds with one shot if that is what you are thinking? What do you think Pieter?" asked Vitali from the FSS (Federal Security Service) point of view.

"We need Oleg to join the expedition, and Inna brings him there. I understand she opposes our president . . ." Pieter acknowledged and nodded his head. *More words not needed now*, he thought.

"Exactly!" interrupted Vitali reinforcing Pieter's point. "No one in the world would condemn us for her death in Antarctica. Shit happens and especially in a very complex expedition like this. And for Nik, alive with success or death if not, he would still be remembered as a hero," Vitali chuckled at his ambivalence.

"It doesn't matter, the world will condemn us no matter what," scoffed Pieter seeing Vitali who didn't like his comment.

"Before we dispatch our troops from mainland, do we have any troops in Antarctica at the present, Vitali?" Rubi asked Vladimir.

Vladimir frowned, which gave him a tough look with cold piercing eyes and scary skeleton cheeks. His officer's hat was too big for his skull. He always wore it sideways and kept it on during the conference call. The perfect persona of a killing machine.

"Let me answer the president regarding the Vostok Ice Station then answer your question, Rubi. For your information, we do *not* keep people at Vostok Research Station during the winter, it is secluded and vulnerable to extreme weather there. They just sent back an ample research team since the station is currently under a major modernization rehab of its living quarter modules. Usually, we keep a team of thirty or forty in the summer, sometimes more, and only ten in the winter, comprised of half scientists and half technicians, no military. The other stations like Russkaya, Mirny, and Bellingshausen are permanent stations as you probably know, all located in coastal areas, and have easier access for our submarines to assist."

"Thank you!" exhaled Rubi.

"Our expedition could be blended with the end of the summer ice station crew for Bellingshausen Ice Station. No one would connect–" Vladimir stopped.

"Figure out a way to send thirty full-gear commando troops disguised as scientists with the white camouflage uniforms. No one would suspect that we have a search expedition in Antarctica, right?" Rubi drilled his Arctic Forces Commander.

"True sir, it's quite normal to beef up the station for the summer. We still have six weeks until winter crew relief. It's a little unusual to do it toward the end of summer, but we have a strong reputation of doing the opposite, so let them laugh. We should have light weapons like handguns." Rubi replied.

Vladimir was not sure where Rubi was going with this. "Concurred. With guns!" Vladimir thundered loudly.

Vladimir, the commanding officer of the South and North Pole special forces, was ready for this mission as he was trained for it all his life. It was a different kind of mission that he thought would be a walk in the park. "Now reports from our agents say the Interceptor landed 100 km from our floating research station at the South Pole."

"If we knew what to search for, we would know already," the president seemed frustrated.

"Suppose we *do* find the Interceptor and suppose we are first; then logistically how would we bring it in? It's heavy I suppose, right?" asked Pieter.

"I thought the same," said Rubi. "What's your thoughts Pieter?"

"I am reinforcing Oleg's participation, perhaps bring more engineers?" Pieter suggested.

"Not sure about that," blurted Vitali from a deep thought. "They should not leave Russia," he was firm. "If we can't bring the Interceptor as a whole, leave it there with our flag sticking in the snow," he chuckled. "Oleg is enough to leave our land, but he must come back, Pieter!"

"We have options. We can fly our Mi26-chopper from the *Admiral Karlinski* research boat, but until you decide, let's start assembling the expedition team Rubi. We always can cancel or change the team members," said the president.

"So, it's all or nothing, Rubi?" frowned Anatoly. "I think it's a good idea, perhaps a couple of mechanics to dismantle the Interceptor into pieces if needed. Think about it?"

"Then we could not hide this mission from the Americans for too long!" Rubi insisted.

"Rubi, then it would be too late for the Americans too. Please think it through, it's good idea." Anatoly pushed and the rest agreed, starting chatter that soon subsided on its own.

"OK, I will consider your suggestions gentleman," Rubi concluded.

"Keep this out of the eyes of the ATS (Atlantic Treaty Secretariat)!"

"The USA officially requested today, permission to retrieve the Interceptor that landed accidentally in Antarctica. The organization's executive secretary in Buenos Aires granted it. No country other than us and the Americans have land marking sovereignty land claim. Other nations have claims with no specific territory and land markings, the rest of the total fifty-four nations' members of the organization have no claim whatsoever," Rubi stated showing a bit of the information he had withheld.

Pieter, flashed back to the London hotel incident between Nik and the woman. He was sure it was a CIA excursion targeting the soccer star and was not comfortable with the event he left behind unsolved. He bribed the hotel security who emailed him the woman's photos and portraits to be analyzed by his SVR agency labs, using face recognition technology. He kept this personal and confidential for his own accolades when it was all over.

Pieter realized that there were a few agendas and everyone in this virtual meeting had a few different objectives, he would try to satisfy them all.

He agreed and encouraged to have Nik and Inna his fiancé on the expedition while he was investigating Lucy's photos, her origin, and how she got so close to Nik? Was it coincidence she was sniffing around him in the hotel at the same time? He didn't want to miss any detail, especially when the CIA was involved. His spine shivered. It didn't matter where he would end his espionage journey, but he must kill Lucy, an ego thing. Furthermore, he determined that if in the worst-case scenario the suspicions swarming his mind proved to be true, there would be no better place than Antarctica to eliminate the two lovers. He flirted with the idea and wanted to make sure to collect the $10M from the CIA which was supposed to be paid to Nik.

CHAPTER 16

March 20, 4:22 p.m.
CIA headquarters, Langley VA

Byron drove Lucy through the special gate directly to the Dreamliner parked on the tarmac before the passenger boarding had started. The cockpit crew prepared the plane, calibrating instruments, and logging the flight plan data on its computer.

Byron and Lucy, aided by an American Airlines official employee, went up the side steps of the passenger loading bridge leading to the terminal on the left, and to the airplane's entrance door on the right. The cabin crew seemed unprepared, asking themselves, "Who is this prima donna?"

They directed Lucy to the cockpit where she would be seated on a jump-seat for many tight painful hours behind the pilots.

"I guess the flight is full?" she joked with the stewardess.

"No," the crew member replied laconically, looking her up and down. Then she took another long look at Lucy's face and explained, "You were assigned to that seat in the cockpit by the airline, if you need anything, please just ask."

"What's up with that bitch?" Lucy asked herself.

Patrick was not in a good mood. The mission was complicated, and he felt as if the entire US defense leaned on his shoulders. What could he have done better, or differently, he asked himself time after time. To his disadvantage, he couldn't use too many advisers if he wanted to avoid intel leaks. He was on speaker phone replying loudly to questions from people on the other end of the line.

The defense contractors, DARPA and General Duke gave him a grim outlook on the final development progress which meant he needed more time to hold off the adversaries from further escalating their vision to expand beyond Ukraine and attack their neighboring countries.

"October?" Patrick roared.

"That's how it looks Patrick. October if everything works well!" said General Duke.

"It's five, six months away, and then two years for deployment. The world will collapse ten times by then!" he screamed. Victoria, his assistant came over and closed the door to his office rolling her eyes. The rest of the agency employees stared at her from their cubicles. "Too noisy," she said smiling.

As usual Patrick was on the phone when Lucy entered and sat on the same armchair, tired, and exasperated from the last couple of days. She looked like she just came out of a blender. Victoria had let her in and closed the office door behind Lucy.

He glanced at Lucy quickly, then he sunk into his executive chair with a loud thud and sighed.

"How have you been?" he managed to put a tired smile on his face.

"Looks like I am better than you!" she exclaimed and scoffed. "What's going on?" she asked.

"Well DARPA, General Duke, and Marcus all rode on my back to delay Russia's escalating aggression and get NATO involved. That means World War III and we are not prepared, at least until we can complete the hypersonic missile and its Interceptor development," he slurred putting the phone on mute. "The president personally watched the development and is not happy with the progress!"

"You can't blame him," she replied. "It's a tough time to be the Commander in Chief in the Oval Office!" she spat the words in his direction.

Patrick took a break from the global catastrophe and got back to his little world of espionage.

"So, it's all done and confirmed. From what we know Nik, Inna, and her father are on board the expedition to Antarctica!"

"Where are you getting the information from?" Lucy asked as she stared at him. "Besides I already predicted that!" She smiled devilishly.

"Marcia!" Patrick answered ignoring her cute little teasing gesture, after all she was mentally exhausted after her killing spree in London. He continued, "And you have a very important part in it, Lucy. We ended operation Polar Protocol. I will explain." He gasped still listening to the howling wind outside.

Lucy tensed and her face froze. She felt that this mission would be very different in terms of its magnitude, for everyone involved; no solo mission, but an orchestra where Patrick was the conductor. It was no longer her cat and mouse game or running after other agents in the stinking gutters of a city in Far East Asia. It was time that Patrick laid out his entire plan, his goals to meet his objectives, though she knew he would only feed her moves to her step-by-step.

"Patrick, Patrick are you there?" General Duke's voice came through the speaker, apparently the line was muted both ways.

"Oh shit, I thought I hung up!" Patrick said and then unmuted, "Yes, yes I am listening!"

"We were with the design team manager, and it seems like there was progress and we will know a more accurate time schedule today," General Duke sounded optimistic. "They worked day and night!"

"Sounds good, General!" Patrick was eager to end the call and get back to his plans.

He shook his head and rolled his tired head. For the next thirty minutes, he clarified his mission objectives. Nik and Inna's functions were planned weeks before Lucy's trip to London. One more issue was the protection of the scientists which was more Dan Schmidt, the director of the FBI's job. The murder of John Gregory was not resolved, and Patrick needed that case closed.

"I could not send you to Antarctica without first meeting face-to-face with Nik in London. I wanted you to be able to judge him, to observe his personality even for a short time; is he reliable? Initially, I made the first move to contact Nik through Marcia, our agent in Russia, to check out his offer. He wanted a few things at once; save his fiancé Inna, sell Oleg to us and get paid. The money goes to Pieter fifty/fifty, who helped him to join the expedition."

"Is this where Marcia comes in?"

"Yes, that was all Marcia. When that was established, I moved to Plan B which was by far more complicated and involved!"

"And it cost the American taxpayers $10M!"

"How much would you pay to get our Interceptor ready and eliminate the Russian military advantage?" he asked and rubbed his eyes.

Patrick went on to explain the main target of his plan and Lucy cut him off to ask, "So Nik and Inna are just pawns in your game?" She was surprised, "Why send me?"

"First, to show we are serious and want to convey that message by sending you. Second, give the SVR a good reason to chase you and get them distracted from our main plans and third, make them believe what we want them to believe."

"I have heard this too many times Patrick, it's not help-ing me or my new assignment," she growled. "What do you want me to believe?"

"You will figure it out Lucy. They will be after you one way or another, and I will assign a ghost agent to tail you for protec–"

"No thanks, he will be more than a concern for me than myself. Pour me a damn bourbon, will you?"

Patrick walked heavily over to his bar and poured two glasses of Black Label.

"Ice?" he asked.

"No, I'll have enough ice in Antarctica."

"Now seriously, I have no doubt that you can complete this mission!"

"Amen," she replied and raised her glass.

Patrick retorted, "People might think we sit in the of-fice and get drunk every day, huh?" Lucy giggled seeing the bottle was almost empty.

"It's our official drink," he laughed. "Let them think it!" he added and then he put both his hands behind his neck and leaned backward in his chair. "You just can't do this business if you aren't semi-intoxicated."

Lucy understood, as she was an expert of body language, that Patrick was satisfied and made his final changes to his plans when he sat back, unwinding.

She smiled.

Then Patrick snapped up from his relaxed position and blurted out, "In two days, you will fly to Arturo Merino Benitez International Airport in Santiago, Chile. A Dolphin helicopter from the Arctic Star Coast Guard research vessel, will grab you from the heliport there and take you to the ship. The Coast Guard ship is commanded by Captain Dave Lucas, and Rear Admiral Jacob Rushbun, commander of the

South Pacific Fleet which departed Pearl Harbor. Two of the best son of a bitch tough guys in our arsenal."

He checked her reaction and she responded, "Granted, but why the big circle outflanking me through the Pacific Ocean? Antarctica is that way." She pointed in the other direction.

"Drama Lucy, to steer the Russians to you and away from what I am doing!"

"Well, they will figure out I am on my way to Antarctica!"

"Exactly!" shot Patrick. "I want the Russians to know that we are serious about protecting the Interceptor. That means for them that we are not bluffing, it's real!"

Lucy nodded, she was being used to distract the Russians and leave Patrick with his plans undetected until the right moment when he would activate her back into action.

Patrick handed her a new passport with her fake identity and said nonchalantly, "Here, a present from Victoria, she destroyed your old coverup story used in London."

"I trust it's from our confidential sources," chuckled Lucy and shrugged. Her comment marked the end the conversation.

CHAPTER 17

March 23
Top secret mission
Arctic Star *icebreaker - 100 miles north, northeast of the*
Pitcairn Island, south Pacific Ocean

Hurricane Mina headed directly to the center of Pitcairn Island, created thirty-foot ocean waves that
crashed over the ship's starboard, swaying it from
side-to-side like a ragdoll. The captain on the bridge deliberately headed directly into the hurricane, still 100 miles west,
to toughen the cadets on board his voyage. "Calm waters do
not make good sailors, there is no better lesson than the real
thing," he used to recite in his daily briefing.

The wind blustered hard, sending water splashes onto
the bridge windshield and the wipers worked hard to clear
the rain revealing the frightening view. It was the first
time crossing the path of an escalating Hurricane, going
from Cat 2 to Cat 3, then Cat 4 storm for most of the cadets; they were freaked out and dysfunctional under the
circumstances. *How many will drop after this?* the captain
asked himself and chuckled.

"Captain, a call from the admiral's office headquarters,
for you, sir!"

A petty officer struggled to overcome the noise of the
wind's violent pounding of the ship as he read announce-
ments on the intercom.

"I'll take it in my cabin," he replied with an icy tone keeping his pipe tight between his pursed lips.

He combed the gray ocean's horizon and mumbled a command only he understood, and then he slipped into the narrow corridor to his cabin. His Beagle dog chased him while he held the walls with his hands to keep from tripping. He entered the cabin marked, "Captain and Ponzy," his dog's name, and locked the door firmly behind him.

A call from the Admiral's office required confidentiality, he thought and was curious. *What was this all about?* He snorted and picked up the call on speaker.

"Captain Lucas here," he said with a fake calm and gently scratched his short white beard out of habit when he was skeptical about something.

"Hello Captain, Vice Admiral Harry Closter here!"

"Hello Harry, what a surprise! Must be boring sitting in your calm office, huh?" his bristly voice sneered and then he chuckled.

The Vice Admiral chuckled and asked with a friendly mischievous tone, "How is it going? I mean the storm, are you there yet? Are your cadets behaving?"

Son of bitch, Captain Lucas thought. "Harry, the cadet's idea was *brilliant*; go on a top-secret mission, when they were still home sick, maybe it was a mistake!"

"You could have come up with another idea, captain. No one stopped you!" growled Vice Admiral Closter in response.

"Most of them are sick in their cabin, when the time comes to erect the two cranes, I hope they will recover!" Captain Dave Lucas quickly lowered his temper, no reason to start a dispute at sea. His mission objective was figured out in detail using top tech and intel for success. The cadet training was a deception that the captain approved during the planning. No one knew the real top-secret objectives other than him him.

"Is the storm an issue?" the Vice Admiral changed the subject.

"Well, Mina, Cat 4 now with 150 MPH winds, is moving toward Cat 5 very quickly. It's hitting us hard right now, but we are going through it teaching our young bastards how to fight and win the ocean." He smiled devilishly and reattached his sloppy captain's hat on his skull and added, "Let the crew sweat!" He laughed and Harry joined in just to keep the call friendly.

He knew Dave Lucas very well. It was a love-hate relationship between a commanding officer and a tough seaman under his command. The best he could have for the mission. Dave was never married, he excused it as a waste of time dealing with women's issues ninety percent of his life. Instead of children he preferred dogs and between missions he took care of three more dogs at home, who were now with a dog sitter at his Seattle home on Mercer Island overlooking the Washington lake.

"Good point Captain Lucas, nothing like learning the job on the job. This is *your* perfect storm!"

"My ass, perfect storm!" he responded. "So what is this call for, Mr. Vice Admiral?" Captain Dave Lucas returned to a more respectful retort by mentioning his high prestigious rank.

"What's your position, Captain Lucas?" Harry asked even though he knew where the ship was and what the synopsis would be even before he made the call.

"About 100 miles north-northeast of the Pitcairn Islands. We are heading into the eye of the storm! What are you getting at?" he asked.

"It's a little excursion. We have an official request to shift your heading to Santiago, Chile." The Vice Admiral sounded hoarse and there was a bit of concern in his voice, even though he knew the new *Arctic Star* was state of the art in coast guard vessels designed for ocean surges and weather abuse. A tough set of metal assembled well for many oceanic duties like the mission it was heading to, and with an experienced captain, it could handle any mission.

"Huh? What is in Santiago for us, Harry?" the captain scolded and sounded puzzled while the ship clanked in the background. "Make sure the Russians take the bait that our mission is looking for the B-2 bomber's missing crew, training our cadets on real events."

"Disinformation is Patrick's job!" the Vice Admiral Closter replied, "Dave, are you confident in picking up someone from the airport?"

"Isn't it going to jeopardize our real mission? Patrick will go berserk!"

"It's his request, he is in charge of the entire plan!"

"Who and why for God's sake?" Dave was frustrated by the sudden change of his assignment. "Is he changing our mission?"

"No, he is not! It's just a small change for a couple days then you will resume your mission in Antarctica. You will assist and collaborate with the agent joining you. The agency mission needs to be accomplished as a matter of national security, once the passenger embarks your ship!"

The intercom distracted Captain Dave with a call from the bridge and alarms sounded to get all seaman back on, "Captain, we are entering Hurricane Mina's eye."

"10-4," he replied to the intercom and then snapped at the phone. "I am about 3,000 miles away from Santiago—"

"I know! I know!" The vice admiral shot back, upset. "I don't need you to make the entire trip to Santiago. We've dispatched the Dolphin Heli for a round trip to save a day or two!"

"In this weather? I am not into these CIA games, Harry. How am I supposed to know who the agent is? Do I need a password?" he said sarcastically.

"I never mentioned the CIA Dave and a password is a good idea!"

"Well, we have no war with Chile, so who else would ask the National Guard to help in the eleventh hour?" Dave amused himself.

"You will be informed later; change your course. Keep it for yourself, tell your crew you are outflanking the storm, but you are right about the CIA!" Harry exclaimed and knew when he mentioned the central intelligence agency, Dave would be easier to work with.

"OK Harry, I am sure the Geotraces science team will NOT be happy. I'll prepare the Heli crew, we have a couple days to digest the new assignment." He sighed and looked in the mirror and said to himself, "Good luck, captain." He moved uncomfortably knowing in-bay intelligence mission things could go wrong and twisted at the last minute. It looked to him as if a rescue operation of a CIA agent who got into trouble. He chuckled and mumbled, "Not again."

As the voice of the vice admiral sounded on the line again, he was reminded that the conversation was not done. His metallic icy voice was more direct now when he said, "We will get you more details later, Dave!"

The *Arctic Star* changed course by ninety degrees toward Santiago, slightly away from the storm that would eventually hit her later.

"Fuck!" he growled and went for his bourbon.

CHAPTER 18

March 24, 5:12 p.m.
Moscow

Nik was very flattered by the airport reception. His fans threw elbows and screamed his name for autographs.

"Next time we will beat Liverpool!" he exclaimed with hope.

The bus drove the team straight to Dinamo Lev Yashin stadium which was named after the legendary goalkeeper considered to be the best in the soccer history.

Nik took a quick shower in the locker room, changed his clothes then drove a few minutes away up to Park Berezovaya, in his Jaguar to meet Marcia. He parked in the Woki Toki Club lot and walked on the wide walkway into the tree-lined park. Light snow covered the walkway for walkers, bikers, and ice skaters. He zipped up his coat all the way and put his hood over his head for warmth; this also helped him from being recognized.

It's still freezing in Moscow, he thought.

In the middle of the park, he took the left walkway toward the ice rink which in the summer turned into a basketball court. He entered the spectators' room, watching the ice skaters and looking at the people skating in the rink, hearing faintly, the cheering and giggling of children.

Marcia was skating with a five-year-old boy, coaching him from behind. They both wore a stocking hat with a warm full-body coverall; she also had a scarf hanging off their shoulders. It was cold out there and another month away from more comfortable weather.

She acknowledged him with a chin raise, and he reciprocated. She left her son to skate by himself whispering something in his ear. She went to the ladies' room and after a few minutes stood by him for a second, whispered something then left.

Nik waited a few minutes looking at his watch and walked after her to the ladies' room and she opened the door for him. He walked in and in utmost surprise he shouted, "Inna!" His fiancé was standing there with excited tears in her eyes, frozen in place.

They hugged and kissed passionately. "Marcia and I helped each other hide from the FSS," she said sadly, and she started to sob lightly.

"I know the entire story," Nik whispered and wiped her tears with his scarf.

Marcia entered the ladies' room and joined them on alert.

"We can't stay here long, FSS is all over, Nikita," Marcia said.

She bundled up and held his hand.

"I was out of the country for three days. What has happened?"

"Things change Nikita. They arrested most of the movement members; I'm the only one at large. Our safe homes were all discovered, we couldn't assemble or plan our next move."

"What are you talking about? They agreed to let you join me on my expedition to Antarctica," he stated in excitement. "We are going to get out of here with the help of the Americans," he tried to cheer her up. She smiled.

"Look, you know I can't leave my father behind doing what he does to destroy the world, right?"

"He is coming with us. He will not pass the opportunity to spy on American technology; it's in his blood. It was discussed with Pieter, Marcia confirmed. Right Marcia?"

"Huh?" Marcia wasn't paying attention.

"Don't trust Pieter too much Nikita. He may be steering the entire thing. It's too risky to join the expedition; he is all out for the money," she was extremely concerned, looking around for peering eyes.

"We have no life here, you understand?" Nik pushed the issue.

"I agree, either way. If my father stays here, he will die in oppression. At least in America he will die as a free man and perhaps totally recovered from his illness! Look, I already mentioned to my father that he should get help in a western country, he refused."

"But if you tell him you are leaving, he will join," Nik said decisively and examined Inna's face carefully and then checked-in on Marcia's expression.

"How can you do that Nikita? You are a soccer star, not the president!" Inna noticed Nik's tense glance and tried to get into his head. Nik paused and inhaled. It was obvious that the plan was not cut and dried. Marcia explained that Inna's father was still working hard to decipher the new weapon's design and she threw out a carrot telling him that the Interceptor, if retrieved from Antarctica, could help him solve his concept for a new generation of missiles. "Scientists are like little children!" Marcia stated.

"I already cleared this with Pieter and his boss. I just have to convince them to release your father. I told them he was sick, and they should use his brain until his last breath. This expedition came at the right time; every scientist would love to get a look at American technology. I am sure he will change his mind and come!"

Marcia went back to the rink to join her son who was still cutting the ice as if he were a new ice skater champion rising to stardom. She smiled a sad smile, kissed Inna and Nik, and then waved her hands behind the glass to join her son.

Inna threw a kiss into the air and dropped a tear. "She is such a lovely woman!" she stated. "How did you two meet?" she asked sobbing.

"Marcia is our contact to the Americans!" Nik said without explanation and sniffed. "Let me call Pieter!"

He walked a few feet away from Inna to a quieter area and whispered on the phone.

Pieter answered right away and sounded fresh and laid back. "Nikita, are you recovered from jet lag?" His friendly tone was warm and welcoming. Nik needed to reassure him that there was no last-minute regret, and the plan was ago. *There are too many pieces to tie together*, Nik thought.

"I am fine my friend. What about you?" he chuckled gently. "Time to meet again!"

"Great, are you up for a drink at my place later? I am free!"

"Sure, it's 6 p.m, now. Is 7 OK?"

CHAPTER 19

March 26, evening
Antarctica

Vladimir's commando troops and the civilians boarded the old Ilyushin Il-76, (NATO code name: *Candid*) a heavy transport plane capable to land on the icy runway of Novolazarevskaya Station in Antarctica. The station is located forty-five miles in and on the Schirmacher Oasis, Queen Maud Land, separated by the Lazarev Ice Shelf. The last leg of the summer on the continent gave the impression it wasn't that bad being there year-round as temperatures rose to the mid-thirties during the day. However, the rugged icy landscape showed signs of the rough winters that attack the land with no mercy.

The four jet engines roared at high altitude leaving a cloudy condensation tail behind. From the windows, at 35,000 feet, they could see the southern Pacific Ocean in its full glory, looking calm and inviting from that distance. Icebergs floated as small white oddly shaped dots, drifting north with the ocean's current.

The long flight came to its end very close to its destination on the other side of the globe. Meanwhile, three Akula class Russian submarines headed to the Antarctic continent to circle around the 60th latitude south line fully submerged and deep enough to avoid thermal wake and stay hidden by the American spy satellites. Any early discovery would end the mission.

The sub commanders' missions had dual objectives, one of them was top secret, the other was to assist the expedition. At any time, in case of a conflict, they must avoid any friction with the American southern Navy fleet.

The Ronne Ice Shelf was under constant satellite surveillance in search of the American Interceptor. Relying heavily on their top agents to report the exact location, it sent the Russian satellites to check every groove, bump, and trench on the ice shelf that may shed light on the mysterious missile spot.

Pieter was restless. He analyzed every piece of information sent to his laptop. Periodically he shot a glance at the soccer player and his fiancé sitting in front of him quietly with tense faces waiting for this to end.

Next to Inna, was her father, Oleg, a middle-aged man whose head drooped; it seemed he was suffering from the unpleasant trip imposed by his daughter, Inna. They shared glances with each other, each one drifted in and out of their own thoughts.

Inna, an idealist, and anti-Russian government activist, asked herself many times what game Nik was playing with Pieter? She trusted her fiancé and got her father out of Russia as she insisted when thinking about defecting. Everyone would take credit after the mission's success; who initiated the defection plan, or who brought the idea to fruition? She only hoped there were no surprises in this plan; of course, she knew nothing about the $10M the CIA agreed to pay Nik for his role in bringing the scientist to the US.

So far all worked well in accordance with the plan, and she didn't understand why she still felt so stressed. Her breathing was heavy due to her anxiety attacks; she tried to control it with a breathing exercise. She was concerned that Vladimir wouldn't let them go and Pieter would not assist. It would be easy to execute them in cold blood if they were considered irrelevant; Antarctica, a land with no sovereignty, would make it easy to do. Or they could just walk off and join the American expedition side since there are no borders.

Nik offered no further details, not even the fact that the Americans already deposited $1M into his Swiss bank account. If this wire transaction was discovered by the SVR, he was a dead man walking.

Inna knew the danger, but safety in Russia was fragile. The danger in this expedition without knowing the end was actually less frightening. President Primankov's secret police already announced a few times that they had a warrant for her arrest. If caught, she may be executed or found dead in a street shooting.

Nik's plans make sense then, she thought. He made it sound like the only plan was for Russian intelligence to recruit Inna's biological father, the lead scientist of hypersonic Russian missile development. Nik convinced Pieter that Inna was the only one who could get her father to take the trip, totally a patriotic move, which made Inna look good. Nik, on the other hand, planned to make this trip his career change and the $10M was to live a relaxing easy life of retirement. Each one had their own agenda.

Pieter was caught in his own thoughts, analyzing the three; he would order a kill if they tried to defect. He wondered if Vladimir had the same order from the top brass in Russia, since he had no intention to follow orders. He didn't trust Nik but respected him enough to be his partner on this mission, but he also needed to show his loyalty to Russia, and side with Vladimir.

Inna sighed in relief and snuggled into Nik's shoulder. She opened her eyes and smiled nervously at Pieter.

"How are you Inna?" Pieter sounded inquisitive with a hint of arrogance.

"Good Pieter, good. Happy we are finally doing this!" She ignored his attitude.

"When we get back, you will be a hero again, Nik," Pieter jeered.

Nik was silent. He knew Pieter sounded hostile since he sided with Vladimir. He wondered if they were still a team. The money would be transferred to his account and therefore Pieter relied on Nik to get his share of the deal. He could not be on the expedition without him.

"I hope so, for our people, Pieter!" Nik responded with a patriotic quip and cheerful thumbs up.

Turbulence hit the plane, putting an end to the perfect rhythmic hum and shook everyone abruptly. The old metal clanked, and the wings rattled like a snake's tail.

"Fasten your seatbelts!" the captain announced on the internal intercom. "We are descending to our destination soon; we have to cross the storm on our way. Ten minutes of bumpy road ahead!" Then the intercom went silent.

"We need to catch up on a few things," Pieter ignored the turbulence and saw Inna fading.

"We still need to confirm the Interceptor's final location. So far, our satellites have revealed nothing," said Vladimir, who was more interested in how they would navigate the troops back and forth alive after stealing the Interceptor.

"Who the hell knows where it is?" Nik sounded polite as he shrugged his shoulders. He hoped that the conversation would not turn political knowing Inna's strong personality would make it hard for her to control her temper.

"I know, you are still searching Pieter!" said Vladimir calmly. "Hope it's not buried in the snow, its stormy over there."

Pieter rolled his head toward Vladimir with a slight smile and said, "Vlad, tell me please, since you planned the military operation portion of the mission, and know the ice stations better than many of us, I am sure you have more options to achieve your objective. What will they carry on-site in terms of equipment to help us navigate?" Pieter continued, "Antarctica is the same size as the USA and Mexico combined, from where we are on the Ronne Ice Shelf, if rumors are correct, it's like crossing the entire US twice. How do you suggest we can do th–"

"Relax Pieter! I disagree with your provocation and it's not your concern we–" Vlad was surprised when Pieter cut him off.

"Not my concern, Vlad? Whose concern should this be? Is it yours only?" Pieter erupted like volcano; his red face breathless.

Vlad flushed angrily and his eyes flickered. He was not accustomed to anyone confronting him, especially in front of his troops, he didn't care which intelligence agency was backing them. "Calm down Pieter, damn it!" Vladimir yelled back, "We shall wait, that's my order. Meanwhile we are here and preparing for our cross-country excursion, we will strike when ready. Understood?"

"Three-thousand miles with a sixty-year-old passenger?" Pieter chuckled. "A Mi-26 helicopter would be nice."

"Helicopter? Where do we have a helicopter here? We don't even have a snowmobile," Vlad spat back, on fire. "I know time is of the essence, perhaps it's not the best plan, but this is it. I don't want to be discovered!"

"Why couldn't we wait until we found the missile and then plan the trip?" screamed Pieter, inches from Vladimir's face.

Vlad inhaled deeply and said, "Because time was of the essence. It was better to wait here rather than in Moscow! You got it through your thick skull, yet?" Vlad's response was furious, and he got even closer, butting noses with Pieter, face-to-face and ready to exchange punches.

"Calm down!" yelled Nik from the side, watching the drama. "Stop it, damn it! We are all in it. Are you both out of your minds risking the expedition?" he crossed to the other side of the plane and sat between the two rivals.

The troops sat at the back of the plane, closed off by a curtain partition, silently obedient to the system, asking no questions. The information given to them when they volunteered was more than enough.

"Well, Pieter has a point," said Nik when they both calmed, not without sending barbed glances at each other. "What if they find it in the western part of the continent?"

"Not according to what we learned."

Vladimir stood his ground and was firm with his decision. He didn't accept criticism from anyone, especially Pieter whose rank was lower than his.

Oleg pouted and joined the tense conversation from an engineering view. He asked himself if the efforts were justified at all. He couldn't figure out how the Americans could resolve the issue to intercept the "Missile that cannot be intercepted" which he designed. No engineer in the world would pass on the opportunity to check this out and it made him feel justified. He changed the subject and made sure both commanders were listening.

"The technology of hypersonic guided missile Interceptors must be very complicated and challenging. After thinking about it, it was worth the effort to check it out. That is why I am here. The less you both fight, the less anxiety the rest of us will have."

Vlad nodded and Pieter exchanged glances with Nik, sharing a moment of silence.

"Oleg, it's a military decision, well-thought out. This is why we dispatched submarines to circle Antarctica on standby, comrades. Understood?" He forced a smile. "We are landing!" he announced and went to the troops in the back.

The plane made a circle around the icy landing strip, which was cleared by the research ice station; extended its flaps and lowered the landing gear.

"I don't see the station!" Nik commented looking out the windows.

"Oh, it's a few kilometers inland," replied Vladimir. "This is the first beachhead. I preferred to wait at the ice station than create a beachhead somewhere remote; here we can plan our steps carefully and have the necessary logistics planned," Vladimir replied with a definitive tone, though visibly stressed from the heated episode. He added, "We wanted to operate confidentially!" His voice elevated a decibel, "Additionally, we wanted to use our ice station's resources first before we jumped ahead."

"I was just wondering Vlad, nothing personal–" Nik nodded.

Inna was stressed as well; her thoughts turned to all her friends she left behind–underground members who resented Primankov's war against Ukraine. Many people in both countries developed severe mental health issues. Now, in Antarctica many psychiatrists, in the seclusion of the ice continent, stayed to write their theses on that subject; especially on how to relieve themselves from personal stress.

Vladimir debated with himself if it was necessary to remind Pieter of his role on this expedition. He didn't give up easily and would not let Pieter run the operation. Also, Vladimir didn't trust anyone he hadn't personally chosen to join the trip, so he kept his cards close to his chest from Nik, Inna, and her father. The last three were the responsibility of Pieter, who also could not be trusted, in Vlad's opinion.

"For all of you, information is on a need-to-know basis. Pieter, you will be informed, of course, when we change plans."

Pieter was not sure he understood the message, and Vlad took this as a sign that perhaps he was not clear enough. "The submarines are equipped for missions like ours. Perhaps, landing on a remote beach in secret."

"Yes, like mini subs that can be propelled on sleds; new machines developed by this man!" Inna pointed at her father.

Vlad ignored Inna and said, "Yes, your father is the head of the 'P.D. Grushin Machine-building Design Bureau' which also developed the hypersonic missile, the horror of the west."

"Yes, I know. I know why my father is here, Vlad. I understand the subs are equipped with machinery to bring the American Interceptor back to Russia. I know everything," Inna mumbled loudly and squeezed herself closer into Nik's rib cage.

"It will be a big victory to bring it home; it will embarrass the Americans. Hopefully your father's trip will be fruitful," Nik commented raising his head.

Oleg nodded his head and so did his daughter. They sat together covered in warm blankets. The Ilyushin touched down and rattled to a complete stop on the icy runway.

Pieter's cell phone vibrated signaling a text message coming via the plane satellite connections. He opened the message, his face froze, downloading to his cell were fuzzy photos analyzed by his counterintelligence face recognition labs.

"Spider!" Pieter whispered loudly. Photos of Lucy's face from the London hotel Hilton Wembley, identified her with 100% accuracy. He continued whispering, "Hello buddy, my CIA colleague." He smiled. It would be his great achievement to eliminate the number one CIA agent who had operated all over the world, but mostly in Asia, particularly Russia and China.

CHAPTER 20

March 26, evening

Lucy prepared for her trip to Santiago through Langley's headquarter office with her new fake ID and fake passport. Her new cover story was that she was an oceanic geography researcher monitoring the ice shelves break-up and separation rates in Antarctica. "Thank you, Victoria," she mumbled with a cold smile. "I wish that it was true, to be someone else for a change," she continued mumbling, examining the documents.

"Take care of yourself. Don't forget that every intelligence agency, friendly or otherwise will be after you since your face was published in London," reminded Patrick with fatherly advice and a reassuring hand on her shoulder.

She nodded. "I know how to protect myself, Patrick!"

The idea of a military plane flying her out to Santiago found to be too conspicuous and expensive, but was kept in accordance with Patrick's mega plans. "I'll manage," she said again to herself smiling when the idea was first disclosed to her. "It would be very awesome if I could have the entire plane just to myself," she commented sarcastically.

Without being able to carry her favorite gun with her, due to regulations, she hoped that its use would not be necessary. The official CIA SUV drove her to the airport with two additional bodyguards who realized, as it was reported by field agents, Russian agents covered all three major airports in and around D.C. looking to retaliate. "Someone talked already!" she exclaimed with confidence. "Must be someone we all know," she muttered softly as Patrick was staring at her.

Traveling as a tourist always sharpened her senses. She was transported to Dulles airport for her 5,000-mile flight that eventually will board her to the nuclear Coast Guard Ship *Arctic Star* then to Palmer Ice Station located on Anvers Island situated on the north side of Antarctica; supposedly this was close to where the hypersonic missile Interceptor could have landed. She was not sure where the landing site was since reports were confusing and non-conclusive, but she didn't let this deflect her focus for the mission. *It all will be clear one day,* Patrick's words echoed in her mind.

The failed mission was quickly blasted on social media with many thousands of wanna-be spy commentators speculating where the Interceptor landed, searching Antarctica's grid on google maps, cluttering social media with fake locations and photos, causing intelligence agencies to create chaos and confusion on purpose.

Lucy was dropped off by her two bodyguards that could not go through the TSA security screening area, so at that point Lucy was on her own, supposedly in a secured and safe area. The bodyguards gave her a thumbs-up as goodbye when she passed through the scanning machines and disappeared into the sea of passengers rushing to their gates.

Her photos were uploaded to every app used by the Russian agents participating in the hunt for Lucy. The face recognition app was much like the Israeli NSO spy program's version, but with a twist added by the Russian software engineers which enabled the cell phone to ding when a match was nearby. This upgrade was originally designed to spy, and hunt anti-government figures, like Inna, Nik's fiancé, and her political underground members.

The tracker could accurately pinpoint the location of the spy or agent. The Russians called their app NSTS (National

Spy Tracking System) and could hack any cell phone, track the individual subject, its location, open its camera and record all sounds, and conversations, just like Pegasus, the NSO program. However, Lucy replaced her phone every mission or at least every two-month interval. Her phone also included a warning tracking sensor, a new technology developed by Apple for military purposes over and above the Russian NSTS and the Israelis Pegasus program. She put her phone notifications on vibrate to signal tracking on and went to the ladies' room on her way to the gate.

Pieter and his boss in counterintelligence made Lucy their prime target: the one who escaped the spy network list provided by the mole to their special execution operation department. The name "Spider", Lucy's CIA code name, was heard many times at the Russian intelligence community headquarters. Her presence was noticed by the blood trail she left behind, typical of her notorious heel kicks, killing the Russian agents with her martial arts skills and expertise as a ruthless death machine.

By examining his dead agent in London, Pieter had connected the dots immediately. He only had to confirm his suspicions proving he was spot on, and the face recognition app confirmed it was Lucy, his agency's fiercest enemy. Like every spy, Pieter dreamed of eliminating Lucy and being given the "Hero of the Russian Federation" medal for his bravery.

Her phone vibrated. She froze, looking at the blinking message that she had been locked and encrypted by a tracking app. She moved to her destination, acting normal, but her sixth sense filled her with adrenalin making her heartbeat quicken and her breath shallow. Then she took a deep breath and exhaled slowly realizing the pressure. "Shape up," she mumbled softly.

Lucy examined the passengers around her gate and didn't see anyone suspicious or a threat. No extra sweating due to stress, no one appearing nervous, no one dressed a little differently; all the signs that she was looking for were not there. All those in the gate area acted normal, *He must be cool man,* she thought.

"This is fucking crazy," she mumbled. "How would they know where I am?" She combed each one of the travelers again with her X-ray eyes; she was taught to look for the smallest detail in human behavior. Her phone kept vibrating obnoxiously. "He must be looking at me, this son-of-a-bitch," she muttered to herself in disbelief. Her head spun around to find someone who was looking and waiting for the opportunity to strike. All she had to protect herself were her skills.

"London," she whispered believing it was the only connection who could make the Russian agency realize she was the killer of the soccer team man in London.

The ladies' room was temporarily closed for cleaning, and she headed to another one along the main passenger corridor, the cleaning lady briefly popped out and let her in with a large smile and in broken English said, "You can go in." The cleaning lady entered the ladies' room again to resume her cleaning and she removed the "No Entry" sign.

A tall man and a shorter woman, both athletic in their late twenties, dressed casually with sneakers, light coats, and backpacks, approached the bathroom from two different entrances in a coordinated effort. The man stood outside the bathroom and put the "No entry" sign back up, holding up users from entry, smiling at them saying it was cleaning time.

At the same time, the woman shared a glance with the man and entered the bathroom pulling her gun with a silencer attached to the nozzle and shot the cleaning lady on the spot, thudding on the floor in a pool of blood that soon covered the floor, and sprayed the walls and the mirrors with blood splatters.

She examined the bathroom stalls under the partitions and doors to see who was there. No one was there, so she carefully lifted her leg to kick the doors open one by one, standing and examining each stall for anyone who might be standing on top of the toilet, hiding. She reached the last door, took a deep breath, kicked it with a mighty blow, standing for a fraction of a second, hoping to watch her target die. She held the door open with one foot and aimed the gun on to the empty stall. She spat out a juicy Russian curse.

Looking up at just the right time for Lucy to react in a lightning speed, she dropped quickly from above, landed on the woman whose foot extended directly into Lucy's rib cage. She heard the foot bone snap and then immediately kicked her in the knee as the women came crashing down onto the cold floor groaning with pain. The foreign agent still held her gun despite the brutal attack leaving her broken on the floor. The result of tough training always paid off in her profession. Just to be able to land no matter what, with no weapon in your hand and neutralize your opponent was satisfying, like a cat always landing on its feet.

The Russian agent stretched her hand out to hold the partition and level herself while she aimed her gun at Lucy's chest, not wasting any time, Lucy kicked her one more time. While she was still on the floor in pain, Lucy aimed at the most vulnerable area on the head, the temple, and instantly caused the agent's death; her body twisted like a dead snake.

From the entrance, a man's voice echoed as he aggressively asked something in Russian, and Lucy understood that the dead Russian agent was not alone. The fact that the bathroom was kept empty from users, Lucy realized the dead agent had someone watching the entry.

Lucy stood behind a knee wall watching the entrance through the adjacent mirrors on the wall. She remembered if she could see them, they could see her, but the element of surprise would be hers.

The man asked the same question again, sounding more annoyed by no response. He peered quickly into the bathroom and decided to move in closer. From the corner of his eye, he saw in the mirror, his colleague dead on the floor. He lifted his gun; aimed and ready to shoot.

People still avoided entering the bathroom, due to the "No Entry" sign.

Lucy bent down, still behind the knee wall. She couldn't see him in the mirror after he passed the curved entrance. He approached with caution, step-by-step, trying to listen to every sound. He looked intense.

As he approached the knee wall where Lucy was hiding, she attacked his feet like a tiger, causing him to crash to the floor. He managed to shoot two bullets that hit the bathroom ceiling as he fell backward. One of the light fixtures exploded showering electrical sparks. His head slammed hard onto the tile floor as his gun slipped away. Lucy quickly stood up before he could gain consciousness and landed her heel kick on his chest, snapping his sternum and stopping his heart for good. She sighed heavily.

Then, she glanced quickly at the poor dead cleaning lady and shook her head in sadness, "Collateral damage," she whispered. Lucy didn't delay any longer. She knew that they did not act alone. She collected the foreign agent's gun from the floor and walked hurriedly from the bathroom. From the corner of her eye, she saw a foreign agent in the distance nervously looking at his watch.

People who wanted to enter the bathroom stopped at the entry sign as she passed them. She said, "They are still cleaning, it's a mess in there."

The next agent wore the same backpack, probably from AliExpress; they were obviously working together. *What morons,* Lucy thought, *they shopped at the same store for backpacks.* The man noticed Lucy and turned around to force her back into the bathroom; a place Lucy had no intention of going back to. Spectators watching had no idea there were three dead people inside the bathroom and all the drama that took place. Before the Russian realized that Lucy had no intention of being forced back into the bathroom, a straight kick to his genitals put a stop to his attempt. He bent over, groaning in front of the horrified spectators who couldn't understand what was going on and backed up.

An airport police officer who was close by, noticed the commotion and rushed to the scene with his patrol dog on the leash and a gun pointed at Lucy, who was seen as the aggressor. He asked Lucy to back up with her face to the wall while he called for backup to join him. Lucy didn't resist. The foreign agent tried to stand up holding his genitals, and the officer pinned him down. "Stay down, sir!" he commanded.

The spectators started to intervene with calls stating, "She started it." Others said, "He attacked her!"

Lucy tried to turn her head to the officer who put pressure on her back to stay glued to the wall. "May I make a phone call?" asked Lucy.

"Wait!" he spat laconically. "Don't move!" he ordered and called again on his radio for back up.

"You have three bodies in the bathroom, two foreign agents, and one cleaning lady who they killed!"

"Don't talk!" he growled.

"I have a flight in fifty minutes, sir; one phone call will straighten this up!" she continued talking.

A few police officers and their captain closed in on the scene with their K-9 dogs.

"What do we have here?" the captain asked the officer still holding Lucy tight after he managed to handcuff her without realizing yet the scene inside the bathroom.

"I saw this lady kick this man down!" he said proudly for his heroic action.

"May I see both your I.D.s?" the captain asked.

Lucy managed to pull her I.D. papers and said, "There are two foreign agents dead inside the bathroom, and a dead cleaning lady. The man I kicked down was after me; he is foreign agent, a member of the Russian Intelligence assassination team. His partners are dead in the bathroom, go see for yourself!"

"Call a paramedic!" the captain ordered as the petty police officer holding his nervous dog, barking loudly, tried to get into the bathroom.

The captain followed with caution into the bathroom and came out looking horrified.

"Horrible!" he exclaimed. He was totally disturbed. "I have to arrest you both!"

The foreign agent kept his mouth shut and did not answer any questions directed to him.

"Captain, lock the terminal. There might be others in his group!" Lucy advised.

Then he signaled his petty police to escort them to the police car out on the tarmac. His gun still pulled for precaution.

"I found a gun on her torso!" said another petty officer following Lucy and the agent.

"It was a massacre down there!" the captain announced.

Lucy kept her temper saying, "It's not my gun, captain; one phone call will clear m-" Lucy was cut off again as she tried to convince the captain.

"Miss Greyhound, be quiet and do not interfere with police investigation," he hollered in reply.

"You are making a big mistake interfering with government work!" Lucy exclaimed clearly. She had no choice trying to confront the captain.

The commotion at the scene was tense as the paramedics and more officers approached the "Do Not Cross" tape that closed the area from spectators.

He looked at her as they got into the police car and figured she was very relaxed; something told him she was telling the truth.

"One phone call and it better be quick!" he said with a threatening tone and handed her bag back to her. With her hands in handcuffs, she picked up her phone and dialed Patrick's confidential cell phone.

"Patrick, I was tracked down by the FSB or the FVR whatever they are; two agents neutralized and a third was caught alive. Police are holding me up, preventing me from boarding the flight!"

"Stay tuned!" his laconic answer sounded mechanical.

She was on hold and the phone line hissed. "What is the name of the officer?" Patrick asked.

"Officer what is your name?" Lucy asked. He ignored her question.

"Here, you better speak to my boss!" she said holding back her rising temper.

The officer took the phone and said aggressively and arrogantly, "YES!" His facial expression turned to an astonished look as his jaw dropped.

"I need a confirmation, sir!" he said, then the line was cut off.

"Start moving!" he ordered the driver who neared the airport exit.

His phone rang and he picked it up.

"Yes commander!" he spat visibly upset. "Yes, I just spoke to him, I didn't realize. OK, will do!"

"Turn around; back to the gate," he ordered the driver, then called the other police car who took the captive foreign agent to custody. "Bring him to the station. He will be picked up by the FBI!"

"Officer, uncuff her and take a quick statement from 'Miss Greyhound' as he called her. Then, release her back to the gate," he ordered the colleague seated next to Lucy in the back seat.

"What about that man?" Lucy pointed at the other car with the foreign agent.

"The FBI is on its way to pick him up!" the captain replied.

The paramedics inside the bathroom informed the captain that the cleaning lady was killed by a wound caused by a bullet and the woman and man died from an injury, perhaps by a sharp object.

The captain who took the gun from Lucy looked at her head to toe to see what killing object she might have and raised his eyebrows.

"Did you use those guns?"

"They belong to the foreign agents I killed."

"I'll keep them for the FBI investigation," he said.

"Makes sense," Lucy answered coolly.

They got back to the gate from the tarmac and went up the passenger jetway stairs escorted by a police officer and the captain, then picked up a call from Patrick.

"Your flight was delayed due to a bomb threat!" he said and breathed loudly into the speaker.

"Patrick, someone assisted them with the guns in the secured area, and the bomb threat means someone is still in the airport preventing me from flying out; probably running this operation from close by. How would they know which plane?" she asked.

"Someone is probably listening. Pack up and return. We made a mistake sending you by a commercial airliner!"

CHAPTER 21

March 26, Morning rounds

"How do you feel?" asked the physician compassion-ately and took a quick brief look at Ron Hill's chart. "Fine," he replied.

"Well, you will be released today. Do you have anyone to drive you home?"

"I'll Uber home, doctor," Ron smiled.

Ron didn't have any known family or close friends on his records. He kept his privacy and his magazine fan page readers who followed his articles and blogs were the only people he associated with, as far as the FBI security clearance showed. He came from a poor family, raised in London, but his background was foggy and not very clear though it didn't flag any conflict preventing him from join-ing the FBI.

"You were very lucky. The bullet only scratched your right-side causing bleeding. You will be fine, just perhaps a little scar, but no worries, women will not notice," the physician explained joking with a chuckle.

Ron nodded his head slightly and thanked the doctor for his concern over his future love life and looked forward to leaving that place. His thoughts focused on Pieter who shot him as he asked himself, *Why? Who was he? How did he know where he lived and which sites he visited? More im-portantly, what was his connection with the test flight that morning?*

Ron ran through in his mind, the events around the struggle with Pieter in his home. The shot caused him to lose his balance and fall to the floor when his head slammed the wall, and he lost consciousness. Pieter thought Ron had died and did not check to confirm, or perhaps he didn't plan to kill him?

Before his flight to London, Pieter reported to his boss that he eliminated Ron Hill, an FBI agent pretending to be a military blogger and writer who was tracking down spy networks for the FBI. Ron had gotten too close to completing his mission to expose Russian spies in the FBI headquarters. Pieter didn't buy it. He had his own reasons, and one of them was that Ron Hill didn't know Pieter's future. Right now, they were both on opposite sides of the spy network fence, each with his own current mission.

Therefore, the Russian FSB counterintelligence agency sent Pieter to the B-2 bomber test flight observation desk to meet with Ron to eliminate him, but not before he got everything he stored on his home computer.

Ron, deep in thought, tried to navigate his position with the FBI. He felt vulnerable if he didn't get full agent status with full protection benefits. Now that he was wounded by a Russian spy, he claimed to discover the spy network was headed by Pieter who should help elevate his security clearance and get easier access to better missions. Dan Schmidt discussed that Patrick Stevenson utilized Ron for the Interceptor rescue mission.

Dan Schmidt, the FBI director, was not as satisfied as Ron thought he would be. It was a good idea to recruit him since he was a social media celebrity and knowledgeable military expert who attracted spies thinking he held a secret or two. J thought it would be a good idea to use Ron's computer to send conflicting misinformation through his desktop to the foreign intelligence agencies, in particular, to the Russians.

"Ron, I read your report about your contact with a foreign agent who tried to kill you and stole your desktop computer. You don't know who your enemies are? Who shot you?" asked Dan.

Ron scoffed, "He was professional; I am sure he would have killed me, but I fought back. Therefore, he missed and just caused a deep cut on m–"

"I know the story, Ron. It was heroic. We thought we'd grant your request for a more meaningful mission, but next time don't lose your enemies, Ron!" He chuckled and repositioned himself in his executive chair.

"I didn't volunteer to be shot," said Ron. "I agreed to assist and join the FBI using my fans and my exposure in social media for the agency's purpose. I think you finally granted me what I deserve, some credit for my efforts." Ron was surprised by his own courage standing in front the FBI director with demands.

"True," Dan sighed. "Look Ron, your fans and exposure can help, of course; your assignment is when you kill your shooter, when Pieter is dead."

Ron murmured something unclear and watched his boss' icy piercing stare.

"And where can I find him? Isn't it the CIA's job to chase international spies?" Ron responded. "I was told he was in Londo–"

"Antarctica Ron. The Russians are planning a South Pole expedition to retrieve our Interceptor from its landing site in the ice and snow. We can't let that happen Ron. I am sure Pieter will be there and it's your opportunity to retaliate; an eye for an eye!"

"So, it's true that the Interceptor landed in Antarctica?" he asked with a bit of relief clearing up the speculations by the head of the FBI himself.

Ron didn't expect to get an executioner mission right after he proved his loyalty to the FBI agency. *If he didn't take this mission, there would be no more opportunities,* he thought. It must be very important if Dan Schmidt himself interviewed and sent him to help the efforts.

"What about the bomber and its crew? Did they survive?" Ron was curious.

"It's classified. The Air Force blocked this information about that in order to attempt to save the aircraft and its crew without intrusion from other foreign agencies, including mine."

Dan lit a cigar and offered one to Ron from the fancy box. The sweet tobacco scent dominated the director's office. He pulled out a bag and put it on the table. Ron figured what was in it and asked, "You want me to kill Pieter?" And lifted his eyebrows then squirmed in his seat like an uncomfortable juvenile asking himself, *What's the catch? Why can't they kill Pieter themselves?*

Dan paused taking his time to reply, observing Ron's body language. He inhaled the cigar smoke and exhaled slowly, "You see Ron, Antarctica is a no man's land. There are no laws, and secondly, if you accept the assignment, you will be operating automatically for the CIA when you set foot outside of this country."

"Doesn't it bother you that I have never killed a man before?" Ron sounded dramatic.

"No, it's easy. In our business it's a question of time and then there is always the first time Ron, it was part of your crash training course," his tone was calm and persuading.

"Well, I never thought–"

Dan sighed again and stopped Ron from going on, raising his hands above his head with his palms stretched open.

"You asked to be considered for a real mission, and here we are. An action position, this is your opportunity and I think you are the right man for it," said Dan in a convincing tone. "From here, it can only go up!"

"Tell me all you can about the mission, then!"

"We expect the Russians to follow us in a race to Antarctica, they know about the Interceptor, it's not a secret. *How* they *get there* is a *secret*," Dan emphasized the last words. "We want to know and want to be there first. I'm sure you might have heard about how many adversary spy agencies want to get hold of our hypersonic Interceptor waiting like a freebie to be grabbed. This powerful and innovative design will be the envy of our enemies; one of a kind, the newest technology ahead of its time. Our engineers at Lockheed Martin worked night and day to get to this point Ron. We can't dismiss it; it's only a shame that our lead scientist was murdered. It's triggered a new war, a war on science."

Ron got a chill. He was at Lockheed Martin representing his magazine as a journalist when the scientist was murdered; he saw the commotion in the parking lot from afar that same day.

"Yes, it was a tragedy for the defense team," Ron mumbled. "Who else is going?"

"Right now, just you," Dan snapped. "Other than kill Russian agents, we want you to defend the Interceptor from falling into their hands. *Boom*!" Dan made an explosion cloud motion with his hands and paused to see how his reaction was received, then he added, "You will be briefed at our ice station research facility there. The area is inaccessible, but we have the equipment you will need to use."

Ron took a deep breath and tried to relax. He saw the Interceptor taking off from NAS Mugu Point Naval air station and remembered every part of it. Now he was asked to defend it. He was lucky not to be killed by the guy who shot him.

"Who am I meeting there?" Ron asked. "Do they know about my arrival; how do I get there?"

"Oh, it's all arranged and figured out, Emily Greyhound is the research facility manager; she knows you are coming and will get you all the assistance you need."

Ron hesitated before but now he felt a sense of adventure calling him to accept this crazy unexpected mission. He was sure everyone he knew would be surprised and happy for his opportunity. He scoffed lightly. "I am in!" Ron replied.

"There you go. This bag has your license to carry a gun and your piece."

CHAPTER 22

March 27, evening

Vladimir Korenko chose the best commando troopers who volunteered for this mission. He was not a man of small talk. Long conversations and chewing over everything many times was not his style; he was a man of action and quick decisions. The troops he chose were like him, experts in martial arts, bare hand fighting, and nonmilitary firearms or other deadly weapon such as knives, tools, and metal objects. Vladimir gasped at the many Russian military failures lately although he understood without failure there was no success, but when it came to this mission, he only chose winners.

The antiquated but reliable, Ilyushin, landed on the icy strip with its disguised human cargo. A state-of-the-art snowmobile cruiser waited to transport the Interceptor's recovery team to the ice station to regroup. It was there they would wait for the SVR and its international branches to disclose to their spy network, the exact coordinates of the Interceptor landing site.

The weather was calm with clear skies but cold with the impending stormy forecast for later that day. Temperatures would drop way below freezing with high winds and snow that would lock them in their buildings for some time. Vladimir trusted the ice station personnel and their equipment, and the area was clear so they could mobilize in a hurry if needed.

The "civilian group"' as they were called by Vladimir, sat in the corner as Pieter walked off the plane first along with Vladimir and his lieutenant.

"I don't know Nik, I have a strange feeling about your friend, Pieter," Inna whispered, skeptical. Nik's hand gesture suggested she ignore her suspicion and put her at ease. They followed the troops down the mobile steps attached to the plane, Inna held onto both Nik and her father by their elbows. Her father, the famous scientist, coughed frequently reminding them all that he was ill; with the free hand he held the rail as he went down the steps.

Nik broke from his group, approaching Vladimir and Pieter, making contact with the ice station manager.

"He looks sick," said Vladimir. Nik nodded and replied, "Yes, we know. This is why the Kremlin granted him the journey out of his comfort zone, his lab. We don't know how long he has to live, but as long as his brilliant brain works, let him help our development design until his last breath." Nik sounded patriotic and Vladimir liked that. Pieter heard that too and stayed expressionless.

Nik regrouped with Inna and her father as she tried to bundle up and stop shivering. She grabbed Nik's elbow and whispered, "He will kill us all after they get what they want!"

"Stop Inna, Pieter is on our side and as a SVR agent he won't let anything happen to us. I guarantee. Besides the Russian people would never forgive Vladimir for killing their soccer hero just before the Mondial." Nik chuckled and put his arm around her shoulders. Oleg heard and did not respond.

Vladimir, in the distance, turned around to Pieter and shot a question at him, "How long have the doctors given Oleg? Six weeks? Six months? We hoped this trip would be productive for Dr. Oleg. It will be a win-win situation!"

There was a slight condescending tone in his voice which was humiliating while his lieutenant organized the troops.

The light wind started to whistle and blow harder, blowing flurries from the last snow fall in circles and into the air. All gathered around Vladimir as he greeted the research ice station personnel. The engines of the two snow cruisers were on nearby keeping the cabins warm. Nik got closer to Inna, close enough to whisper in her ear calmly.

"Inna don't rock the boat; The Kremlin knows the only way your father would join this expedition was if you came along. You would not come unless I came, and my celeb status helps. Pieter is an important piece of the puzzle, and yes, there is a chance Vladimir has his own orders that no one knows what the final objectives are. But I trust Pieter since we made a deal he could not refuse."

Pieter noticed the chatter and came closer. "Is everything OK?"

"Oh yes!" replied Nik.

Vladimir introduced everyone to Victor Michaelovich, the lead ice station manager and lead scientist. Victor shook hands with everyone, keeping his gloves on and welcomed them to his station. His skeletal face was cheerful and curious from the surprise visit. He was informed of the expedition twenty-four hours earlier which was not much time to prepare for visitors to stay a couple of days or more.

"Weather is still holding, comrades, we need to takeoff before it gets worse," the captain hollered and asked everyone to clear the area. Vladimir shook the captain's hand and signaled everyone to load into the snow cruisers.

"What's all this about the weather?" asked Pieter.

The ice station manager gladly spoke up. "Weather here is not predictable," he said.

Vladimir agreed, "Forecasts are as good as the prediction of the stock market in Wall Street," he laughed with disdain. Vladimir burst out in laughter.

"Forecast says a huge storm is brewing, right?" Pieter persisted. His concern for delays was obvious. He was eager to get this mission behind him with all its complications. He thought he needed to poke Vladimir to find out his objectives. *Was it just to find the Interceptor, or was there more to it, or perhaps it was connected to the failed North Sea test which recently failed?* Pieter did not share his thoughts aloud; he kept them to himself. He was sure that everyone on this expedition had their own reason why they joined this dangerous and difficult journey. Vladimir's objective could also be, as he commented a few times, to get revenge on the CIA for stealing the K-129 nuclear submarine from the bottom of the ocean.

"Always a storm is brewing here!" Chuckled the ice station manager as he scrunched up his face.

"Once we confirm our Interceptor coordinate point, we are out of here," Vladimir said decisively. "Time is of the essence for us!" he added dramatically.

The ground crew, who also served as cooks, mechanics, and scientists, assisted in many other ice station chores, removed the steps from the plane.

"Amazing scenery, quiet like a graveyard" Inna marveled at the surreal landscape and held her father's elbow, both with expressionless faces.

Vladimir peered at Inna's five-three athletic solid body, which covered by an insulated heavy coat hid the contour of her feminine body. Her light blue eyes were hard to miss, with her round, beautiful face partially covered and her long blond hair escaping from her hood. Her posture indicated she could handle the rugged remote place due to her athletic training as an Olympic gymnast, a dream she dropped when Russia refused to send her to international competitions to represent the country.

Vladimir questioned himself as to her role in this expedition other than convincing her father to examine the American Interceptor missile which would advance the Russian military machine. Something in this puzzle was missing. He understood Nik's deal with Pieter who said Inna wouldn't leave without Nik and her father wouldn't come without her. It was still a complicated twisted scenario, and it confused him. *He would need to keep his eye on them,* he thought.

Inna's father, the central interest of the team, had the same round face as his daughter when he was her age. His long white hair, resembled Einstein's rather than his daughter's blond hair. "Seems like all brilliant scientists have the same hair style," Inna said few times.

He was taller than his daughter and was slender like her. He walked straight on his own merit with only some difficulty, but he was ready for his patriotic task. More importantly for him as a scientist, was to know how the Americans managed to lock on to the frequencies and intercept the hypersonic missile and its coordinates. Oleg's case was easy to convince to add him to the expedition. He would be an important factor since they could not retrieve the Interceptor or bring it back to Russia without him to disassemble the parts and examine them in his labs in Russia.

Pieter and Vladimir were dressed in the white warm arctic uniforms with the ice station insignia patch on their upper left chest, rechargeable battery-equipped boots, and a white helmet with a transparent acrylic wind shield to block the arctic wind from freezing and damaging their exposed skin.

Vladimir's troops, with disguised handguns "no one knew about", made him comfortable. The guns would only be used in life-threatening situations if Vladimir found them necessary. He was aware of the additional troops in the Akula submarines who were equipped with weaponry should they need to become involved. That was the commitment from the military.

"It's a beast," said Vladimir seeing the colossal snow cruiser they called "Kharkovchnaka."

Vladimir ordered his troops to board the snow cruiser and they followed the other two heavy monstrous diesel vehicles, carrying the ice station team back to their camp.

The diesel engines sounded loud and growly, and definitely not fitting of the new environmental policies for climate change with their black soot pumping into the pure Antarctic air.

"Pathetic," whispered Inna.

Nik responded whispering back, "Should be electric vehicles not diesel."

"True, but the generators' fuel to charge the electric vehicles pollutes too," she sounded sarcastic. "Perhaps solar paneled vehicles could be developed for places like this."

"OK Inna, we are halfway there now; keep your defiance for better times. Let's get out of this situation alive and then join the anti-global warming groups on US soil," he whispered back in her ear trying not to be heard by others despite the roaring diesel engine.

The short trip took them through crevices and rugged icescapes caused by the pressure of the glaciers and movement of the sea below.

The vehicles approached the main white building with an orange roof in the center of the research ice station camp. It was the largest building surrounded by many other small, prefabricated structures distinguished by their various functions. Many had unconventional shapes, most with communication towers, antennas, and weather measuring equipment on the rooftops. A green dining room building was connected to a few sleeping quarters with generators producing electricity in a harmony of chaotic sounds.

"You'll get used to all this." The station manager seemed to read their minds. "Living this way year-round can cause mental health issues and trauma so if you feel you need therapy, we have a therapist on staff," he added and pursed his lips. "You know?" he added like he was keeping a secret.

"We are not going to be here that long, comrade," scoffed Vladimir. "We won't need therapy!"

"Well, that's OK. In our cases, commander Vladimir, our government requests we are evaluated by the psychiatrist and provide a report on how the isolation is affecting the crew, so you may take advantage if needed." The manager thought he was helping but Vladimir gave him an icing look.

"They think of everything don't they?" he said sarcastically.

The vehicles moved slowly in a carved ice patch with signage along the way to prevent accidents.

The camp's rugged land, which spread wide, required the installation of many steel handrail supports to assist when the icy conditions, especially in the wintertime, made it a challenge to walk from building to building.

Oil tanks and flexible pipes exposed on the ground connected diesel generators which provided the buildings with heat and propane tanks were for cooking. Empty tanks awaiting removal and replacement were scattered chaotically all around the camp like a huge junk yard. The main building was equipped with the most satellites antennas, weather monitoring equipment, and sensors. Security cameras were placed all around to watch for emergency situations and record events in nine-day intervals.

"It's fucking chaos," murmured Pieter rounding his shoulders.

Nik concurred as he lifted his head, "Yeah, this land is free and wild."

"Did you see the others? The other ice stations? The Americans? They are all the same, you don't use an urban architect here!" Vladimir scoffed defending his team members and rejecting the criticism. "It's actually very organized," replied Vladimir and Pieter softly shook his head seeing the snow tractor vehicles and parts junkyard on the way.

"They are scavenging parts from one vehicle to another," said Pieter.

The station manager was quick to defend the strategy. "Yes, it's cheaper that way, these two tractor trailers are old; hundreds of old vehicles die due to the harsh conditions here, especially in the winter when we can't get out to maintain them in minus eighty degrees Fahrenheit," the manager explained the rationale behind the "junkyards".

The manager directed them to the green building that looked like the central space to congregate. It was the main dining room, recreational room, and assembly room; whatever was needed at the time was its function.

This was not Vladimir's first time at the station. He visited a couple times to evaluate and assess its security needs. He looked where the sun hung beautifully a little above the horizon and the station manager saw Vladimir's gaze and volunteered an explanation to everyone, "The sun rises in September, and each day it climbs higher above the horizon, and in December it reaches its solstice at 23.5 degrees."

"Beautiful," murmured Inna to herself.

"Patches of snow thawed during the last month so there are many pools and muddy conditions," added the manager apologetically. "The mountain tops all around the station camp keep their ice caps throughout the year making the scenery pastorale."

The troops were not part of the discussion, as they were busy organizing for a long night's sleep. Vladimir and his lieutenant got the troops gathered and entered the green building. He didn't let his team forget why they were there and called them to adjust quickly to the environment and the conditions.

"You all have sleeping bags and warm meals on the counters," said the manager, satisfied.

"That's all we need for now. I hope we are not staying here very long," declared Vladimir and Victor nodded.

"OK, feel free, but know it's temporary," said the Vladimir to everyone.

Victor had little prep time in advance to arrange accommodations for his guests. He was happy they brought their own food supplies and a few commodities since many times supplies from the mainland took a long time to arrive due to weather or availability. Hunting seals or penguins was always on the menu he told them. "Is this an environmental mission?"

Vladimir chuckled and took another look at the manager seeing him with the heavy polar coat, helmet, gloves, scarf, and goggles, looking more like a cosmonaut who got lost in space. *They are all strange people with a sense for adventure,* thought Vladimir to himself. *Dreamers that never grew up.*

"OK then, buffet dinner is served. Get it before it gets cold," Victor announced and moved on without asking more questions.

"Holler if you need anything Commander Vladimir," he shot over his shoulder and left for his lab.

Vladimir watched the middle-aged guy disappear into his research lab. "What makes people leave a comfortable life in the modern world come here year after year to measure data that no one cares about?" Pieter asked Vladimir and both rolled their eyes.

"Don't ask. I was just thinking the same," replied Vlad.

"He's probably still wearing his pajamas under that heavy coat," said Pieter and Nik could not hold his laugh. He also felt sympathy for those scientists who thought so differently and cared about the world to make it better someday.

"He well may be!" Vladimir replied and joined in on the laugh. "They are being evaluated by a psychiatrist weekly he said."

"I can imagine why!" erupted Nik with a laugh.

"The Kremlin won't pass up the opportunity to analyze their brains," Oleg got involved in the conversation defending his colleagues.

One camp inhabitant stayed behind to assist Vladimir's crew if they needed help or had any questions; another scientist who wore many hats.

"Hey, I forgot to ask Victor a couple of questions," Vladimir stopped the man. "Do you have any idea of the ice sheet thickness in the Wendell Sea next to Berkner Island this time of year?"

The man stopped and scratched his head. "Oh yes," he was so glad to be asked a scientific question. "It varies, comrade. It is between 2,000 to 7,000 feet thick. Why?" He was curious, then tried to pry into the subject. "Is Berkner where you need to go?"

Vladimir raised his cell phone and showed his lieutenant the message he got on the screen. His second in command nodded seeing the coordinates on the screen.

Pieter knew why Vlad asked that question, even though he also knew that the Russian Navy was not informed of all this. He realized that Vladimir just got a new coordinate for the American Interceptor. *That keeps changing all the time*, he thought and was not sure who was pushing those buttons.

The subs could not poke through the ice shelf to assist if needed, thought Pieter and now the final location was not a mystery, well, at least until the next update.

"Sort of," Vladimir answered without explanation and shot a few quick instructions to his team.

"The ice sheet there is unstable. Twelve years ago, a huge ice sheet broke off the mainland and within twenty-four hours the ice sheet broke off again into many small pieces. You need to know what you are doing in this area," the man sounded like a grumpy professor intimidating his students. "Global warming, you know?" he added without being asked. "Damn too many people, you know?" he mumbled.

They laughed. "Got it, thanks for your advice. We will remember that!" Pieter replied and made a signal to Vlad that the guy was unstable.

"I guess I understand why shrinks are part of the station team," snickered Vladimir.

The dining room temperature was cold despite the heating elements being on. The thermostat registered 68 degrees in the room which was the rule to save fuel and made sure it was warm enough to keep pipes from freezing in the facilities. Inna was cold and stayed in her arctic coat feeling comfortable in it. *The cost for freedom,* she thought.

"OK, soldiers, find a comfortable sleeping spot for tonight and let's go eat," called Vladimir.

"Vlad, see this, it's important!" Pieter hollered as his face flushed. He read the message on his cell phone and cheered. "We have the landing point," he exclaimed and sighed in relief. "Berkner Island between Ronne and Filchner ice shelves, a bit of a long way from here."

"Yes, I know, I got that info too," Vladimir sounded skeptical. "It's close to the Americans."

210 • WILLIE HIRSH

"Satellite images will be downloaded shortly." Vladimir connected his Samsung tablet to the station WiFi encrypted line to examine the area via his satellite mapping program.

Vlad nodded his head and added, "It saves us a lot of wasted waiting time. Let's get the show on the road gentleman. Let's seriously discuss our next move." He sounded content and relieved as well.

"Let's start with the difficult thing first," said Pieter. "I mean planning the trip and checking for any possible cracks in the ice sheet that could pose a threat to our team."

Vlad ignored the statement. He had his orders to execute, and he kept his focus on *his* mission. He knew the biggest challenge ahead would be on the mysterious Berkner Island and minimizing the danger of the ice sheet breaking off. He looked at the photos supplied by the Antarctic geographic society showing the ice sheet that broke off in January. The collapse took only a few hours and surprised environmental scientists around the world. "Global warming in effect," muttered Vladimir.

"We need to add the American factor into our equation too. The trip to Berkner Island will require a different kind of strategy and logistics," Vlad said, heavy thoughts whirling around in his head. "Pieter, you may assist my lieutenant in drawing our trip path from here to that point. Let's see what we need to deal with, plus how long it will take."

Vladimir stretched the Antarctic map on the dining room table and asked the lieutenant, Pieter, and Nik to join the meeting.

Pieter opened the satellite photos, and they examined the Ronne ice shelf conditions from the images while examining the map.

"It's a few thousand kilometers to get there!" Nik was astonished to see the vast distance that reminded him of

Mother Russia's size; probably the first time he realized the vastness of Antarctica.

"See the Trans-Antarctic mountains? They are impossible to cross," intervened the lieutenant pointing to the line on the map over the mountain range.

"We can't rough it across that continent. It's 2,500 kilometers in a straight line! Holy Mother of God! This is pure torture. Steep rugged mountains, thousand-foot-deep valleys below the sea level, see thi–"

"I know!" Vladimir cut off Pieter's unnecessary evaluation. "We are not equipped for that journey; not sure if it was a mistake to fly here rather than join the K-317 Pantera Akula fleet that now circles the continent."

"I know what you are think–" Pieter said and was abruptly cut off again by Vladimir who he was ready to choke him if he could.

"We need to change our mission. Only the subs could bring us close to the Interceptor rendezvous point; I'll contact the headquarters," Vladimir caught his breath. "I personally know the captain of the K-317," he added proudly.

"If we know where the Interceptor is for sure, be sure that the Americans know that too. They will try to be there first." The Lieutenant called his shot and kept his piercing eyes on his commander.

"No brainer!" Pieter exclaimed and exchanged angry glances.

"Calm down both of you," scolded Vladimir. "Our agents sent no other info of activities related to the recovery of the missile. Plus, they might have the same obstacles. I am not sure if the Americans could get there first even though it's closer to their ice research camp since the ice sheet is broken. The Interceptor might be on one of those small ice sheets." Vladimir took back the helm and shrugged his shoulders.

The lieutenant added his own theory without hesitation hoping not to be ridiculed by Pieter and said, "Using our subs makes the most sense, and we should get there fast. In the meantime, we should lock our satellites to monitor the Interceptor's drifting location."

"Sure, it's drifting; it's a moving target!" said Pieter, amused. "I don't know which of our agents got the Interceptor's location information. Do you have names?"

Vladimir scoffed and smiled, "Pieter, if you are with the SVR and don't know, why should I tell you? Besides I am sure it's top secret anyway. Why are you asking?"

Pieter had to recalculate his response. He was close to trapping himself in a corner and could be seen as suspicious as an American collaborator. He tried to ease the tension. "As SVR, I want to authenticate the info," he said confidently and raised his head.

Oleg jumped in, ignoring the last cranky conversation. "Strong currents over there, Pieter is right, it's a moving target!"

"Thank you, doctor. OK. Stand by all," Vladimir concluded sinking into deep thought. *What was next?* The weight of the entire expedition pressed on his chest. Decisions needed to be on top at all times, one wrong step and the Americans would be there first. How the CIA managed to raise the K-129 in complete confidentiality he would never know, therefore he kept his moves to himself. No one here knew the second most important reason for this expedition.

"Lieutenant, have the troops eat and go to sleep early. Lieutenant, I need to poke yours and Pieter's brains next," Vlad said and hoped he would not regret giving them more information. As the troops dined on frozen and canned food prepared by the camp cook on duty, Pieter and the lieutenant joined Vladimir in a secluded corner away from the rest. Inna's worried eyes followed them with concerned glances hoping nothing would escalate.

"We will use our Pantera submarine to approach the Berkner Island coast through the Weddell Sea, hoping we can create a direct beachhead on the ice," said Vladimir. "We should be good, sailing submerged underwater passing the Southern Temperate Zone undetected into the Antarctic no war zone circle. Right here." He pointed on the map while the others were impressed that Vladimir did his homework. He understood the implications as well as the restrictions. He stood up straight, calming saying, "No one will know we are there!"

"Don't we have Plan B?" asked Pieter skeptically.

"This is Plan B, Pieter, at that point we will connect with *Admiral Karlinsky*, the whaler conducting research. We might not be the first ones to see the Interceptor if we hesitate and waste time; this is why I requested the submarine as a backup the first place, to transport us to that point for logistics and add more tools to our toolbox. Perhaps recovery and rescue later, which I hope we do not need. It was all thought out before you all joined us."

Pieter looked at Vladimir with more respect. He had thought of everything, only he didn't share it with them. I wonder why? Did he suspect anyone was a whistle blower? Was that also on his objective agenda to resolve? Pieter knew he had nothing to hide and if someone was a traitor, he wondered who he would suspect? Inna?

"I didn't know that *Admiral Ka*–" Pieter was cut off by Vladimir.

"Pieter, hold your comments for a second. The only concern I have is that we don't have enough intel on the island's terrain, cracks in the ice, any ice caves, and the list of equipment we need to cross–" Vlad held off from losing his temper when Pieter cut him off, too.

"Vlad, even if the Interceptor is only about 15 or 20 kilometers inland on Berkner Island, it's covered by a thousand feet of melting ice and very unstable. The Admiral Karlinsky has an M-26 on board that can hold all of us in its belly. You must ask for accurate satellite imaging; without it we can't go!" Pieter stared at Vlad and cocked his head like he was looking for a different opinion.

Vladimir smiled faintly, shrugged, and said, "Pieter, that's Plan B. We trained for surprises and are not letting fear hold us up. I agree with you, using the M-26 is one of my plans." Vlad frowned and asked his lieutenant, "What do you think lieutenant?"

The tall and heavy-built lieutenant turned his long face and pointy nose to Vladimir and pursed his thin lips. He was only in his late twenties, but combat experience filled his chest with medals having fought in Crimea and Chechnya, and recently was pulled off the war in Ukraine for this expedition. The lieutenant said, "I do the hard work first and the impossible later! So, I think we can do this in phases. The hard part, get to Berkner Island; combat the Americans, that's the impossible, but all doable!"

Vladimir looked at his lieutenant with admiration. He reiterated his statement on a different level, "So, we board, we sail, we land, we conquer!" His intimidating voice sounded as if that was the final decision and mobilization in one step.

"Very nicely said!" exclaimed Pieter backing up Vladimir and his second in command. For him it was important to see that they were moving along and not stranded in the camp for too long drinking coffee all day. Inside his heart he knew he did not want to scrap the mission and was careful not to show any sign of resentment. He was still a SVR officer.

Vlad was busy sending encrypted messages by satellite radio, while the troops, Nik, Oleg, and Inna enjoyed eating on the long wood bench. From time to time, she stole a quick look at Vladimir and Pieter to get a feeling of what was going on.

The lieutenant followed the route on the map with his finger, pointing out possible obstacles that could cause delays when taking the journey to the Pantera Sub. "Add one more day for delays beyond our control and you have a four-day schedule to the final mission destination," he said sounding confident. "Did you make contact, Commander?" asked the lieutenant. Vladimir nodded his head and gave him a tired thumbs up.

"The sub is eleven hours away from us," Vladimir said. "It's eighty hours sailing underwater to Berkner Island. I just communicated with Captain Igor Brodiesev, a tough guy from my neighborhood. My troops are ready for any assignment. They crunched into submarines before and slept on floors when needed; not so sure about your civilians?" asked Vladimir and added with a low tone, "Still not sure what role the civilians hav–"

Pieter didn't wait to respond and wanted to put this to bed before the opposition grew and the suspicious tension tore them apart. He cut Vladimir off again, "They all have SVR intelligence roles under my command, Vlad. It's confidential, sorry but even to you. You work for the military and have your top-secret objectives that you don't share with us. We work for the SVR with specific orders, and we are committed to work together." Pieter inhaled and released the tension in his chest. He refused to clash with Vladimir and wanted to keep his mission separate and in his control.

Vladimir remembered the verbal fight on the plane and shrugged his shoulders in disbelief. "A soccer player and his side kick work for the SVR," he mumbled.

"You are crossing the line, comrade." Pieter raised his icy tone putting Vladimir back in his place. "You are in charge of your troops only, comrade!" he added.

The lieutenant backed up his commander and the argument escalated again. Vladimir, along with the lieutenant were ready to fight Pieter, physically pushing him back while everyone in the room looked on in shock but kept silent.

Nik quickly approached the men and separated them before they cracked each other's noses; a fight they would regret later.

"Calm down! Stop it! I know it's difficult. No hard feelings, Vladimir. We all need to work together," said Nik loudly. "I volunteered to work for the propaganda intelligence department. If we are caught, then we can say we are civilians and if we succeed, it will be a triumph for all of us. Think of our motherland, comrades!" He held Vladimir's and the lieutenant's hands with his strong fists.

"You need to calm down, comrade," the lieutenant added with sincere intention to diffuse the tension.

Vlad ignored his lieutenant's last words and kept going, "We should ask Victor about the climate in those areas, to be more prepared."

"Good point. What the hell? Right now, they expect a storm," said Nik. "It's gonna be a huge storm engulfing the entire north side."

"If we stay, we will be locked in for the next three days. We need to leave no matter what tomorrow!" Vlad decided. "Storm or no storm!"

The wind rattled the windows, to the breaking point which reminded them of the upcoming struggle. The snow hit the ground accumulating in a fresh feathery layer. They looked outside with concern.

"The snow tractor will take us to the submarine rendezvous safely. It should be an easy trip." The lieutenant tried to cheer them up.

"The weather in the west is different from the east; we might be lucky or buried under snow," said Pieter and scoffed. The lieutenant gave him a dirty look.

"Remember that most important decisions in life start with, *'What the hell'*!" Vladimir laughed showing his human side when he was in a good mood; he waggled his finger at Pieter.

Pieter shared a glance with Nik who was listening then shot back at them, "Remember Vlad, we didn't come here to die."

"We all are going to die someday, Nik, but not today, it's too soon," promised Vlad and tapped him on the shoulder.

At the same time the wind started to pick up more speed, howling outside, lifting and swirling snowflakes from the ground causing zero visibility. The temperature dropped rapidly, and they felt it even indoors.

The standby sub redirected its course to rendezvous with Vladimir and his crew. In the meantime, the Intelligence department reported that the Interceptor was floating on a two-mile ice sheet separated from the mainland heading north with the current and wind.

"Tomorrow is another day!" Vladimir muttered.

CHAPTER 23

April Fools' Day

Lucy was one of the few agents in the CIA Asia spy network who survived the Russian counterintelligence ambush a little more than two years ago. She had the pleasure of eliminating the double agent responsible for exposing them to the cruel SVR execution department.

Her failed departure along with the long trail of blood Lucy left behind at the Dulles International Airport, got her thinking how the Russians could find her so easily. *Why were they spending so much time and resources to eliminate her?*

Patrick acted immediately and instructed Lucy to report to the United Polaris Lounge at the Airport and wait for new instructions.

"Let them think you are on board the flight as planned and perhaps they will wait for you on the other end," Patrick said.

For three hours, Lucy nibbled on the light snacks offered by United Airlines when she was dispatched over the loudspeaker using her fake name, to come to the VIP reception.

"I am called!" she introduced herself to the lounge attendant.

"These gentlemen are looking for you," she pointed at two police officers carrying M-16 machine guns waiting at the entrance. She nodded toward them, and they reciprocated.

"We are here to escort you," the short officer said without explanation. At the same time, Lucy got a text from Patrick to follow the two MWAA officers and he would be in contact soon. They exited a door leading to a set of stairs down to the tarmac and a police car waited for them with the engine running.

"Where are you taking me?" she asked as her senses sharpened.

"To Tarmac R-22," said the short officer with the green eyes. Then the driver shot straight ahead across the taxi way to Flight Line Road. Lucy saw two all-white Boeing 739s parked without any insignia or an ID calling code. She gambled that they would stop at the closest plane which was fueled and ready for departure with its front entry open and a set of stairs still attached to it. She understood what those planes were; she called them "no man's land planes." The CIA used them to carry prisoners away from American soil where the constitution does not govern and interrogate them. This way torture and severe interrogation would not hold up in the Supreme Court of the United States.

"Good afternoon, ma'am!" An anorexic looking man in uniform greeted her and politely said, "Follow me please!"

"Yes, good afternoon!" she replied with a slight delay, thinking to herself, *How the hell does this man manage to stay alive being so thin?*

"1-A!" he exclaimed then asked, "Do you want a drink before take-off?"

"Thanks, I'll take a rain check." She hunkered down into her seat.

"Sure ma'am! You have a package in the bin above!"

Lucy opened the bin and opened the package. "Oh," she mumbled. "I thought Patrick was sending me to a mission without my Glock," she murmured and examined her handgun like she was a little girl who would do the same with her doll.

The man, whom she didn't know how to refer to, came back saying, "Welcome to our special express flight to Chile."

A few minutes later the captain announced, "We are clear to taxi in sixteen minutes. We will try to beat the Pacific Hurricane Mina before they shut down air space."

Resume mission to meet with the Arctic Star icebreaker. Patrick's text was his way of saying, "Have a pleasant flight." *The dolphin helicopter will land next to you.*

CHAPTER 24

Patrick handled Lucy years ago when he was the Iranian and Asian East Region desk manager in charge of missions one-on-one, directly with her. He knew her very well, and they worked together very well. She was excited to be on this mission with so many uncertainties that made her body shiver. Adrenalin was her supplement to oxygen. *It was a matter of national security and there was no better way to serve her country,* she thought.

She opened her laptop and downloaded the document that Patrick emailed her. Some other docs were uploaded by Victoria, Patrick's loyal administrative assistant. He made sure she knew who uploaded what and personally went over all the materials. *A little in-office spy game Patrick plays,* she thought. A photo of two young refugee children in England grabbed her attention. *Who are they?* Since she knew how Patrick operated, she knew he left it for her to solve. The photo looked old, with Downing 10 in the background and the shape of the vehicles at that time. *Must be about twenty, twenty-five years old*, she assumed. *How are they related to the mission? Was it a hint?*

Patrick and she believed that adversary spy agencies around the world smuggled their agents disguised as refugees through the porous American border, especially to Europe via Turkey. "They are welcome," said Patrick who advocated vetting just like Victoria.

Victoria, a beautiful, smart woman, lost her husband in a car crash a few years ago and that added to the passionate sympathy toward her. The car that hit them was stolen, and the criminal driver was never found. She decorated her office nicely and was involved in all social events the CIA performed behind closed doors.

"It's getting harder and harder to vet the refugees and check the background of each one of the millions pouring in without control," she overheard Patrick saying.

Patrick was an expert of using people against people, recruiting from different countries and different ideologies, a few with retaliatory urges against their enemies. The feeling that every move he made or said was heard by dangerous people bothered him and his sixth sense urged him to investigate further.

Patrick's ideology centered around making peace with enemies. Someone who was a bitter enemy yesterday could be a great collaborator today, for a common cause. Especially, Patrick disliked double agents. For him, if an agent betrayed his country, one day he would betray you too. A double agent who worked for the CIA always had an expiration date.

Patrick collected data on the lead Russian scientists. He copied the Mossad from the early 1960s, when Nazi missile scientists were hired by Egypt to develop missiles based on the notorious V-2 technology used to attack London in WWII. The Mossad sent bomb envelopes to each one of the scientists. Some envelopes exploded, injuring and killing a few. The message was clear, they understood it, and then the German scientists packed up their suitcases and returned home, back to Germany. The same with the nuclear Iranian scientists, their lives are shortened by deadly attacks to prevent the nuclear program from advancing to a point of no return.

Patrick was not ready to act the same way, it was premature, an action that could act as a boomerang on his own agency. However, the Lockheed Martin murder started that war and the only way to stop it was to retaliate.

Massive planning sometimes took an army of agents to help execute a mission. Patrick always preferred a single agent operation which was usually enough to complete the job. It all was dependent on the assignment and mission goals; a single agent could penetrate deep without being discovered.

Patrick tailored this mission around Lucy with a specific objective, keeping it confidential even among his own closed circle. "Some walls have ears," he recited occasionally.

Leaving behind tracks for his covert agents was the last thing a CIA director wanted to do, but this was not an ordinary espionage hide-and-seek game. He wanted to lure his opponent, to exhaust their mental strength, make them want to quit and abandon their mission. The CIA was aware of the three Akula submarines dispatched on their way to envelop the Russian ice station. He hoped there would be no military collision with the Pacific fleet training in that area.

Patrick's chess move was to dispatch Lucy to Antarctica. She left a trail of clear tracks to lure the Russian Intelligence away from the real purpose of her trip to Antarctica. He knew they would try to stop her from joining the American's Interceptor rescue operation on behalf of the CIA.

His intercom signaled an incoming call from Victoria behind the shared wall.

"FBI director is on the line, Pat." Victoria sounded firm and confident with her pleasant voice.

"OK, thanks," Patrick closed his office door and went back to his speaker phone.

"I'll call you right back on my private line, Dan."

Pat dialed back on his private line and Dan immediately said, "Ron Hill is on board; he is all yours."

"That's great Dan, any info regarding the Lockheed Martin conference guests?" Patrick asked.

Dan sighed, "No, they are all clean as a whistle. No one is suspected of killing John Gregory. Pat, it's a foreign agent's job, perhaps the SVR like you suggested. Those guests were defense contractors, engineers, and programmers with the highest security clearances."

"Ok, thanks. We are moving on!" Patrick concluded and hung up the phone.

So far, the Russian master of disguise made sure the sub's mission was not exposed. But not now! Any military operation required some cover up, disinformation, and deceptive actions depending how much the Russians were willing to invest in retrieving the Interceptor. Patrick made sure to spread fear using "conscious engineering" which he was an expert in creating.

Although the Russians made a confidential attempt to hide the Antarctic submarine expeditions that departed from their new submarine base Rybachiy, heading across the Avacha bay in Kamchatka, it was hard to hide it from the spy satellites roaming space even in a secured network. Satellites recorded every minute of where the enemy vessels may be at any moment, and technicians specializing in the art of underwater hunting figured out from satellite photos using before and after imagery to pinpoint where they submerged for the rest of the voyage under sea.

The Russians were not rookies in sabotage or spy games. The three old and loyal Akula sub expeditions were sent to deceive the Americans as to their true mission, which was used as a new cadets' training expedition. The real nuclear sub force, the Russians kept close and around the Antarctic Circle, was present to keep the Russian's interests in the south continent even though they have no territorial claim. One of those submarines, the newly designed Yuriy

Dolgoruky class, was ready for the complicated mission to transfer the Russian troops to Berkner Island undetected. With the coordination of the US Navy's South Pacific fleet, Patrick seemed to slow the Russian's expedition until his team was ready to intercept them.

Lucy learned the plan just before she left Patrick's office with instructions about her objectives. The last few words Patrick said still echoed in her mind, "A C-17 Globemaster will wait for us at McMurdo Ice Station to return via Falkland Islands." She remembered Victoria's smiling face as she left. But it was the word "us" that sank into her mind. *Is Patrick planning on being there too?* That was something she couldn't grasp. *And why had he kept it to himself? Why was she traveling to the* Arctic Star *rather than taking the* Globemaster *plane?* This was an open question, and she was sure she would find out what Patrick's mind was thinking.

Lucy on the other hand, was more interested in learning her obstacles for her journey, especially from the ice station to the Interceptor landing site. *The Berkner Island is covered with barren rock and lies in the McCarthy inlet of the Weddell Sea*, she learned.

She spoke to scientists who were concerned with the unstable icy landing strip conditions that prevented heavy planes from landing on the strip as they had done for many years previously, especially after the gigantic A6a Ice Shelf broke off from the Antarctic mainland. *One more issue to worry about,* Lucy thought, and her adrenaline rush hit a cord in her chest; a strange feeling of excitement mixed with fear of the events of the unknown.

She checked the time zone differences between the American and Russian Ice stations and realized that each country decided its own time zone based on its country of origin and she scoffed when hearing that crazy idea.

CHAPTER 25

The next day, early morning

The wind was still pounding the landscape at the Russian Ice research camp. Winds gusting to 60 MPH brought low visibility that scattered snowflakes off the ground from the last storm. Without a guide helping them to navigate the rendezvous with the submarine, they could get lost or even worse, they could lose their life.

"Should we wait for the storm to calm down?" asked the lieutenant with sleepy eyes and a rasp in his voice due to the lack of sleep. He was not the only one. The uncomfortable accommodations, canned food, and howling winds kept most of them up all night.

"We must be going!" Vladimir replied laconically, then paused watching the storm through the hanging icicles from the windows. He added, "The storm will not stop us lieutenant. Time is of the essence here; we don't want to be second after the Americans."

"Both snow cruisers are ready, sir," said the driver of the vehicle with a brooding expression. "We travel in tandem close to each other in bad weather," he added.

"Do you have your full crew or just you?" asked Vladimir.

The man answered skeptically even though he had made many trips in bad weather before, "Full crew, radio operator, my diesel mechanic and me. I was ordered to transport you to your designation point."

"It's six hours away."

The driver looked at the lieutenant and replied to him, "If all goes well, we can do better. I hope the storm will not slow us down."

Vladimir checked on his team before they boarded the snow cruiser vehicle camouflaged with white and cream patches to blend with the ground.

"It's a long trip," said Pieter to Nik who overheard the conversation and was anxious to complete the mission.

They chose their route carefully using satellite imaging to outflank obstacles, ice cracks, and crevices they would not be able to cross.

They packed into one cruiser and the troops in the second one, both were ready to go. The windshield was covered with snow and the blowing snow made it hard to keep it clean.

"We use satellites to navigate," said the driver seeing all the anxious faces. "We need to outflank obstacles," he added with confidence from his years of experience.

The first started to move and the driver identified himself on the internal intercom, "I Am Lubov. Alex Lubov. You have a bathroom in the back of the vehicle. In case of an emergency, you have a rear exit. Feel free to use the bunks and the small kitchen room for seating."

"Thank you, Comrade Lubov," replied Vladimir satisfied with the mobilization.

"These two cruisers are the last ones to retire and survived the last sixty years in the harsh arctic conditions. They made the historic journey to Vostok South Pole Station and from there to Amundsen-Scott, the American station, and back. We should get our new snowmobiles soon."

"The kumbaya is over comrade. We are back in cold war mode!" spat Vladimir as his eyes sparked.

They passed a hanger with no windows and a unique shape. Pieter asked the driver, "What's that building for?"

"Oh, we house two Mi-16 Helicopters," he replied proudly.

"So why are we not using them to fly to the submarines?"

"Not in this weather" replied the driver.

Vladimir intervened and scolded Pieter, "Yeah, let's tell the Americans we are coming, right comrade?" He yelled, "Whose side are you on anyway?"

"So, if we must meet the submarine, why didn't we join them in the first place, Comrade Vladimir? Isn't it you who designed the mission?" Pieter did not hold back.

"We have a secret mission other than the Interceptor, that SVR is not a part off," Vladimir shot back coldly. Then he checked the reaction of the call. "I know your mission is also to eliminate the CIA agent, Lucy the Spider. Do you know where she is, comrade?"

"No!" exclaimed Pieter.

"Well, I do, and we are on top of her."

"How do you know?"

Vladimir scoffed, "We do have our ways. She is on her way to the American ice station. Do you need better proof than what I tell you and how important the Interceptor is for the Americans?"

Vladimir undermined Pieter in front of his colleagues who kept quiet and wondered what Vladimir's real mission was.

CHAPTER 26

April 26

T he captain's tinny voice on the airplane intercom came
over loud and clear.

"We are starting our decent to the airport. We are
clear to land shortly," he announced to the only passenger
he carried. "We have a heavy crosswind from Mina. We'll
try to land or seek an alternate airport if necessary."

"Oh no," mumbled Lucy as her body tensed.

The plane struggled to stay on course. The turbulence
shook it badly. The pilot's ex-military experience skillfully
managed the roughest landing of his career. The plane tax-
ied to a secluded tarmac on the north side of the airport
and stopped.

A text message from Patrick gave her direction to stay
on the secured plane while fueling and wait for the *Arctic
Star* Dolphin helicopters to show up first.

Hurricane Mina reminded them it was still a dangerous
storm and Lucy was skeptical of the Dolphin's arrival. The
captain walked toward Lucy shaking his head murmuring
something unclear; he was just happy he landed safely.

"That was a brave landing, Captain!" she hollered, and he
acknowledged her with a shy nod.

"Mina is a powerful storm; we will be grounded for the
time being. Not sure of your destination but as the only passenger it means it's important!" He was curious and then
took the seat next to her. The plane door was still closed,
and the cabin crew member offered them drinks.

"Sort of," she responded with no feeling and wondered again for herself, *how would the Dolphin manage to meet her?* Then she said, "We have two fully equipped agents seated in the back disguised as cabin crew."

Gusty winds from one of the huge storm's spiraled arms, shook the plane. The airport was shut down for all takeoffs and landings just after the CIA plane landed safety.

A white van carrying an airport border police authority struggled to walk up the mobile steps, knocked on the closed door, and peered through its small window. The stewards examined the officer's badge and opened the door with the captain's approval. Then the captain joined the co-pilot in the cockpit.

"We need the passports of all travelers," the airport officer commanded and the stewards who spoke fluent Spanish concurred.

"I am the only passenger, sir!" said Lucy decisively. "No one else on board will set foot on land."

"Your passport, ma'am!"

"Can I see both your badges please?" Lucy was authoritative and examined their uniforms. So far, the uniforms looked legit, a white shirt with black tie with the agency logo. At the top left it said "international" in yellow letters and Lucy asked to see their badges for authenticity.

"We don't take our badges off our shirts."

"Let me remind you officers that according to international law, you are in United States sovereignty aboard this airplane, sir."

"Give them the passport!" insisted the steward and called the captain.

Lucy moved her arm behind her back to feel the cold handgun for assurance. Then slowly, she opened the small bag and gave them her passport. The second officer went to the cockpit to ensure no one else, other than the pilots, was there. He came back and shook his head.

Lucy noticed through her window, the van downstairs. The driver was looking up all the time and looking at his watch with anticipation. He seemed nervous and uptight, and he tapped his hand on the steering wheel. Then he turned around toward the back of the van and said something she could not make out and realized he was not alone. Perhaps a few guys were in the back awaiting the right moment to react. She naturally stiffened and her brain ran crazy scenarios. As the back doors opened, three other uniformed border police with loaded machine guns came out of the van rushing toward the steps to the plane.

The on-board officer examined the passports and looked at his cell phone to match the face image reported to them. He knew the name was fake.

"You need to come with me, ma'am!" he commanded with an authoritative voice and started to draw his gun.

Lucy's sixth sense processed the situation as the three disguised border officers started to climb the steps.

"Close the cabin door!" she screamed.

The stewards jumped like a cobra toward the open door pushing one of the border officers on board.

"Shut the door!" Lucy screamed again and the steward struggled with the first border officer trying to get into the plane calling for his partners inside to shoot Lucy and the crew.

The two CIA agents in the back of the plane who were monitoring the situation from the windows, moved forward to the front cabin with guns drawn.

Miraculously the Dolphin helicopter from the *Arctic Star* ship, swaying from side-to-side from the high wind, landed a short and safe distance from the parked Boeing. Lucy was too busy to stay alive. The steward managed to lock the main cabin airplane door and dove to the floor to get out of the way of the second airport officer who drew his gun.

The Dolphin's rotor distracted the foreign agents who thought Lucy was getting reinforcement and that was all Lucy needed. That brief moment was priceless, and she took the golden opportunity to shoot the closest guy point blank in the head. The force of the bullet threw him into his buddy behind him who was about to shoot the steward on the floor. He fell dead with a loud thud.

The two CIA agents finally got into the scene as the three foreign agents on the top step landing tried to open the door. They started shooting the door with their machine guns, breaking the windows, and damaging the door mechanism.

While all the shooting was going on in the front galley, Lucy shot out her window and with her hand over the fuselage started to shoot the foreign agents who stood on the landing. Two fell dead onto the hard landing floor, the third one tumbled and rolled down the steps, stopping near the van's wheels. He was only wounded.

The driver zoomed away and left the wounded comrade dying on the tarmac asphalt as the wind pushed and rolled his body toward the Dolphin.

The two CIA agents rushed to Lucy. "Are you OK?" the first shouted.

The captain and copilot got a signal from the stewards that all was clear, and they came out; their pale faces examining the dead men and the damages to the plane.

"I'm alright, there are two dead on the steps, all fake border police. How the fuck did they know all this shit?" the CIA agent hollered, tense and frustrated looking through the window.

"They were shooting the plane those assholes," shot the steward in post-traumatic panic. "They are crazy!"

Mina poured rain as she started to hit the tarmac. Puddles formed then immediately drained into the airport's underground infrastructure. The Dolphin's rotor still turned. "What chaos," cried Lucy focusing on the situation. "I need to board the helo, before the real local airport police arrive. I can't stay here."

"I'll open the right door and emergency sleeve," offered the steward.

"We can't stay here either; we will be arrested for espionage," said the first CIA agent.

"Join me!" cried Lucy.

Lucy opened the plane door, and the steward activated the emergency slider to let Lucy slide down with her bag first. The rain hit her face and soaked her clothes. She was not prepared for this kind of welcome to Chile.

"Get out of here," cried the captain urging the two CIA agents to roll down the sleeve.

All three rushed to the helicopter and Lucy was first to bang on the side door. The flight engineer opened the door a crack and tried to raise his voice over the sound of wind. "Password!'

That threw Lucy, she could not remember the password in all the commotion. Then her face lit up and she screamed in joy, "Arizona! Arizona!"

The flight engineer nodded and opened the door wide and assisted her to get in.

"We are picking up only you," he added.

"Get my colleagues on board sir. That is an order!" she commanded. Her voice was sharp.

"Let me speak to the captain!" he responded and turned around.

Lucy grabbed his flight overalls and pushed him back. "We have no fucking time, we all will be arrested by the police!" she screamed, the two CIA agents had already climbed on board with no consent and Lucy screamed "Go, go, go!" Many airport security vehicles approached them from all directions.

The helo captain climbed up immediately and turned west, toward the Arctic Star facing the storm.

CHAPTER 27

Three days later

The Globemaster C-17, an extended range military transport plane, was ready at Andrews Air Force Base in George County near Washington, DC. The cargo uploaded the night before was confidential, without any manifest or computer log to avoid tracking. Three crewmen entered the plane with six civilian-clothed passengers all carrying the same kitbags.

"Looks like they are familiar with short trips," Victoria scoffed to herself. The two-pilot crew entered the cockpit, nodding their heads toward Victoria with polite acknowledgment without asking any questions. The third crew member was the loadmaster who completed his task and took his seat next to the monitoring instruments.

Patrick surprised Victoria by granting her first field mission with the simple task to join the Interceptor search crew. She was ecstatic and accepted the new role immediately then went to a ten-minute session on how to handle a gun. "It's the same Glock as Lucy's," she commented during the session.

Victoria held her holster at her hip like a cowboy and proudly walked into the plane taking her seat directly beside the loadmaster in the cockpit jump seat.

"What's the load?" she asked, but the loadmaster changed the subject.

"We will be in the air eighteen hours with midair fueling," he said.

"Wow, exciting, have you been to the ice station before?" she asked.

"Yes, a couple of times."

"How is it?"

"Cold!" he exclaimed and laughed.

"No, seriously!" she insisted.

"We will sit in the cabin; the cargo bay is off limits. Here everyone serves themselves. There is coffee, snacks, water, and soft drinks. Enjoy the flight," he pointed to the storage area where each of the items he mentioned was kept.

He grabbed a couple of sandwiches and a coke and strapped himself in.

It's odd, Victoria thought, *they save words here, not very social.* She assumed it would get better once they landed on the icy strip. She wondered what kind of a welcome was awaiting her.

The six civilian passengers were sitting in a secluded compartment like a first-class section behind the galley and the loadmaster's instrument niche. *What could the confidential cargo be? Perhaps I'll get a look when we unload,* she thought.

The main cabin and rear cargo doors closed, and the composed voice of the captain announced, "There is an ice storm in our path, and it is affecting our landing site, however that's not the worst news. Hurricane Mina took a sharp turn to the south and turned back into the Pacific Ocean along the shores. Looks like she won't go away," he chuckled. "So, expect heavy turbulence until we cross Costa Rica, the flight will take about eighteen hours at 45,000 feet."

Victoria's thoughts drifted as the plane started to taxi, then she realized that she would be sitting in that seat all by herself with one unsocial guy which made her a little queasy. She took comfort in the fact that this was her first mission, something she waited for a long time.

The four jet engines roared, and the metal monster started its takeoff run lifting the heavy bird. She busied herself by thinking of global issues to get her mind off the pressure she felt. Her thoughts drifted to the war in Ukraine. She openly supported Russia claiming Ukraine was always part of Russia, the Motherland, a stance that surprised her friends and colleagues. She was the minority in her group on that subject but kept the compelling argument smoldering. She felt bad for the many soldiers on both sides who had no home to return to after the war ended. She always hoped she could help in one way or another.

Victoria wondered why Patrick chose that mission to be her first. *Perhaps time and opportunity,* she thought. The ice station crew was still at its summer capacity, slowly reducing the team of researchers for the winter. Patrick explained that the Interceptor should be found quickly and disclosed the location coordinates to her confidentially.

Where is Lucy? she wondered as the Globemaster reached its cruising altitude then she fell asleep.

CHAPTER 28

The helicopter took off before they had a chance to grab Lucy for questioning. She left a mess, and Patrick's political superiors would need to clean it up with Chile's government. She remembered what Patrick said once, "Let us complete our mission and have the politicians clean up the mess." Well, that's nice. She murmured, "Someone knew where I was, and that is more disturbing." Greg and Bill, the CIA agents who joined her, asked themselves the same question.

"Who are these people?" Lucy asked loudly, sitting comfortably in the helicopter. The two CIA agents made themselves comfortable as well both with no idea how to answer her. They all knew the consequences of staying behind on Chilean soil.

"Terrorists!" said the tall agent who called himself Greg.

"OK, but which group? Who do they represent?" Lucy insisted. "We left behind a few corpses, and they knew the crew wasn't involved. It's a problem."

"Let Patrick deal with diplomacy," hollered the short agent who called himself Bill.

The flight engineer listened through his headset to the conversation and intervened, "The control tower is asking us to return!"

"Tell the captain, don't you dare!" Lucy yelled decisively. "No take off clearance pal, you know what is waiting for us down there!" She exclaimed loudly.

"We are still in the territorial sovereignty of Chile, and they can shoot us down!" the captain said.

"How far off the coast are we?" asked Lucy and the rest bit their lips.

"Eight miles."

"Do what you need to do. Get off their radar and get them off our backs. Skim the ocean if needed, but don't go back!" Lucy replied.

"High waves and strong wind. It's very dangerous to fly below 100 feet," the captain explained.

"I know all about it, Captain. You don't want three CIA agents on your conscious rotting in a Chilean jail, right?"

"The *Arctic Star* is about 300 miles south, south-west. We have thirty to fifty knots wind speed, not the best day to fly especially when fighter jets took off to intercept you!" The captain sounded concerned. The visibility was murky, and the captain was sure no fighter pilot would be crazy enough to fly in this weather by chasing a helicopter 100 feet above sea level. A few minutes later, using the ship beacon to navigate, they passed the Chilean territorial waters and sighed in relief.

"Damn SVR! Live another day," she mumbled.

The Dolphin bravely struggled the storm and flew as fast as possible to the safety of the landing platform of the research ship.

• • •

Patrick strapped himself in and connected his headset to the cockpit crew, calling Lucy across the continent to the *Arctic Star* now close to the ice station. Perhaps if the weather was not critical, she could use the Dolphin to reach the ice station, he thought trying to save a day.

The boat sailed through Hurricane Mina which was going in wild circles in the Pacific Ocean, due to a high-pressure cell heading south with forty-foot crashing waves. Lucy ran out of curses for every ocean wave crashing over the stern.

"Storm over?" asked Patrick mischievously and chuckled.

"You owe me Patrick, for sending me on board the *Arctic Star* in this storm!" she scolded her boss. "OH, and how could the SVR know where I was in the airport? How did they know where and when I landed in Santiago, Patrick?"

She heard Patrick exhale. He paused and made sure his line of communication was encrypted. "OK, it's time to tell you. I used you to distract the Russian intelligence tracking so they would follow you and avoid tracking me then I could join you at the station aboard a National Guard plane!" He inhaled and held his breath for ten seconds, a way to calm down. "I asked them to plant a chip in your passport!"

"Fuck, Patrick! I thought someone in the office was controlling the information from us to the SVR; they know every step we make Patrick!"

"True, for the reason as we discussed in the offi–"

"We discussed shit, Patrick. You never told me that I'd be the guinea pig to coax the SVR away from your whereabouts? You put my life in danger!"

"I told you; I trust you. You manage situations well, sometimes you leave a trail of blood and that is the collateral damage. It was important for me to complete our mission by being there with you and the rest of our team!"

"I was your guinea pig!" She was furious and scolded with disbelief, "What would happen if I had been killed in the Dulles or Santiago Airport? Would you write me off as collateral damage?"

"Calm down, you are too smart to let Russian agents take you down. I didn't want the Russians to know where I was.

They knew you were on the way to protect the Interceptor and it made the whole idea legit and worth the risk," Patrick paused and watched the pilots communicate with the controllers heading south as the jet engines hummed steadily. "That was all part of my plan Lucy, I could not disclose all my intents. You did very well, in fact, they chased you around the world."

"I got it, after al–"

"It was all planned, on purpose, a small deception. Victoria is on the plane as well, so act surprised when you see her a–"

Lucy cut Patrick off. "What?"

"It's complicated. Ron Hill, the FBI agent, was assigned to us as well. He was almost killed by Pieter; Victoria knows the Interceptor's coordinates and will lead the team there."

"Ron? Where is he now? There, here, where?"

"On the plane with me, sitting in a secluded compartment in the back. No one knows I am in the plane's cockpit."

"I don't know what your twisted mind planned now. Victoria sits in the front, Ron sits in the back, both alone?" she asked somewhat sarcastic but also showed her admiration for her boss. "I think I know what you are thinking. I'll wait till the end to confirm my thoughts!" she added. "What are the coordinates?"

"Wait for that–"

"Won't you trust me with the coordinates? Damnit Patrick!" she yelled. "Do you trust anyone? How will I know she is taking us to the right place?"

Patrick snorted a short laugh. "Think Lucy, think hard. You'll know of course, in time, Lucy."

"Pat, did you find out which terrorist group attacked us in Santiago?"

"Yes, international freelance terrorists for hire, perhaps the Wagner group PMC or something like Baader Meinhof.

They are experts in cracking and sabotaging the most difficult cases of espionage for the SVR without leaving any trace leading to their patron, the Russians."

"The boat captain announced the ice station is in range of the Dolphin helicopter. The weather cleared, whom shall I report to over there?"

"The ice station manager please, also bring Greg and Bill, both agents with you."

"OK, no more tricks mister!" she scolded lightly and cut the transmission off.

CHAPTER 29

"Y ou have the latest coordinates. Any satellite images?" Pieter approached Vladimir questioning him angrily in the tiny officer's dining room on board the submarine.

"I am in charge Pieter!" he growled back "It's a need-to-know basis!"

"So, the SVR is not entitled to know if you have a positive confirmation as to where the Interceptor landed exactly?" Pieter growled in response and frowned, then looked at the troops who were protecting their leader.

"Those who need to know . . . KNOW!"

"Why don't you trust me?"

"You are not part of the military mission; therefore, I am not allowed to share information that might be transferred to the citizens."

A loud metal clanking stopped them from arguing. The sub rattled gently, but they wondered what the cause was. They both looked at each other, understanding each one had his own mission to complete.

"Strong current. We are deep under the surface sailing along the curvy shore of Droning Maud Land into Weddell Sea," said the lieutenant calmly watching the maps.

The clanking increased as the sub reached its cruising depth under the ice sheet and when the clanking stopped, a gentle hum took over. The sub crew was trained to keep silent when it was a cat and mouse underwater chase during the cold war. They considered this mission to be on high alert.

The Russian sub sonar officers detected the sounds of the Pacific fleet carrier engines thrusting the vessels forward from many miles away, informed Vladimir.

"Thanks, lieutenant," Vladimir replied and then turned to Pieter. "The captain has his instructions to bring us as close as possible to the Interceptor coordinates. I pointed out to him that once we are out of the Brunt Ice Sheet, we will be exposed to the British Halley and the Belgrano Argentinean research stations. He recommended sailing deeper to avoid thermal break until we get to Berkner Island." Vladimir gasped.

Oleg, who kept silent most of the trip decided to add his two cents and said, "At this time in April, it is important to know the coordinates and follow the breaking ice sheets. The Interceptor might float toward us!" he coughed lightly with a pained face. "Also, for your info, something good came from Halley Research Station, the discovery of the ozone hole in 1985, so it's not all bad!" he coughed again and covered his mouth with his palm.

"Oleg are the rumors of your sickness true?" asked Vladimir, concerned.

Oleg and Inna nodded, and Inna whispered in Vladimir's ear, "It's getting worse. It's Leukemia!"

"He needs to be treated," replied Vladimir in a whisper as Oleg took his seat away from them.

"When we return back to Russia," she concurred.

"I see why he wanted to join us; time is of the essence for him, right?"

"Oh yes, he is of the Russian old school, loyal to the end!" Then he got closer to the scientist. "Good point Oleg!" he exclaimed and shrugged his shoulders. "We will request new satellite imaging and locations; hope someone is monitoring, the–"

"Did you actually see an image of the Interceptor coordinates, the actual spot, Vladimir?" asked Pieter and clenched his jaw.

"A reported storm might cover it with fresh snow. As much as I know from photos that were sent to us by our agents in the field, the Interceptor is painted black. It should be easy to find it when we are close to the coordinate points."

"Agents?" asked Pieter curiously. "I was the one who sent the documents to our headquarters after shooting and killing a double agent in LA. I sent his entire desktop to our embassy, and they sent it to our homeland through a diplomatic bag!" scoffed Pieter. "Ask *me*! I was there when the B-2 bomber took off!" he growled inches from Vladimir's face, raising the tension between them again. "Why do you think I am here commander?" he slurred.

"Yes, we know you killed a comrade Pieter, but miraculously he is alive," he chuckled. "No thanks to you!"

Pieter was stunned. He was not sure why this important information was not disclosed to him. The rest kept quiet. The tension reached a point where Pieter didn't trust the agency or the people he worked for.

The sub pushed forward, close to the island with ice sheet thousands of feet thick. The captain joined them in the dining room quarters, their grim faces looked at him with anticipation.

"What's going on?" he asked and raised his eyebrows as he leaned on the door jam. Then he went to the bar, unlocked it, and pulled out a bottle of Stolichnaya Vodka, glasses, and poured a round. "Soon we will say goodbye once we find a spot to land. You can return with your secret cargo. *Admiral Karlinsky* research ship is nearby."

"Disguised as a whaler!" added the lieutenant and chuckled.

"Yes, disguised as a whaler," laughed the captain and raised his glass. "Nostarovia! To success, and you Nik, try to bring the European championship to Moscow next year!"

"I'll drink to that!" replied Nik with a big smile, happy to be acknowledged.

"You bring a lot of respect to our country," the captain added and gulped the drink in one shot.

"Sure captain, thank you," Nik responded humbly.

"After all, if you bring the Interceptor home, we will advertise Nik's face on every banner!" the captain said and poured another glass to the rim.

"Are we planning to return with the *Admiral Karlinsky*?" asked Pieter with a bleak expression. "Why didn't you plan on coming here with it in the first place?"

Vladimir's face got tense. "Deception comrade. Do you think the Americans are sleeping at their post? We went to our ice station as global warming researchers, under a snowstorm we boarded a submarine, we disappeared from their radar, then we show up at the Interceptor with the *Admiral Karlinsky* research boat, which has all the equipment we need to retrieve it and bring it on board. This plan was confidential, so NO ONE knew about it, just a few closed circle admirals. A deception was always the plan, sorry I didn't report to you, Pieter!" Vladimir slurred in disdain and then cheered loudly, "Lazarovia!"

Then he followed the sub captain's lead and poured the entire glass down his throat and shook his head, trembling. "Whoa!" he growled and gazed at Pieter. "Good stuff!"

Pieter didn't realize how complicated Vladimir's twisted plans were, so no one really knew how they would reach the lost missile.

"Captain!" the intercom flashed.

"We received a transmission through our buoy. We are under the *Admiral Karlinsky,* connecting."

Vladimir blinked and nodded in confirmation. "Get the team ready for transfer to the boat," ordered Vladimir and the lieutenant went back to prepare his troops.

"How are we getting from the *Karlinsky* to the Interceptor? The ice sheet is 300 feet high?" Pieter asked.

Vladimir grinned and clarified, "The boat has two helicopters, comrade; all was thought out, you seem too skeptical!"

"We were supposed to work together Vlad. Your attitude has changed, and I don't like it," responded Pieter.

The troops and the expedition team transferred through a connecting tube from the submarine to the disguised whaler floating in calm waters. Vladimir made sure his troops and the civilians transferred safely and were distributed to their quarters. He was greeted by the boat's captain, a solid 220 pounds of oceanic gorilla with a long black beard, wearing a white officer's cap and a white tight jacket full of medals on his inflated chest. His small gray eyes blinked quickly as he asked Vladimir to join him in his cabin for a quick briefing.

Vladimir's lieutenant supervised his troops and Pieter organized the rest. The sun over the horizon beamed weak light; it would hold the same position in the sky until the end of summer.

They sat down in the captain's cabin and Vladimir asked, "Do you have anything to drink?"

"Sure, the best!" his deep hoarse voice thundered.

He then put two glasses on the small corner table and grabbed a semi-full bottle of Beluga Gold Line Vodka.

"Wow, better Vodka than the sub's bar cabinet."

They poured the drinks; it appeared it wasn't the first one for the captain.

"*Hah*," Vladimir enjoyed the drink and pursed his face.

The captain pulled his shoulders back, "I have some bad news for you!"

"Shoot!" Vladimir was impatient.

"I was briefed of your secret mission. I know this area better than my own back yard, and I was asked to report to you that the American Pacific fleet is circling the area 100 miles from here. In addition, it was just reported that our satellite photos show that a cargo plane landed at Palmer Ice Station a few minutes ago." The captain was skeptical on how that info would affect Vladimir's mission and added, "I think, they are watching you; I think this complicates your mission!"

Vladimir was not bothered by this intel and replied, "Comrade, I see it a different way. To me it means the Americans are protecting their expedition by protecting their Interceptor, you, see? The rumors that this might be a fake story, or a trap have now disappeared. I will love seeing the American's next step." Vladimir cheered, "We are on the right track, comrade!"

"Tell me, what's so important with the Interceptor that we are ready to go to war with the Americans for it?" he snorted waiting for an answer.

Vladimir frowned. He paused and helped himself to another drink. He didn't rush the answer and looked at the captain's cold eyes, shaking his head gently. He cleared his throat and coughed lightly after pouring the drink down his throat. "They developed something which is a combination of sophisticated Artificial Intelligence gyro technology that can lock onto millions of frequencies in one second, like the AI is running the missile."

"I don't understand comrade!" he waved his hands.

Vladimir waggled his finger at him. "We were using our hypersonic missile in Ukraine, and the west had no answer to counter our technology. It could not be intercepted because they changed the frequencies millions of times in one second, so no missile could lock on it and intercept it to destroy it. In a lack of competence, the Americans lost one of their newly developed Interceptors on Berkner Island." Vladimir sounded as if the trophy was already in his cabinet.

"I am afraid that stealing the American Interceptor will only prolong the current war and lead to a direct collision with NATO. We should develop our own!" the captain shrugged and poured the rest of the bottle into his glass.

"We are behind, but right now we have the military advantage. If the American Interceptor is deployed, we will lose it. We are at war, captain!"

The third officer walked in and handed the captain a message. The captain read the note and tightened his lips as he forwarded it to Vladimir. The lieutenant asked permission to join.

"It's from our agent. It says the Interceptor landing site on the ice sheet broke off a couple hours ago and is drifting into the Palmer Basin."

"Crap," growled the lieutenant. "We need more info, like photos, etc."

"They sent us the satellite images lieutenant; we need to prepare the Mi-26 now."

"I thought they had two helicopters," the lieutenant replied.

"The Mi-26 can transfer all of you in one shot!" The captain jumped in.

"We need to get our troops up there, Vladimir!" The lieutenant kept pushing.

"It's a heavy lift chopper, lieutenant," scolded the captain. "It can load ninety people. You are only thirty-five men with light weaponry. There is enough room for your Interceptor!"

"How would we load the Interceptor?" The lieutenant wanted all the details upfront.

"With two pilots, you get one navigator, one flight engineer, and a flight technician. They are experts and have the tools to bring in the Interceptor." The captain of the boat dismissed the lieutenant's skepticism and glanced at Vladimir. Vladimir shot a quick command surprising them both, "We go now!"

CHAPTER 30

T he heavy compacted snow that created the landing
strip had a layer of fresh snow a mile away from the
US Palmer Ice Station on the north side of the Palmer
Peninsula.

Temporary goosenecks marked the landing strip and its
thresholds due to the dim light of the pale sun hanging in
the horizon. The visibility was low and without the proper
ILS precision navigational systems, the captain needed to
use his skills to land his heavy load on the runway using vi-
sual flight rules protocol. The midair refueling took under
account the ability to fly back for refueling in the Falkland
Islands and from there to its home base.

The captain communicated with NZ12 airport station
with a request for ATIS information. After a turn 2,000 feet
above the ice, it aligned with the landing strip for final approach, and touched down in a cross wind that required
another set of skills to navigate the heavy plane safely. The
wheels blew snow high into the sky on touchdown, and the
thrust reversers covered the entire plane with flurries until it stopped just 100 feet from the people waiting for it;
there were a few snowmobiles and a snow cruiser equipped
with communication antennas there as well.

"Victoria Harper?" asked the young lady in front of the
steps since she was the first to get off the plane.

"That's me, I am the only female on this flight," she replied in a grumpy tone and then flashed an apologetic smile.
She added, "Long flight you see."

The young lady nodded with some compassion. "Tell me about it! I did that flight nine times and it was never fun. Come with me. By the way I am Gail!"

Victoria remembered she was on a CIA assignment, and she needed to keep her profile low, and her mouth shut.

"Where are we heading, Gail?"

"To the camp, your team will join you there, but first, you will get a hot meal. Then I'll take you to our guest dorm building up the hill with a beautiful bay view."

"Good, I have been eating snacks for twenty hours and the only view was the Pacific Ocean with its icebergs." Victoria giggled waiting to remove her heavy clothing and freshen up.

Temperatures were mild for early April at 33 degrees Fahrenheit, the beginning of winter. "Now until October it will get colder and colder, sometimes the station will be shut down for supplies or inaccessibility due to heavy snow and ice in the Palmer Basin," explained Gail enthusiastically.

They both got on the snowmobile, wearing helmets attached firmly with straps. Gail ignited it with pro skills and started the short trip to the ice station camp, leaving behind the plane before she had the opportunity to see for herself what was the secret cargo that the crew kept confidential from her sight.

"Well, you will like our chef's chicken soup." Gail smiled from under the strap. Her face was covered.

"That's all I want to hear right now!" exclaimed Victoria and held Gail tight around her hips, rubbing her gently to look for a weapon. *She has no weapons,* thought Victoria. *Precaution? Who knows?*

"What about the rest of the people on the flight? Are they joining us soon?" Victoria's curiosity bothered her. She checked the Glock handgun Patrick gave her for personal use and it comforted her. Then she asked another question without waiting for the answer of the first, "Have you heard anything about the lost Interceptor?"

Gail gasped and quickly thought before replying. "Oh what?"

The snowmobile's engine noise disrupted the conversation and Victoria raised her voice loudly, "What about the guys that we left behind in the airplane?"

"Sorry, I didn't see anyone from the crew. I was asked to help you; I am only a researcher!"

"What about the Interceptor? Did you hear anything?"

Gail turned her head letting her long hair escape from the helmet and wave in the wind. She replied loudly, "Oh the plane? It continues to McMurdo Ice Station on Ross Island. That's all I know; they always do that!"

"Have you heard about the Interceptor?" she asked again infuriated.

"What about it?" she replied.

"Have you heard anything? Rumors, commotion, anything?"

"No, not really. As I said, I am only a rookie researcher, what about you? What are you specialized in?"

Victoria mumbled something that sounded like search or research as Gail cheered loudly, "We are here!"

Victoria saw the first building from around the corner. All the camp's small buildings were centered along the slope of the rocky low hill, no snow, overlooking the Bismarck Strait and the Palmer Basin's spectacular view.

"We are south of Anvers Island. We call this point, Gamage Point. You can see the basin is in full view with small or broken ice sheets. Soon in the winter, when sub temperatures drop into the minus twenties and thirties, they form a solid ice sheet you can walk on; it goes from here to Cape Monaco and Cape Lancaster–many miles across." Gail was informative showing off her area geography she learned during her stay the last six months.

The snowmobile headed to a light blue two-story building with a sign marked "Bio Lab Building" which also served as the dining room, labs, and offices and if there was room, it could be considered a storage facility.

"From here, we will walk," Gail said and parked the snowmobile next to the main building in the corner. "You will be lodging in our guest dorms in the building over there." Gail pointed her finger toward the top of the hill which was on the edge of the camp.

She held Victoria's elbow and momentarily felt her stiff cold gun in her holster. She ignored it and didn't ask any questions, instead she added calmly, "Your dorm is called the GWR building." She smiled and exposed her bright white perfect teeth.

"What's GWR?"

"Garage, warehouse, rooms." She giggled. "There is the boathouse, with a couple of inflatable boats we use for research at the sea. We hang out there sometimes and have drinks. It's fun."

Victoria wondered if with all the fun, fun, fun, they are getting any work done, and she chuckled softly.

As they were about to enter the Bio building through the building's insulated blue door, Victoria noticed the big red ship named *Laurence M. Gould*, an ice breaker which entered the area through the Hero Inlet while a bunch of station researchers and service employees hollered and cheered, waving hands and later would help dock it.

"Wait a minute, Gail. This is cool, what is that ship?" Victoria held the door open shortly before stepping into the Bio lab building.

"Oh, that's our supply ship, it takes four days to get through the Punta Arenas Passage. It comes here periodically from the supply stations in Chile and Argentina," Gail said, happy to explain.

CHAPTER 31

The Dolphin helicopter from the *Arctic Star* ice breaker research ship landed next to the parked *Globemaster* that Lucy was to board. Patrick greeted Lucy and locked her in the cockpit for a quick chat while the pilot performed preflight on the plane for his next flight out.

Ron Hill was in the back of the plan. He didn't question why he was sitting in the back all by himself, but thought it was weird CIA protocol. The loadmaster was instructed to show him the snowmobile cruiser on the ground and asked Ron to board it. "This vehicle will take you to the Interceptor soon," he informed Ron who nodded and kept quiet.

"I see Ron!" said Patrick, who saw him through the cockpit windshield.

"What's going on Patrick. Isn't it time to get me up to par with your plans?"

Patrick pulled back his shoulders and gazed at her. He paused with a reply and Lucy continued, "It looks like a serious military operation here!" She gasped nervously trying to figure out the whole enchilada.

"You are right!" Patrick sighed. "No point keeping this confidential from you anymore. You were not the only subject we used to distract the Russian intelligence. Do you know why the Pacific fleet was on its way?"

"NO!" she replied loudly, and her eyes wide open. "Tell me!"

"Did the *Arctic Star* captain tell you anything about his mission?" he asked again.

"Other than to pick me up from Santiago, NO!" she inhaled deeply, and she brooded.

"The *Arctic Star* is equipped with special equipment and technology to retrieve objects from thousands of feet under water and–"

"What are we retrieving now?" Lucy cut Patrick off and stared at him.

"Poseidon!" Patrick said whispering like anyone could have been listening.

"What the heck is the Poseidon?"

"It's a Russian nuclear torpedo, the same concept as the hypersonic missile, only it worked underwater and could not be intercepted."

"Holy cow!" Lucy thundered and understood why Patrick tried so hard to clear the CIA's tracks after his plans of running her from place to place having the Russian intelligence wondering where she was, and what her mission was. A living moving target. She got over it and wanted to know more. She raised her chin saying, "Next!"

"Three Russian subs conducted a test in the North Sea, and the Poseidon test failed!" Patrick still sounded dramatic watching if anyone around was listening.

"What has this got to do with the Interceptor?"

"The Poseidon crossed the entire western hemisphere and landed deep in the Bellingshausen Sea across from Palmer Land and the Interceptor coordinates were reported not far from there. The three Akula subs circling the Antarctic 60-latitude are searching for the Poseidon and assisting the Russian expedition to get to our Interceptor first."

"No wonder everyone is so confused, I am confused." Lucy ran through her thoughts analyzing what Patrick disclosed and how she fit into all this when she was not a target anymore. She said, "SO, if I read this correctly, the entire Interceptor test and its loss was bogus? Its landing coordinates are fake?" she blinked her eyes.

"Sort of." Patrick was serious. "It was all planned to get the Russians busy looking for it and out of our way. Our main goal is to retrieve the Poseidon!"

"Gosh, Patrick, I understand why you could not share this with me in case I fell into their hands. So why mobilize the Pacific fleet, military choppers, and—"

"To make it look real, Lucy," Patrick said. After a short paused added, "Plus, we need to meet our next objective!"

"Oleg?" Lucy raised her eyebrows in question.

"Yes, Oleg. He designed the Poseidon and the hypersonic missile for the Russians, and he will be inches from us, so you fit right there to take advantage!" said Patrick.

"You want me to hijack him?" she laughed.

"No, I want you to make sure he doesn't change his mind!" Patrick said. "He wants to defect!"

"Well, I know some of those details from my mission in London."

"Nik, Oleg's daughter Inna, are all in on the plot. The Russians will watch intently, and they don't know that yet, the defecting, understood?"

Lucy frowned. "But without the Interceptor they will figure out it's a bluff and retreat!"

"A week ago, confidentially, a C-130 landed there and unloaded a black missile that looks identical to the one that flew on the B-2 test. Let them get to it first, we will join!"

"You have multiple objectives, Patrick? Hope we don't lose one. Are the three Russian subs in danger of our mission? Are they the ones that tested the Poseidon?"

Patrick shook his head and smiled. "No. The ones closest to us are the Akula class. The one that tested the Poseidon is the K-329 Belgorod and the B-90 Sarov, special purpose submarines. They headed back to Russia with their tails between their legs. The Akula's searching for it as I said!"

They watched Ron looking around, taking photos of his surroundings, and then boarding the snowmobile.

"First, I have no love for the Russians even a bit, when the first hypersonic missile test exploded two years ago, the west cheered and laughed, now they are landing on the Ukraine's asses. So, if the Poseidon is deployed in the near future, then we will chase our military developers to develop a response. Same shit every time like now, every time they are ahead of us, we chase our own tails."

"That's the whole point, the burden of our slow development landed on the CIA's shoulders," Patrick got very serious and mumbled something short when listening to Lucy's concerns. She was right, he thought. He stared at her as she brainstormed the issues and felt the sincere worries that flooded her mind.

"We observed the Russian Navy's entire Poseidon test. Remember our agent, Marcia? She helped, plus we have a ton of sensors that monitor the oceans for the special torpedo characteristic sounds. We used everything we had in our arsenal, including, satellites radars, sonars, submarines along Doomsday Alley to find the torpedo's location. Its sounds stopped and we recorded its coordinates by an AI master computer that also computed its projection, taking under consideration the ocean currents and the ocean temperatures, etc."

"So, are we mobilizing?" she poked his rib cage.

* * *

We need to move now, no more delays," Vladimir commanded his lieutenant. Tension on his face was visible. The man replied with a salute and prepared his crew to board the Mi-26 helicopter. The pilot was conducting a preflight at the same time.

The troops checked their weapons and equipment not knowing how long or what to expect out there. The lieutenant checked each one of them and tapped their shoulder in support and encouragement.

"We are ready, commander," he reported to Vladimir on the radio.

"Send the drones ahead of us and watch our path," commanded Vladimir staring at the captain.

The "whaler" captain nodded and instructed the helicopter pilots to get ready for the worst-case scenario and obey the commands issued by Vladimir.

Two drones launched to provide real-time videos of their destination area. The light flurries stopped and changed to clear visibility.

Pieter was close to Vladimir and saw the gravity of the mission and stress on his face. *What was going on in his stomach?* asked Pieter to himself. It's time to end this exhausting expedition. He got the signal for permission to board the helicopter from Vladimir.

The Russian "whaler's" energetic captain briefed them from the bridge and watched them boarding the plane. He wished them good luck via the vessel's exterior loudspeakers. He sat in his captain's chair watching the huge rotor turn and the helicopter back ramp retracting to close. The pilots saw his thumbs up through the windshield and the chopper became airborne with a loud roar leaving the boat behind.

"I locked in the coordinates on the computer!" responded the pilot to Vladimir's question. "It's a short flight; we'll be there in twenty minutes."

"Thank you, comrade, stay vigilant. Let me know of any extra activity ahead of you."

266 • WILLIE HIRSH

"Sure, commander," he replied.

Vladimir sat in the cockpit behind the pilots with his headset on and scouted the blue water below as they approached the broken ice sheet. It seemed small from afar, but when they approached, Vladimir realized the monstrous size and height of it. "Like an island," he mumbled.

The helicopter rattled and flew close to the surface of the ocean creating tiny salty droplets on the windows by its rotor draft; it was a combat mission flying below enemy radar. The troops and Pieter were tense with stoic faces. Nik and Inna appeared worried and concerned, but Inna's father seemed calm with no expression. She held Oleg's hand and leaned on him for comfort.

The helicopter got close to the icy island floating separately from the mainland. It had broken off into two pieces, each one was the size of Moscow itself and as high as three times the Eiffel Tower in Paris.

"We are very close, commander, but which one of the two ice sheets?" hollered the pilot.

Vladimir stretched to see outside. "Ask your navigator! He should know, Holy Mother of God, he is the one with the drones, comrade!" Vladimir yelled.

"Do you see anything?" the pilot asked his navigator who was still looking at his instruments.

"Climb to 500 feet above the ice sheet and fly in a circle around the left ice sheet, captain!"

"Nothing from the drones?"

"*Nitchvo!*" he replied (nothing).

The pilot concurred and navigated the helicopter as instructed, climbing just above the surface of the ice sheet but well-above the ocean to scout the surface.

"All white, I see no Interceptor. Are you sure we are at the right place?" Vladimir was furious.

"Oh wait, I see something!" yelled the navigator. "I am taking control of the drones!"

The drone's long-distance cameras spotted a partial black spot and were directed to that direction to investigate. They buzzed quickly over it at a low altitude. "Yes, this must be it!" The navigator sounded excited and yelled loudly like a child.

"Yea!" they all cheered in the cockpit. The pilot directed his helicopter to the Interceptor and announced in the cabin victoriously, "We have the Interceptor!"

"Get ready, Oleg!" yelled Vladimir. "This helicopter can lift it and transfer it to our boat."

The pilot raised his hand. "Comrade Vladimir, my radar spotted aerial activity twenty miles from here!"

"What? Do we have company?"

* * *

"Damn," Lucy murmured. "What a monster!" She referred to the snow cruiser with its diesel engine on.

The loadmaster held the Apache helicopters and its crews inside the plane awaiting a call on the radio from Patrick.

Ron Hill sat alone in the snow cruiser. He started to get anxious, touching his Beretta handgun; the piece given to him by none other than the FBI director himself when interviewing for his new role.

Ron looked a little disoriented and combed the area from the window with amazed glances. The Globemaster was parked like a snowbird, and he saw the crew checking the wings to make sure they were cleaned from snow that could dislodge during takeoff.

He saw Patrick, whom he recognized from photos he shared with the FBI before joining the CIA.

Patrick greeted the military cargo plane crew and joined Ron in the snow cruiser with Lucy, both wore their winter coveralls, goggles, and hoods. Ron shook his hand without removing his gloves, Patrick and Lucy reciprocated. "Patrick Stevenson, cold out here, huh?" he introduced himself.

"You need no introduction, Mr. Stevenson!" replied Ron as he shivered. The occasion to meet the CIA director himself was overwhelming.

"Ron, you met Lucy?"

"It's my pleasure," he said politely and asked, "What's your last name?" Ron was curious.

"You can call me the Rose of Jericho!" she laughed.

Patrick signaled the Apaches to be on standby and dictated the snowmobile cruiser to mobilize.

"Time to get on our way!" Patrick tapped on Lucy's shoulder gently as he sat next to Ron.

"How far is the Interceptor?" asked Ron.

The snow cruiser was not a comfortable luxury vehicle, its hard seats made the trip feel longer as it moved slowly over the rugged ice.

"Not far, it may take an hour or so. We are picking up Victoria from the camp. It's on the way," replied Patrick and his radio clicked. "Patrick!"

He recognized the ice station manager's panicked voice, "Victoria and Gail left on a snowmobile; I assume they know where to go!"

A *hisss* sounded on the radio. Both Patrick and Lucy looked at Ron like he had the answer. Ron froze.

"I told Victoria to borrow the snowmobile from the station," Patrick clicked the radio. Patrick looked at Lucy for advice and then looked at Ron who kept silent.

"I acknowledged!" she replied and sounded stressed. "I guess they both know where they are going, just reporting!"

"Gail was not supposed to join Victoria. Patrick out!" Then Patrick hollered to the driver, "Step on it, Pitcher."

Lucy shaking her head could not resist asking Patrick a question, but his face signaled her to change her mind. Patrick did not want to hear any questions.

"Who is Gail?" asked Ron dramatically.

"My junior and newest CIA agent on her first mission. You know Victoria?" Patrick asked.

Ron shook his head. "No, I don't know either of them!"

Patrick analyzed his face like an X-ray machine.

"I hope no one else needs to die today!" added Ron and Lucy and Patrick nodded with agreement. Then he looked at his smart phone compass app using its own sensors to determine the magnetic north and asked calmly, "Are we going in the right direction?"

* * *

"Here it is!" yelled the pilot and directed Vladimir to a long black cylindrical object half-covered by the snow.

"What about our company, comrade?" asked Vladimir calmly to keep everyone at ease.

"I see three helicopters hovering in the distance. They are on hold, just hovering!" said the pilot.

Vladimir commanded the navigator to send the drones to buzz close to the hovering helicopters in the distance.

"I see a snowmobile with one person quickly reaching the Interceptor!" called the pilot.

"Get us down there fast!" Vladimir tensed.

The heavy Russian Mi-26 landed carefully. Everyone got out, surrounding the Interceptor, about fifty yards away.

"Go check it, Oleg!" commanded Vladimir losing patience and his troops made a circle around them all signaling they were claiming the area and its special cargo.

"I'll go with him!" said Inna and waited for Vladimir's permission.

"Have the troops circle us and we will all go!" suggested Pieter encouraging them to leave as a tight group so he could walk toward the American side by himself.

Vladimir nodded and they started to walk toward the Interceptor to get close to Oleg.

"I know your days are numbered and the leukemia is eating you alive, but as long as you breathe, I want you to die as a devoted Russian top scientist. Don't make any silly moves, I have your daughter with me!"

Oleg nodded and stole a glance at Pieter who stood there looking like the battle was lost.

The snowmobile with the single person on it closed the distance hurriedly and the snow cruiser was on their tail and approaching the Interceptor.

In the distance, the two Russian drones approached the hovering Apache.

* * *

Patrick's radio clicked again when he saw the snow cruiser chasing the snowmobile that was closing in toward the Interceptor.

"Two unidentified drones in attack formation, permission to fire!" sounded the chief helicopter in formation on the radio, calm as ice.

Patrick looked at Lucy and she nodded her head as to encourage Patrick to react. Patrick did not need encouragement.

"If they possess danger, splash them!" Patrick commanded back on the radio.

"Roger that sir, they do seem aggressive."

"Your call!" replied Patrick.

"Splashed!" the pilot in command responded.

The navigator reported to Vladimir that the two drones were splashed by the American helicopters. "Yes, I see! We are walking to the Interceptor now. I guess our American comrades are looking for a war," Vladimir gasped and signaled his troopers to get their guns ready.

"A snow cruiser is approaching from the west, Vladimir. Do you see them?"

* * *

The snowmobile stopped as did the cruiser behind it. Patrick urged Ron and Lucy to stay together since it could become deadly. Patrick joined them and approached the Interceptor. Oleg, Inna, and Nik were in close distance on the other side while Oleg checked access doors and sensor components.

The snowmobile person walked closer with goggles and scarf covering their face. The person stood twenty feet from Patrick and his crew while the Russian examined the Interceptor.

"Get your rotors hovering in combat position. It's getting hot here!" whispered Patrick into the radio and the Apache helicopter leader acknowledged.

Ron was restless and Lucy watched him rubbing his holster.

The snowmobile rider came over to Patrick and pulled off the goggles and scarf. "Hello strangers, remember me?" asked Victoria with an unnerving smile.

"Who is the commanding officer here?" asked Patrick loudly and waved his hands high above his head.

Lucy was ready to pull her gun, but Patrick held her hand down. "It's not necessary!"

In the other direction, Vladimir called loudly in reply, "I am Major General Commander Vladimir Korenko, Commander of the Russian Federation, Spetsnaz Arctic forces and you?"

"I am Patrick Stevenson, Director of the CIA and I see that you found our Interceptor, you can take it with you if you like!"

Pieter quietly asked Inna, her father, and Nik to move forward closer to the American side.

"I see you have reinforcement of three Apache helicopters fully equipped. They killed my drones!" called Vladimir.

"And I see your Spetsnaz Arctic troops, expert in Arctic warfare with guns ready to attack as well. Your drones approached in attack positions with dangerous maneuvers around my helicopters!" Patrick replied.

"True, we don't trust your country, Comrade Patrick."

"We don't trust yours either. I suggest you take your helicopter and your troops back to your ship and we go our way as well!"

Oleg slowly walked around the Interceptor and laughed. "What a hoax!" he looked at Pieter who sealed his lips. "It's an old WWII Mark 14 torpedo, its motor buried in the snow, you can just see its middle."

"Well, it looks good from above," Pieter whispered back.

Vladimir approached closer to Oleg as he touched the fake Interceptor, opening and closing the access door panels and looking inside and smiling. Vladimir held him by the elbow with a firm grip and asked everyone to join the troops in the outer circle and did not let Oleg walk away.

"Don't touch my father!" Inna yelled and Pieter moved to stand between them firmly and stopped Vladimir from hitting Inna; Nik did the same.

Vladimir pulled the gun from his holster and placed it on Pieter's temple. "Oleg, come back, last chance to obey me. Your daughter will be the first to die here. Nik you stand aside!" Vladimir sounded frustrated.

"We are not going back," cried Nik and tried to get in between Vladimir and his fiancé as Pieter took position to block Vladimir's line of fire and shoot Oleg.

"Push back!" yelled Pieter and looked at Patrick for support. "Patrick! Inna, Oleg, Nik, and I would like asylum in the United States of America, NOW," he continued shouting, with one hand warning Vladimir from opening fire even though the Apache helicopters threatened to shred his troops and himself if he executed his threat.

Patrick was sure that Vladimir's threat would not be realized, and his troops would not open fire despite their threatening appearance.

"Vladimir, let them go. I'll trade the Interceptor and your FSB agents with you!"

"No!" Vladimir yelled in anger and his face crumbled. "They are standing on Russian federation claimed land and as a Russian I have the authority to open fire on my citizens!" Vladimir hollered waving his gun.

"There are no borders here, Commander Vladimir! The United States claimed that piece of land too, you are thousands of miles from your closest ice station and with no military support, even from your three Akula submarines monitoring our Pacific fleet closely in the area. Do you want to start a war? Then you will be the first casualty!" Patrick demonstrated his situation calmly and raised his fist high to signal the Apache helicopters to hold fire.

Nik pushed Inna gently. She held her father and walked toward Patrick's position with hesitation. Vladimir aimed his handgun at Pieter's temple. Inna was walking away, back and forth.

"Stop or I shoot!" Vladimir yelled, losing control, and cocked his gun, a step closer to the point of no return. He had no one to ask for advice and consult, the heavy burden was all his. The lieutenant stood with the troops and decided to assist his commander who was not happy with the situation they were trapped in.

Patrick realized the escalation of the situation and warned Vladimir and his second in command. "Let me remind you, Major General Vladimir Korenko, that first, my helicopters are ready to defend us and destroy your helicopter and troops, your spy whaler *Admiral Karlinsky* anchored not far from here, and your three submarines, will be destroyed. If you want to personally survive, you will have no home to return too!"

Seems the threat hit a chord in Vladimir's nervous system. He looked at the three Apaches hovering steady in the cold sky with their rocket launchers and threatening heavy machine gun under the fuselage. Heavy-duty fire power compared to his vulnerable troops holding handguns. All he needed was a graceful exit without humiliation to show a victorious picture from this grave situation and Patrick realized that. *That would be a win-win situation,* Patrick thought.

In the time it took Vladimir to assess the scenarios and determine his next step, Patrick called out loudly with confidence, "Asylum granted!" which encouraged Oleg and his daughter to walk faster toward him.

Lucy watched Victoria and Ron, restless after the announcement, spring into action which was not a surprise at the moment.

Suddenly Victoria yelled loudly, "Stop right there, no one move!" Pulling her gun at the same time and aiming it at Oleg's forehead who was approaching the American side. Inna and Nik following closely behind him, stopped. At the same time, Ron pulled his gun and placed it to Patrick's neck from behind. He moved uncomfortably.

"Well done. Well done comrades," yelled Vladimir cheerfully and signaled his lieutenant to grab the defecting party and bring them back by force.

"Oleg, come back to Mother Russia. You still have a lot of work to do!" The lieutenant pulled his gun for the first time.

The tense situation was ready to explode, and Lucy hoped that Patrick had it under control.

"Did you know that? Ron and Victoria?" asked Lucy and Patrick nodded firmly thinking, with sarcasm, it was great timing to ask questions now.

"Shut up bitch!" yelled Victoria frantically, pistol-whipping Lucy's face then aiming at Lucy's chest.

"I knew you never liked me, Victoria!" cried Lucy, holding her hand on the wound as blood poured from her upper left cheek and was absorbed by her winter scarf. "It's all compiling in my head now!" Lucy growled and automatically reached for her gun.

Vladimir and Pieter watched the drama on the American side with horror, both seeing from their position the escalation rising to an armed conflict.

"Major General Commander Vladimir, set Pieter free, in return I will trade your FSB agents. It's your last chance," Patrick offered and seemed apathetic to Victoria and Ron's armed threats.

Snowflakes started to fall. "Will the world be the same tomorrow?" Patrick asked aloud.

"You mean our Russian federation traitor?" laughed Vladimir and waved his gun in defiance.

"Don't listen to him Comrade Vladimir!" Victoria screamed desperately. I'll blow his head off with his first move!" She was agitated and Ron repeated after her, both threatening to blow Patrick's skull to pieces.

"Victoria, remember who gave you this gun?" asked Patrick and Lucy froze keeping her gun in her holster.

Victoria noticed Lucy. "Don't you dare, bitch. Drop it unless you want another scar on your perfect face!" She

276 • WILLIE HIRSH

ignored Patrick's question in the heat of the moment. "Ron, take the bitch's gun!" she ordered.

Lucy analyzed Patrick's question to Victoria. *Was he saying Victoria's gun was shooting blanks?* She tensed even more under her heavy winter clothing.

Patrick turned his head slightly toward Ron and pushed his gun away from his neck while Ron tried to keep it where it was, tight on his neck.

"And you Ron, your 9mm Beretta, or should I call you Alex Alexandrovich, FSB agent reporting directly to Semyon Kratzki, your brutal boss, who executed your biological parents in London some thirty-five years ago. Then sent you both to a sleeper cell to teach and prepare you to be super agents. Neither of you were, and it didn't matter how sophisticated your journey plans have been, your bullets are blanks too, just like your sister's Glock!"

Lucy immediately drew her gun. She read Patrick well and trusted he was telling the truth. Now her gun was aimed at Victoria close enough not to miss if she shot. But Victoria squeezed the trigger a few times to eliminate Lucy first with no reaction. Ron tried to shoot Patrick at the same time from the back, but Patrick and his driver jumped Ron and struggled him to the ground.

Victoria realized her gun carried blanks, throwing the gun at Lucy she jumped on her with a commando knife and with tiger instincts was ready to slash her throat. Lucy tried to repel her first by grabbing her hand away from her body, but Victoria was apparently too strong. Lucy had no choice but pull the trigger. The shot pierced the crisp air and echoed far mixing with the light wind's gentle sounds.

Lucy hit Victoria in her chest and her body collapsed on the icy surface with a loud groan. She was hardly breathing.

"Victoria!" Ron let out a loud cry while being held on the ground.

"Speak up!" yelled Patrick "Speak up! Who knows the coordinates? She did? Your sister? I saw you watching your compass on your watch. That is not all Alex Alexandrovich," slurred Patrick. "Your parents immigrated from the Soviet Union to London seeking asylum. They were murdered shortly after by the KGB with plutonium in their drinks, sound familiar huh? Well, they died in agony whispering your name until their last breaths!"

"Stop . . . Stop!" yelled Ron and his eyes tearing and his hands shaking.

"Now you remember who gave you your gun, Alex? Dan Schmidt. We knew you would not exchange the Beretta with your SVR service GSh-18 piece we found in your apartment." He inhaled and went on while tacking down the driver from moving and added, "The Department of Health and Social Care in London cleared you for adoption by your uncle who changed his name to Isidore Cain, another English name, but he was not your bloodline uncle, he was a brutal SVR sleeper cell agent. Their entire mission was to train you to be a super spy agent, a military blogger. Brilliant plan but also because the real Ron Hill disappeared without a trace and later you adopted his name and his background."

"You American bastards, you think you own the world!" Ron gasped almost choking then yelled, "You think you are so smart, Mr. Director?"

"Don't make any silly moves Ron, I know all about you!"

"Brother and sister!" Lucy was amazed spitting the words slowly. "How long has this been going on?"

"Trained to be FSB agents from childhood!" added Patrick. "Long story, I'll patch you in later." He pulled his gun and said, "This gun has real bullets!"

Patrick didn't let the episode engulf him emotionally and tried to stay even keel. In his age, he was not cut out to fight physically someone twenty years younger than him.

He called for Vladimir. "Take your agents and go, Oleg and his team will join me. Start walking Pieter!"

"The traitor stays with me!"

"We are trading Vladimir, have your lieutenant escort Pieter and my driver will escort Ron. No weapons!"

Vladimir nodded his head to his lieutenant, and he grabbed Pieter by his arm whispering in his ear, "I'll find you pig; I'll kill anyone you ever knew in Russia. Fucking traitor."

The driver reciprocated and pulled Ron from the ground. "Let's move!" he ordered.

"Victoria needs urgent medical help. We can send her to our research station, nearby."

"Don't bother Patrick, we will fly her to our research boat," Vladimir replied.

The lieutenant squeezed Pieter's arm hurting him badly. He pulled it back with force and hit the lieutenant in his face. The lieutenant grabbed Pieter's throat, he fell to the ground and started choking him.

"Help him!" Lucy cried.

"Let them struggle!"

Pieter rolled back and landed on the lieutenant's belly, hit him in his face several times quickly in a row, and then relaxed his deadly hold. Pieter took control and the lieutenant became lethargic, then he stood up looking at his opponent in apathy with no emotion.

The driver holding Ron stopped and looked at Patrick for a signal. "Leave him!" Patrick said and asked the driver to back up a few yards. Pieter left the lieutenant to his comrades and joined Oleg, Inna, and Nick.

"Get to the vehicle!" ordered Patrick and the driver joined them. Vladimir did not react, instead he signaled with his finger to the Mi-26 pilot to start the engine. He directed two troopers to get the lieutenant, Victoria from the ground and pick up Ron and have them all join the transport helicopter.

Then Vladimir, the last to stay there, turned around and asked Patrick, "Do you have an operational Interceptor, or it was all a bluff?"

Instead, Patrick replied, "It's all real, and it's right here!"

Hurriedly, the Russians boarded the helicopter. Vladimir was the last on the helicopter ramp before closing, took off his hat and saluted Patrick. Patrick reciprocated with a salute. "Goodbye comrade," he whispered and was sure that Vladimir heard him.

Patrick's radio clicked. "Will cover for you until they are gone!" suggested the Apache commander pilot.

"Yes, wait until they are gone, then have your boys shred the torpedo."

"That will be fun!" he replied and once the cruiser was in a safe distance with its live cargo, the three Apache helicopters emptied their machine guns until the torpedo was buried under the ice in a heap of hundreds of small, twisted pieces of metal and electrical wires.

Safe and away from the standoff in the warm cruiser all were cheery, happy, and hugging each other. Patrick's radio clicked again. The research camp on the radio cried aloud, "Gail was found dead, Patrick!"

"Victoria killed her, she was the last one with her on the snowmobile," said Lucy.

"Sad!" replied Patrick and laid back in his seat exhausted, mentally, and emotionally. Lucy and the rest felt the same.

* * *

The cruiser reached the camp, and they all went to the dining room for a quick meal before flying back to Washington.

"Welcome to America," announced the camp manager in a sad voice.

"Where is Gail?" asked Patrick.

"Transported to the boat. Set to sail soon!"

He shook his head gently. "She was a good kid!" said Patrick sadly.

"I want to board the Russian's *Admiral Karlinsky* and finish the job if Victoria survived!" exclaimed Lucy emotionally.

"Our mission is complete Lucy; we are going home soon."

"But Patrick, you are leaving without clarifying everything with me. For example, how did you know they were brother and sister?" she asked.

"Only two people had the fake Interceptor coordinates, Victoria and me. That was her test, after I investigated everyone in Langley to accept her. Victoria disclosed the coordinates to Ron, and he forwarded it to the FSB, his agency. When we got news of a Russian expedition to the same exact fake coordinates, I knew I hit the lottery but needed to confirm. So first, I moved them away from our state, therefore the FBI recruited Ron, and I promoted Victoria to the agent she always wanted to be.

On the other hand, I recruited Pieter with a bonus of $10M to convince him to bring Oleg, the Russian top scientist, to no man's land, Antarctica. From here it should be all clear."

"Yes, so far it's clear but it's not the whole picture," said Lucy.

"Dan Schmidt, the FBI director linked the murder of John Gregory, our scientist, to Ron, but he had no supporting evidence. He looked into his past since he came to the US as an exchange student with Oxford university. There were a few missing links he needed to connect the dots. The FSB built him step-by-step, and constructed a whole new past life, including one as an expert weapon blogger. How convincing right?" Patrick paused and inhaled.

"Brilliant!" gasped Lucy.

"So, I was working on that at the same time that the president started to panic and hit me with the Russian dominance of the hypersonic technology. John Gregory, the murdered scientist, worked on the development of the hypersonic missile Interceptor and was murdered at the eleventh hour before the real test, not the fake one I planned!"

"So, the B-2 and its crew are safe?"

"Sure, the Vandenberg mission control flight test was a show directed at the Russian Intelligence. The B-2 and its crew landed safely in Diego Garcia."

"Oh cool. It was speculated all over social media," said Lucy.

"Yes, and I couldn't share that with anyone. I wanted to know who briefed the FSB with information like, how to stop our military technological development program. That was Ron's job but as the big fish he was, I wanted to capture the entire cell and I could not believe they worked alone. It seemed like someone was sitting in my office, listening and briefing all our activities to our enemy. Therefore, I asked Pieter to take his laptop, insinuating he stole it for the Russians, and in the heat of arguments he shot Ron by accident. We kept Ron alive to lead us to the traitor in the agency. This is where you fit in, to distract the Russians knowing you are on their blacklist, and then run you around!"

"Marvelous, Patrick!"

Patrick smiled sadly and continued staring at her. "Our intent was never to kill Ron, just to provoke and convince his agency to allow him to take the offer from the FBI. From there he'd join the CIA expedition, the Russians just took the bait, all of it. They didn't realize that I spared him to trade him off for Oleg who will assist Lockheed Martin to complete the design of our Interceptor expeditiously since we need to dominate the world militarily."

"Yes, it's always our goal."

"And more importantly was to confirm Ron's sister was the leaky faucet."

"And Victoria, how could you see that from the begging. She was right next to you?"

"I monitored and silently wondered about Victoria. Something with her past didn't sit well with me from the day she was hired. Her husband was a powerful senator and her background from London made me suspect there was the same pattern as Ron's. Both came about the same time as students with the help of her husband who was a B-2 bomber pilot then. Victoria studied fashion design at FIT and became a successful decorator who was very involved with our military society gala nights. I watched her despite my predecessor's objection to put her on the pedestal. So, when the Russian Poseidon test failed, I noticed that Victoria did not forward me the briefing a–"

"And the famous car accident?" Lucy asked.

"True, her husband died in a car crash accident!" Patrick continued. "It was deliberately planned!" exclaimed Patrick.

"She claimed she was in the car with him at the same time!" said Lucy.

"She was not!" Patrick shot back. "Police reports mentioned her husband was in the back seat when he crashed, the driver's head was smashed into the windshield with a failed airbag deployment, which did not activate. She claimed she was sitting in the passenger seat next to the driver and the airbag deployed and saved her life."

Pieter moved closer when he heard the conversation, concurring from his perspective, and added, "I was trying to get some inside info for Patrick and expose the SVR and FSB plans that killed the senator. I am sure they will be after me until my last day alive!" he said, concerned.

"Ron and his sister Victoria are not their real names. They were domesticated in London, learned the British accent, schooled at home, and brain-washed with the soviet era ideology," Patrick disclosed. "I decided to stop the scientist killing spree program and threaten with abduction," he chuckled.

Oleg joined in as well and said, "It will be easy to abduct them, they all would want to work here. The CIA spread the disinformation to convince President Ilya Primankov to release me to go to Antarctica because I have leukemia and my days are numbered. That was another bluff to let them give me up easily!"

"They hallucinated stopping the US military and NATO from reaching a point of confidence and participating in the Ukraine war," said Pieter.

"That was another reason but not the last," Patrick said.

Lucy grunted and scolded, "If I knew Ron's history, I would have shot that son of a bitch!"

Patrick looked at her and said, "There are two ways to shape history. One way is by the sword, and the other way is by vision. In the long run the vision will win, that wasn't my vision, that was Napoleon who said it."

* * *

The *Arctic Star* did not look like the *Hughes Glomar* explorer, the ship that raised the K-129 last century in a top-secret CIA operation. Only when the two tall cranes were assembled overnight by its competent teams of cadets, did it look like it was ready to be an underwater recovery boat. The commotion on the vessel's upper deck was obvious as the excitement and concerns of the young sailors prepared for a nice calm journey.

"I hope we are not too obvious," said the young navigator bluntly.

"Don't worry, no one is watching us, no satellite flying above us. It's not entirely about the Interceptor. First, we wanted to direct the attention from what we do now, elsewhere, and second, we need more time to get our hypersonic and Interceptor clear for deployment. We need to complete this with the full summer sun light, darkness in this area lasts eleven weeks from May to end of July. That's a whole big operation of deception. Now I can tell you this!" Captain Lucas sounded proud to join and to be part of the small forum who knew all the mission's objectives. "They came to steal our Interceptor while we are stealing their Poseidon, fair game," he giggled softly.

"How big is the Poseidon? Weight? Length?" the crane operator asked as the sonar unmanned underwater robot searched the bottom of the sea for the lost torpedo. They all understood why Captain Lucas kept the *Arctic Star*'s mission confidential to avoid unnecessary leaks that could abort the mission.

"It's like a small submarine, last we knew it should be visible with its white and red checkered colors painted along the cylindrical shaped object." Then the captain displayed photos of the Poseidon taken by collaborator field agents before it was loaded onto the Russian Doomsday submarine before the North Sea test.

"Ok we know what we are looking for!" said the sonar technician relieved.

"How are we doing with the crane towers?" asked Dave and squeezed his pipe between his lips. His Beagle dog,

Ponzi, wagged his tail every time his master talked as if he was talking to him.

The crane operator responded, satisfied, "It's making progress captain. Your cadets are doing a great job erecting it fast, like pros!" he smiled.

Dave Lucas smiled and looked at the monitors, the unmanned underwater robot searched the sea floor at around 1,000 feet deep. "We got an alert that the Pantera Russian sub is in the vicinity. Watch carefully and let me know immediately," hollered Lucas.

"I'm sure they will know why we here," the first officer said.

"Of course, they are searching for the Poseidon too!" the captain thundered. "We monitored it from the second it was launched!"

"We are lucky, the south ocean floor has one of the deepest ocean floors on the planet after the Pacific Ocean," said the navigator seeing the depth registered on the screen of the unmanned robot. The strong projector flashlights and cameras all around the robot gave a very dark picture of the cold ocean depth. Creatures you usually do not see elsewhere on the planet, explained the biologist are like the ghostly looking ice fish and others. The creatures are attracted by the light of the camera distracting them from looking for the Poseidon torpedo.

"Sonar picked up something," the sonar technician called calmly on his speaker.

"OK, direct me to it," the robot pilot instructed using the intercom line on his headset.

"Ten-Four," he clenched his teeth.

The cameras projected six small screens on the master monitor. Something attracted Dave who was holding his cognac-colored beagle in his arms. "Go back. Go back. See camera six!" cried Dave.

The sound of the robot's electric engine faded, and the underwater vehicle stopped.

"Direct camera six to three o'clock," fired the navigator and the robot pilot gently moved all the side cameras to various positions.

"See!" cried the captain who almost broke his pipe between his clenched teeth. "Right there, red and white checkered cylinder, that's it!" he pointed with one hand toward the screen.

"I see it!" replied the pilot. "Current is very strong here!"

The screen showed the torpedo intact laying peacefully on the sandy ocean bed, held by a rock from sliding down the steep edge of the ocean floor shelf which dropped dramatically several thousand feet into the abyss.

"We hope the current won't push it over the edge!" said the pilot.

"We need to act quickly; I am sure it landed elsewhere, and the current pushed it until it was stopped by that rock," said the biologist.

"We will need to cope with the elements guys. We didn't expect it to jump like a fly fish onto our deck. We have a little junk down there compared to the K-129 submarine the CIA raised from about 16,000 feet deep, get serious!" scolded the captain.

"It's humiliating to think that we have a problem," added the navigator.

"Let's get to work and bring it home guys!"

The commotion on the upper deck to prepare the straps took some time and effort working in freezing temperatures and strong winds. The crew worked in short shifts of thirty minutes each, in and out to give the young cadets time to rest. The deck master stayed the whole time directing them, coordinating with the underwater vehicle pilots below.

"How the hell did the Russians have no idea where the missing torpedo was?" asked the first officer, skeptical.

"It doesn't matter, soon enough they will find out. Lately they are using their brain power in the war against Ukraine," joked the captain.

The *Arctic Star* was anchored motionless on a leveled sea about 500 miles away from the Palmer Land Long Peninsula and another 500 miles from where Patrick and his team were on the land.

The Pacific Fleet, cleared from circle latitude 60, was in a combat alert and in range of its airplane squadron of 'Super Hornets' F-18, to support the *Arctic Star*.

Lucas was called to pick up a call on the bridge. "Yep!" he called with his pipe he kept in his mouth since early morning.

"We have a positive location 3,200 feet down, sir?"

"Great dude, how long will it take until you are on your way home?" the tinny voice on the other side of the line asked.

The unmanned underwater robot tightened the Poseidon with ropes. The entire operation was conducted from a control room behind the bridge. The captain recorded every move seeing the pilot doing a marvelous job with the robot.

"She is secured!" the pilot cried, and the robot slowly lifted the Poseidon up to lock it under the ship's hull for its long journey home to San Diego.

"Will call you when we get home!"

"Thanks, and have a great trip, Captain. All our objectives were accomplished," declared Patrick satisfied and ended the call.

He turned to his group and stared at Lucy. "Now all we need to complete our mission is our military hardware development, and the unsuccessful Lockheed missile test to adjust the strategic imbalance. With Oleg's fresh set of eyes and his experience resolving bugs, we should be back in the front row. The stage is yours, Oleg!" Patrick sounded dramatic.

"By the way, I think I know why the Poseidon failed. I'll fix it for you and don't forget my daughter, a member of 'Liberty, Freedom and Democracy' in short, the LFD that opposed Primankov's policy to go to war with Ukraine. She opened my eyes and exposed me to what my scientific developments were doing to our homeland, otherwise I would still be a prisoner of the soviet concept and ideology."

"Patrick, the president is on the line for you, sir! You can take it in my office, it's a secured landline," said the camp manager proudly.

Patrick relaxed on the ample chair, picked up the phone, and greeted him cheerfully, "Mr. President!"

"Patrick, are all your objectives complete?" Rufus went straight to the core subject.

"Yes sir, the Poseidon is on its way. I have the top Russian scientist here with me, and we killed a sophisticated Russian spy cell!" he exclaimed and released a deep sigh.

"You left a big commotion in the south seas, and Russia dispatched submarines, etc. It was not the Silk Road Plan you introduced to me in the situation room. It was supposed to be a small little routine CIA operation as you said, aided by our military," the president scolded.

"Mr. President, it was a slippery slope. I know what I said, but I don't know what you understood. I am guilty by association sir!"

"Mission accomplished then. Let me call President Primankov. It's good you avoided humiliation because it's time to stop the madness in Ukraine and the mad race of a future doomsday weapon," the president moved to his wish list agenda. "Well Patrick, when the US is on the top, we just keep climbing!"

They both chuckled.

ABOUT THE AUTHOR

Willie Hirsh has published four novels: *Regicide: The Shadow King* (second edition, 2020), *Amongst and Above All* (2020), and *Constellation: The Final Leap* (second edition, 2020), which was an American Book Fest Finalist in 2018, *Doomsday Alley* (2022).

Willie currently spends his spare time traveling, photographing nature, and painting landscapes in oil. He loves writing spy and political suspense books after a career in engineering.

willie@williehirsh.com
twitter-@WillieHirsh
Instagram
Facebook-The Odyssey of Art by Willie Hirsh

ALSO BY WILLIE HIRSH

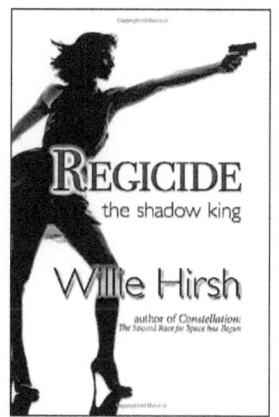

Regicide - the Shadow King
2020

Amongst and Above All
2020

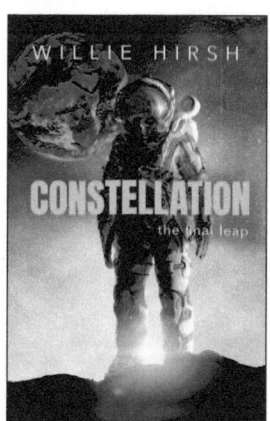

*Constellation - the
Final Leap*
2020

*Doomsday Alley -
Countdown to the
Apocalypse*
2022